Totally Bound Publishing books by Jayce Carter

The Omega's Alphas
Owned by the Alphas
Shared by the Alphas
Saved by the Alphas
Protected by Her Alphas
Caught by Her Alphas
Tamed by the Alphas
Claimed by the Alphas
Exposed by Her Alphas
Trained by the Alphas

Ready or Not
Fake It 'til You Make It
Opposites Attract
Third Time Lucky
Enemies Closer

The Omega's Alphas

TRAINED BY THE ALPHAS

JAYCE CARTER

Trained by the Alphas
ISBN # 978-1-83943-930-8

Interior text design by Claire Siemaszkiewicz
Totally Bound Publishing

Published in 2020 by Totally Bound Publishing, United Kingdom.

Totally Bound Publishing is an imprint of Totally Entwined Group Limited.

TRAINED BY THE ALPHAS

Dedication

To the woman in the grocery store line who
bought a big bottle of wine and goldfish crackers
at lunchtime.
I aspire to that level of no fucks given.
You are my hero.

Chapter One

The gazes pinned to Alison made her want to lift her lip and snarl. Instead, she shimmied her hips again to the cheers of drunken, horny men.

This isn't exactly where I planned on my life taking me.

Then again, when had plans ever taken her anywhere she really wanted to go? Alison floated from one emergency to another like some attention-deficit avenging angel.

That life suited her, though. No distractions. Nothing to tie her down. Just her and her sometimes warped sense of justice.

And the who knows how many men currently staring at me.

She lifted her hands and toyed with her curly blonde hair, knowing it would lift her shirt and show off a strip of skin between the top and her tight leather pants.

"Come on, baby, show us something good!" one of the men called out.

Alison offered him a mocking smile, playing the line between tease and whore, while reminding herself to keep her eyes on the prize.

She wanted to entice. To lure someone into a chase. To do that, she needed the faceless men to covet her, to want to not only have her, but break her.

It was a difficult line to walk, but she had no other choice.

She'd tracked down every lead she had, every shady contact and blackmailable asshole she could find, turned over anything she could follow up on and called in all her favors for what little information existed—her friend Anne had been abducted by local scouts looking for omegas to sell off. It was the only thing that made any sense, but the time to find her was running out.

That thought threw off her rhythm, but she disguised it as an alcohol-fueled slip before she crawled off the table and sauntered toward the back area of the bar where she had her things.

The music pounded in her veins, so loud she felt as though her heart followed its pace. This was the third night she'd pulled this stunt, and still to no avail. Plenty of offers for quickies in the bathroom, a few who'd suggested paying her for the night and one man who had even wanted to become her 'sugar-daddy'. She'd turned them all down.

She would have even if she didn't have a job to do. The last thing she needed was to get involved with anyone, let alone the drunken filth at a place like this, the men who thought she was the floozy dancing on the bar top, the ones who saw her as some wild, slutty woman in need of their firm hand.

I'd cut their hand off if they tried.

If they spent five minutes with her—the real her—they'd realize their mistake.

This was a game she was playing. It had started with the tight pants, with the shirt that read *OMEGA: BETAS NEED KNOT APPLY,* and had continued with the face she knew was a trap.

Her wild, curly hair, her full lips—those things had always made her look young and innocent. A gift from her mother, she supposed, from what she could remember. Not that it mattered. While she didn't care about looking pretty, she wouldn't deny that her features had helped her more than once. Men turned complacent when there was a pretty face across from them. They started thinking with their dick, and that always helped Alison.

She opened her water, listening for the click to show the seal was intact, before gulping down nearly half the bottle in one go. Her normal exercise routine didn't involve things like dancing, and she'd woken the morning after each time with a deep ache in her muscles.

Tomorrow would be no different.

"You look good out there." The man who spoke stood just beside her table.

One inhalation let her know—*alpha.* It required a person getting rather close for her to tell, what with all the bodies packed in so closely in the club, but once she found that sickly-sweet smell, it couldn't be denied.

It was always like tasting fake sugar to her. Something she wanted to like, something she should enjoy…and yet something that she knew to be artificial. One taste and she'd regret it.

Which is why I've stayed the fuck away from alphas all my life.

"Thanks," she said, sliding back into her 'I'm a bad girl who needs a strong man to put me in my place' persona. "I just *love* dancing."

"I can tell. This place is a little loud for a good conversation. Want to head out? Find somewhere quiet?"

She fought the urge to roll her eyes. Why did men always try such stupid tactics? Instead, she curled her painted red lips into a smirk. "Thanks, but I don't go home with strange men—at least not on the first night."

He returned the smile, then nodded. "Sure thing. Well, maybe next time?"

When he walked away, Alison's smile dropped. They normally didn't give up that easily. Maybe he wasn't as certain he could close the deal as others?

Or is it something more…

Was he the one she was looking for? Could he have been one of the scouts using this club as their hunting ground? She could say the one looking for her, but she didn't care for putting herself in the prey category.

Alison was *not* prey. She was a predator through and through.

All she had to do was lure something in by playing the drunken, defenseless omega, and when the asshole tried to pounce?

Alison would show her teeth.

Kyle tried to ignore the omega swaying to the music on the bar, the one with the curly blonde hair and no sense of self-preservation.

He wasn't a victim blamer, but after all he'd seen, there were times he wanted to grab a few women and make them look at what happened to those who weren't careful enough. He wished they lived in a world where that wasn't true—he'd lived his life trying to make that world—but a person could only see so many crime scenes of murdered omegas before they had to accept the reality.

In their world, a woman alone, drunk and making a spectacle of herself was at very high risk.

Don't think about it. You have other things to worry about tonight.

"Anything interesting?" Daniel took a sip of his drink—a dark glass to disguise the fact that the cup held water rather than liquor. Funny, because Daniel still looked out of place. No matter what the man did, he always looked like someone's best friend. Short, soft brown hair and earnest, almost honey-colored eyes kept him from fitting in somewhere like this.

How the two had become best friends was the sort of mystery people couldn't solve. Daniel was kind but a worrier. Kyle? He tended to make a joke of everything, never taking life too seriously. Daniel looked like a cop and Kyle like someone Daniel might arrest.

Opposites attracted, though, and they'd been friends for so long, he couldn't recall much of a life without the man who was more than a brother to him.

Kyle shook his head. "Nothing yet. A few familiar faces, but that's it."

Daniel huffed before leaning back in the booth. "Felicity isn't going to make much of an impact with Blondey up there doing her one-woman show."

"Maybe the scouts would rather take an easier prize." Kyle let his gaze shift to the woman at the bar—long black hair, dark eyes, high cheekbones. Felicity was, without a doubt, pretty.

"I don't like her here," Daniel offered for what had to be the millionth time.

"I don't like it either, but we don't get to make all the rules. Besides, do you have a better idea than bait?"

A soft growl was Daniel's response at first. "We're supposed to be keeping omegas safe, not dangling them in front of the bad guys like carrots."

Kyle wanted to argue, but he'd been about as comfortable with the entire plan. Despite him and Daniel running the task force who searched for the slavery ring, they still had bosses, and those bosses had thought some undercover work—in this case having Felicity pose as a flirty omega to entice a scout—was the best in for them.

Catch the scouts when they moved in, then leverage that to find the information they needed.

And all of it in time.

Kyle rubbed his eyes, the lack of sleep getting to him.

How was he supposed to sleep when all he could think of was the fucking calendar? He'd see the days passing, the weeks, and that huge box circled in red two months away.

The final slave auction.

The last chance to take down the people he'd chased for years, the last chance to get those in charge, the ones who would have the names of the slaves already sold, who could help them recover so many omegas who had gone missing over the years.

But to do it, they had to find an in. They knew the date, but the location would only be revealed to buyers and scouts with *merchandise.*

Which left them exactly nowhere. Just grasping at straws, which had a young, inexperienced FBI agent like Felicity wearing a short skirt and corset top, hoping like hell someone took the bait before they ran out of time.

Because time was not on their side.

Trent lifted his lip and snarled softly at the men that surrounded him in the club. They all stunk of sweat and lust and made his temper worse than usual.

He *hated* places like this.

He'd much prefer to be home with a good show on and a pizza than out here, with the loud music and drunken idiots.

Unfortunately, home wasn't an option right then. Instead, he'd been forced to go out in order to pick up a delinquent minor who thought heading to a place like this was a good idea.

Trent rolled his shoulder as he tried to ease the tension that held all his muscles rigid. He pictured little Kat, the fifteen-year-old daughter of one of his clients. The girl, like all teens, thought she knew everything. What she thought most of all was that she was dearly in love with an idiot, predatory twenty-five-year-old, the same one who had wanted her to meet him at this club.

Her mother had called Trent in a panic, and Trent, being the nice guy he was, had agreed to go get her. Her uncle was just outside, ready to bring her back after Trent had found her.

It seemed her uncle, while being a caring and loving father figure, might not fare well against the sorts of people who frequented this place.

Which was fine with Trent. He didn't mind playing the scary one or convincing people to do as he said, because he looked like the type of person who'd slit someone's throat without blinking.

Sure enough, in the corner, Trent spotted the girl. She wasn't smiling, her eyes large and wary, as though she'd realized what a huge mistake this had been.

Poor girl. People ought to learn things from others instead of having to live through the lessons themselves.

Trent had lived through his fair share of them, so he knew what the fuck he was talking about.

He walked over, and the relief on her face when she spotted him about made up for ruining his night. Hell, at least she thought of him as a good thing.

"I'm so sorry," she started to say before her asshole 'boyfriend' held his hand up to her face to silence her.

"Quiet, Kat. Who is this asshole?" The man who was way too old to have anything to do with a fifteen-year-old eyed Trent as if he might be willing to take him on.

That was when Trent saw it, the way he could always spot it. The man was an alpha. Kat was a beta as far as they knew—she hadn't had a heat, but she was still young enough that she could—but the man? Alpha through and through. He was the worst sort, too, the kind who thought that because of his designation he should be given shit, that he deserved whatever he wanted, no matter what anyone else said.

"Her mom asked me to get her home," Trent responded, not giving the man an inch of space. He sure as hell didn't cower to twenty-five-year-old self-important pricks.

"Yeah, well, she isn't ready to go home. When we're done with her, we'll send her on back." The man cast a suggestive look Kat's way then laughed with his buddies, as if that were the funniest thing he'd ever heard anyone say.

Well, guess I'm not walking out of here without bloodying something on this asshole. Kat letting out the saddest little whimper and curling her shoulders in solidified it.

It reminded him of when he'd met Kat's mother, of how the woman had stepped into his gym, her shoulders curling in just the same way, a shaking little thing who was terrified of the world.

Kat had played in the gym while Trent had trained her mother, when they'd spent week after week, then month after month working on self-defense. Now, at fifteen, Kat had started lessons as well.

Still, he hated to see that same fear.

"Look, asshole," Trent said. Even using something passive-aggressive like 'buddy' didn't seem right. Nope, he wanted no question about exactly what he thought of the fucker. "Kat's coming home, now."

"And if I say no?" The man grinned wide, his entitled bullshit spread out across his face.

"Well, then I'm thinking I'll make it so that pretty face isn't too pretty anymore. Then? I'll make sure the police know you're picking up fifteen-year-olds, because last I checked, that's statutory rape."

He snickered, setting a hand on the back of Kat's neck and pulling her in close to him. "She wouldn't turn me in, would you, sweetheart?"

Kat pressed against his chest, but it didn't budge him. "I want to go home," she said in a voice that lacked the strength it should have had.

"Don't be like that. We haven't even started having fun. Bet you I can get you moaning in no time." The man leaned in to kiss her.

Trent drew his hand into a fist, ready to nail the fucker and teach him in no uncertain terms what 'no' meant.

Instead, Kat moved. She did it so quickly, as though by muscle memory. She stomped down on the man's foot, which made him step backward and loosen his grip. Next, she brought her knee up into his groin, rewarded with his howl, and finally set her hand on the back of his head to yank him down into her rising knee.

The crunch of his nose might have been the best thing Trent had heard in a long damn time, though the wail the fucker let out when she'd gotten his goods had been up there.

Still, before anyone got any stupid ideas, Trent put his hand out. Kat grasped it so he could pull her to his side, then pressed her behind him.

"That fucking bitch," spat the man as he stood, blood pouring down his face. He took a step forward, as though he planned to do something, but one look at Trent seemed to make him reconsider.

The man might think he was tough when it came to a fifteen-year-old-girl, but facing off against a fully grown alpha like Trent was an entirely different matter.

Trent had spent his life being the alpha people watched carefully. Standing at a touch over six and a half feet and with the sort of physique he'd built up through a hell of a lot of work, he was used to making people nervous. Add to it his shaved head and sharp features—well, Trent was good at intimidating people. Some thin pup barely out of his teenage years wasn't much of a challenge, and it seemed they both knew it.

"Whatever," the man muttered, taking a step backward. "The bitch isn't pretty enough to be worth the effort anyway."

Trent huffed a soft laugh at the lie. Why did men always try to use that? They sure as fuck thought the girl was pretty enough if they had a chance. They thought she was worth chasing after, but the moment they got turned down, she became ugly.

Kat went willingly, and the hand-off to her uncle didn't have any issues. It seemed she'd had her taste of trouble and had realized maybe it wasn't worth it. She gave Trent a hug and a muffled thank-you spoken against his chest. He hugged her back, awkward as ever, and told her how proud he was of her for using what he'd taught her.

As they drove away, he grinned. *She'll be just fine.*

There was nothing better than watching a girl go from a scared thing and grow into a person who knew what they were capable of. He'd watched it—helped it happen—with so many women over the years.

He shook free the thought.

He needed to head back in, to settle things with the owner, smooth over any bad feelings. The last thing he wanted was cops showing up at Kat's place because the asshole in the club tried to press charges just to ruin her life. He seemed the type to do it, too.

Trent made his way through the crowded club, toward the back where the staff door sat. Just before making it there, though, he caught sight of the last thing he ever expected to see.

In the back booth, just beside the door, two alphas sat. He didn't tell that by the way they sat, by their demeanor. Instead, it was because he knew them—or had known them.

The two alphas who had been more than brothers to him for so long, the ones he hadn't seen in eight years.

Knew I should have stayed home.

Daniel didn't bother to hide his surprise at seeing none other than Trent standing there, by their booth, looking similar to how he had before. Same ungodly large physique, same shaven head, same sharp features that seemed permanently carved into a scowl. Sure, he looked a bit more haggard, but that wasn't really a shocker.

Trent had never taken care of himself well and living alone hadn't done him any favors. Guilt gnawed at him, but Daniel refused to let it take hold. Anger made that easier.

Maybe it would be a good meeting, though. Maybe they'd see each other and laugh and let go of the past.

"What the fuck are you doing here?"

Or maybe not…

Kyle snorted softly, not seeming to take Trent's downright antagonistic tone to heart. "Last time I checked, you didn't own this town."

Trent's hands drew into fists. "You sure moved away quick enough. Thought that was you conceding this town to me."

Daniel spoke up, because they didn't have time for the back and forth. "We're not here to step on your toes. We'll be out of your way just as soon as we can."

Trent narrowed his eyes, the way he always did when figuring something out. He might look stupid—a side effect of his hard-ass attitude and his physique—but he was far from it. "You working?"

Daniel nodded once, sharp. Trent might not be with the FBI anymore, but he sure as hell knew what *working* meant to people who were.

Trent twisted, and he seemed able to follow their line of sight perfectly. Across the way, Felicity still sat alone by the bar. "She looks like a cop. Since when did they throw newbies out into field work?"

"Since we needed an omega," Kyle answered.

Trent made a disgruntled noise in return, and it wasn't as if Daniel could argue the point. The longer they watched Felicity, the more obvious it became she wasn't ready for the assignment.

Which left them with few options, none of them good.

Without meaning to, Daniel's gaze went back to the omega they'd seen before, the one in the tight leather pants. She was gathering her things to leave.

Good. She needs to get her ass home and safe.

"Fuck," Trent muttered and nodded toward the other side of the club.

Three men were eyeing the omega, and Daniel could read that sort of look. It wasn't anything good. They nodded, as though something had been decided, gazes pinned to her.

"We're on a job," Kyle reminded them.

"So you're going to let her just walk out into whatever they have planned?" Trent asked.

Daniel gritted his teeth. *No.* That wasn't going to happen. He used his nearly invisible earpiece to tell the agents in the van outside to keep a closer eye on Felicity.

Not like it matters. She's drawn no attention.

The omega rose, slinging her purse over her shoulder. She wasn't wearing heels, but she stumbled around as if she was. The girl was so drunk, he had no idea how she intended to get home. The need to take her aside and lecture her hit him.

Well, they'd probably get the chance. The night was a bust anyway, and he wanted to make sure the woman made it somewhere safe. When they got her into their car, they could make it clear her behavior was high risk, and exactly what could have happened.

Daniel eyed the woman stumbling their way—meaning she'd take the back exit to the parking lot rather than the front to the street. Another bad choice.

She really is a trifecta of horrible decision making, isn't she?

When Daniel went for the door ahead of her, Kyle on his heels, he was surprised to find Trent following. "This isn't your problem," Daniel bit out.

"This is *my* town, and I don't much like women being targeted here. So, yeah, I think I'll stay until I know she's fine." Trent wouldn't budge. Daniel recognized the steel in his voice, the fact that this was one of his hot-button topics.

It was hard to argue. He might not be happy with Trent, but he trusted him more than he did those other three men in the club. What if they headed out, too? What if they came looking for the omega? The last thing Daniel wanted was to end up outnumbered.

Besides, what if *they* were the scouts they were looking for? An extra set of hands was always useful.

When they walked out into the back parking lot, it was dark, with only one dim light above the door to illuminate anything. Few customers used it, since it was mostly employee parking. A front entrance went to the street, and a side to the parking lot customers used.

The van with the other agents sat in the parking lot of a bakery across the street, but Daniel didn't worry. Felicity was capable, even if she'd turned out to be terrible bait.

The woman stumbled from the door, laughing and looking as coordinated as a dog on ice skates. She stumbled, pressing a hand to the wall of the building to keep herself upright.

She was pretty—hard to deny that—but in her current state it felt wrong to even notice that. Not to mention that an omega, especially one like this, who seemed determined to become a statistic, was a horrible bet on his part. He'd worked enough cases to know the risks to omegas. Not to mention he had no desire to try to see one through the trauma they always seemed to have.

Nope. I'll stick to betas, thank you very much.

From the side of the building, around the corner, two of the men who had been eyeing the girl appeared.

Well, this just got worse.

Chapter Two

Alison didn't care for playing the drunken damsel. She'd worked so hard to become strong that making herself appear weak felt like a huge hit to her ego.

However, that didn't matter when she felt as though she had finally made progress. She'd spotted the man who had hit on her, and how he'd gone back to another two men, all three looking her way. In addition, another trio, who been sitting in a booth near the back door, their staring less obvious yet more intense, had left the club just in front of her.

Either could be nothing—just men looking for an easy target—but Alison doubted it. Both had studied her differently.

Lust, that she understood. She'd seen lust play across the features of so many men that she could spot it from anywhere. These two groups, however, had something else, something more clinical, more detached.

Since only one scouting group appeared to hunt in this area from what she had been able to find out, the odds were good that both sets of scouts worked for the same people. The larger groups took swaths of territory and hired nobodies to actually snatch the girls. It limited their risk. That hadn't been easy information to find, but Alison was nothing if not tenacious.

If she could just get taken to the general holding area for omegas, she'd find her friend.

"Hey, sweet," one of the men closest to her said, the one with the short, soft-looking hair and dark brown eyes. "You doing okay?"

"M'fine," she slurred, giving him a grin that was all tease. "Heading home."

"Right, well, maybe we should give you a ride there. Not sure you're sober enough to make it yourself." This time the larger alpha spoke, the one with the buzzed hair, square jawline and amber eyes.

He was *exactly* the sort of alpha to avoid, the kind far larger and stronger than anyone needed to be. Despite his nice words, his voice was deep and rough.

"Hey!" called a man from the other group.

Come on, let's play nice. Just abduct me and get this over with.

"We saw her first," said the man who had hit on her earlier. "She's ours."

"Fuck off," responded the large, scary alpha, who didn't sound nearly so sweet when talking to them. "If she was yours, you'd be here."

Group two shifted, as if not sure they wanted to go up against the others.

Alison couldn't blame them. Group two seemed like the everyday punks who thought they were tough because they'd gotten used to scaring people who couldn't fight back. Group one, though? They struck her as men who not only could defend themselves but had no issue doing so—especially the one with the shaved head.

"But—" a man in group two said.

The man with the short dark hair and kind eyes gave the other group a chilling look. "You're going to have to decide if she's worth it, because it's going to get very costly for you in a minute."

The other man took a step backward, though he didn't seem entirely cowed. "Yeah, well, don't get comfortable here. I haven't seen you before, and this area is already spoken for. This isn't over." With that, they backed off.

So, looks like group one is the winner.

Once the others had scurried off, and the winning group surrounded her, they seemed rushed. *Probably want to get me out of here before the others come back with more.*

She played her part perfectly, trying to look nervous, to back away until she pressed against the wall of the building and could go no farther. When she dashed forward, to break through them, the one who hadn't spoken grabbed her and hauled her against his solid chest. He had brown hair, long enough to brush the collar of his shirt, pushed back. She flailed, making sure not to fight hard enough to *actually* break his hold.

"We're not going to hurt you."

Liar. She'd seen enough to know exactly what happened to omegas who were sold, and they most definitely got hurt.

Except then the alpha kept speaking. "We're FBI. Just relax."

Shit.

Suddenly the way they'd moved, the way they'd watched the club, all made sense. They'd picked the spot that best overlooked the club, had seemed to know immediately where all the exits were.

Yeah, they were trained, and FBI made as much sense as anything else.

Being brought in by the FBI was about the last thing she needed.

Which meant this little interaction was officially over.

Kyle held the omega tightly and tried to ignore how good she smelled, and how perfectly her body pressed against him. Sure, with her being drunk, it wasn't as if he'd actually act on it, but he was a man, after all.

Not just a man but an alpha. What alpha could be expected to entirely ignore a squirming omega?

He'd whispered to her the truth, hoping to calm her. She was panicking as if stressed—something that annoyed his alpha side—but oddly he scented no fear on her.

Then again, scent was a tricky thing. He'd learned it wasn't always reliable.

When he said they were FBI, that fight drained out of her.

Good.

He loosened his grip, not wanting to frighten her any more.

She swung her head backward, nailing him in the nose with a sickening crunch. His eyes watered before the pain registered, and he let go of her immediately.

What the fuck? Finding out he was one of the good guys was supposed to calm her, not set her off.

Kyle brought his hands to his face, the wetness telling him he was bleeding, his vision blurry. Anyone who said getting hit in the nose wasn't a big deal was a liar.

He was pretty sure she'd broken the damn thing.

"Hold up," Daniel said in that 'I'm a good guy' voice he had. If anyone could calm a panicking omega, it was Daniel. Except, then a grunt that Kyle would have recognized anywhere as Daniel's said that he hadn't quite succeeded.

Kyle blinked away the tears in his eyes, that damn automatic reaction, in time to see Trent barring her escape. He had his hands up, palms out. "Already told you that we aren't here to hurt you."

The omega didn't back down—not that he was suddenly believing the whole ploy. She'd gone rather quickly from so drunk she couldn't walk to surprising two trained FBI agents.

It seemed she wasn't exactly what she'd pretended to be.

The omega dashed forward, but Trent countered, able to avoid a strike to his ribs and twist her body until she leaned against him.

While Kyle and Daniel both knew about fighting—they had to in their line of work—Trent had always been the best at it. Suddenly he wasn't quite as annoyed about Trent staying.

She swung her head back, but it seemed Trent had learned from Kyle's mistake, because he tilted his to avoid it. When she tried to stomp on his foot, he quickly shifted it. The two seemed evenly matched.

At least, that was what Kyle thought until the omega lifted her foot to stomp again. Trent moved to dodge the hit, but doing so meant he had to shift his weight. The omega threw her body in that direction, unsettling Trent's stance and bringing them both toppling down.

It was almost beautiful, in a twisted and violent way.

Trent put his arm out, trying to stop his fall from crushing the much smaller omega beneath him. That seemed to be exactly what she'd been waiting for, because she rolled when she hit the ground, avoiding Trent's attempts to grab her again. She was quick, small and a few steps ahead.

That gave her an advantage, because before Trent could rise, before he could pick up all his bulk from the ground, the omega got her feet beneath her and took off.

She rushed toward the back of the parking lot and scaled the chain link fence as if the fight hadn't winded her at all.

Kyle kept his hands over his nose, despite the stickiness of blood leaking down over his lips. "Well, damn. Can't say I expected that."

Daniel and Trent both grunted softly, as if in agreement.

Then again, who would ever have expected a tiny omega to lay out three full-sized alphas?

If he'd been attracted before…it was nothing close to now.

Chapter Three

Alison threw her shirt into the laundry basket much harder than she needed to, but damnit, she couldn't help it.

She'd been planning for weeks. She'd had everything in place.

This was supposed to be the night she finally got some real information, the night everything paid off.

Instead, some do-gooder FBI agents had butted in—thinking they were white knights, as all men did—and she'd walked away with nothing.

The scouts had seen her face now, which meant she couldn't just go out and hope to catch their attention again. If she showed up at the same club, it would be far too suspicious.

She stripped out of her clothing, wanting to wash away the scent of the club, the sweat from her dancing, the smells of the alphas. Maybe after that she'd feel better about it.

Not likely.

The hot water relaxed her, but it didn't solve the problem. She was still fucked.

She didn't have a lead. Her one shot had been entirely ruined.

Worse? She couldn't seem to scrub the alphas who had messed everything up from her mind.

The one who had grabbed her, with his smooth voice and warm body. The one who had tried to grab her, his eyes far too kind. Lastly, the one she'd tangled with the most, the one who had nearly bested her, the large one who had barred the door.

Why had they been so interesting?

Because no matter how much I fight it, I'm an omega at the end of the day, and tough alphas are my weakness.

She snarled softly at herself. No. She was so much more than an omega. She'd worked hard to become more.

There was no way she was going to let herself be distracted by some trio of assholes who had caused her nothing but trouble.

Still, their scents…

She slid her hand down her body, gliding over her skin because of the pouring water. She thought about fighting that need, but she knew better.

Living as long as she had on her own had taught her that ignoring needs didn't fix anything. She couldn't ignore a heat and she couldn't ignore the reaction she had to alphas. All she could do was refuse to give in to it, and that was easier when she wasn't wound up and horny.

So she let her fingers dip between her thighs, telling herself it had *nothing* to do with the three men.

But as they filled her head while she brought herself to climax, she knew that was a damn lie.

* * * *

Daniel took a beer from Tiffany, laughing at a joke her mate Marshall had made.

Even on days when frustration ate at him, when he could find no good in his job, he needed only to take a look at Tiffany to remember *why* he did what he did.

He lost a whole hell of a lot of the cases he took. Often, he showed up at the end, and all he could do was find those who'd left bodies. When he had those images in his head, when they kept him up at night, it took seeing the ones he'd helped save to remind himself there was a point…some of the time.

Tiffany was young—barely more than a kid herself—and Daniel shuddered to think of what the slavery ring he was after would have done if they'd managed to catch and keep her.

Instead of that fate, she was happy. She had three mates who adored her, and last he'd heard, they were looking at opening up a coffee shop. She had a future, a family.

It didn't take away the sting of his failures, the hurt at the lives he couldn't save, but it helped him tell himself it was all worth it.

"Kyle seems testier than usual," Tiffany pointed out, nodding at where Kyle stood on the back porch with Kieran, another of Tiffany's mates.

"Well, you saw his face."

"Isn't getting bruised up part of your job?"

"Sure, but I think when it's a five-foot-tall omega who does it, his pride gets a bit wounded."

Tiffany laughed hard enough that she spat some of the water out and had to use her hand to cover her mouth. After that, there was some choking, but when she finally regained her breath, she smirked. "Please tell me she had blue hair."

Daniel snorted, thinking about the omega thief Tiffany referred to. "If Kara had been involved, she'd have gone for his balls, I'm sure." The viciousness of *that* omega was well known, especially now that she and her mates were helping in the slavery ring investigation. It had been their efforts that had gotten them their first inside contact, as trustworthy as any slaver could be when he'd turned only to reduce his eventual sentence. "This omega was different. Shoulder-length curly blonde hair, green eyes."

Tiffany's back went straight, and Kane groaned.

"Do you know her?"

"You just saw her last night? You're sure?" Panic bled through Tiffany's voice.

Daniel nodded. "Close enough for her to break Kyle's nose and put down another friend of ours. I got a shot to the ribs, but I'm pretty sure that made me the lucky one."

"That sounds like Alison all right," Kane muttered.

Alison. Daniel tried to pair the name with the face, to see if that could have been the girl.

Then again, she was an enigma to him. She had the face of some sweet, mythical creature, like a sea nymph. Of course, she hadn't looked so innocent when she'd attacked.

Even sexier, though…

"Tell me about this Alison."

Tiffany pressed her lips together. *Right. Omegas always stick together against the big bad alphas.*

"I don't want to cause her any problems," Daniel said.

"*If* it's her, she busted the nose of an FBI agent. I don't feel like that's something you'd track her down just to give her a pat on the back for."

Daniel rubbed his hand over the back of his neck. "We don't blame her, because she had no reason to trust us. That's all good." He'd love to say it was square because they'd both gotten their licks in, but the truth was that he and the other two alphas had had their asses handed to them by that one little girl. *And there goes that totally inappropriate erection again…*

Daniel clearly had terrible taste in women.

"There are scouts looking for omegas right now, and she needs to understand that. I don't want to bring her in on charges. I don't want to get her into trouble. I just want her to understand that this area is dangerous right now, and she needs to be more careful."

Kane snorted hard. "Right. *Alison* needs to be careful."

Daniel gave the other alpha a withering look. "If you have something useful to contribute, go for it."

"Let's not bullshit. You seriously think you aren't throwing off some really aroused scent right now? Don't pretend like this is some fucking nobility shit."

Daniel's jaw popped as he ground his teeth together. "Fine. She was attractive. That's not why I'm looking for her." *Does a half-truth still count as a lie?*

"Doesn't matter," Kane said. "Trust me, if anyone is in danger, it's anyone stupid enough to tangle with her. She doesn't need your help."

Daniel's annoyance slid away with this new tidbit of information. "Who is she? I looked for any records of an omega matching her description. Nothing. I figured anyone running cons—"

"She doesn't run cons," Tiffany snapped.

Daniel lifted his hands, palms out, to placate her. "It was just a guess, Tiff. She pretended to be drunk, which seemed an awful lot like a great scam to rob guys. I figured when she realized we weren't good targets, she bailed."

Kane shook his head. "If that girl was there, it wasn't to pick up a few bucks off drunken idiots. She had bigger fish to fry."

Daniel frowned. *She couldn't be after the slavery ring…*

"But you don't know what she was doing?"

Tiffany rested her elbows on the counter. "She's been missing for a few months, and no one's heard from her. I don't know what she's planning, but it's got to be important. She wouldn't fall out of contact otherwise."

"What was she doing before?"

"She's a fucking harpy," Kane said. "If you think Kara is a headache, she's nothing compared to Alison. That girl is some avenging angel who fucks up people who screw with omegas."

Fuck. Daniel growled softly. She *had* to be after the slavers. He couldn't think of another damn thing that made any sense.

The door shut as Kyle entered from the patio. "About that omega—"

"Alison. Yeah, I just heard."

Kyle took a seat beside Daniel. "You know…those scouts saw us nab her."

"Yeah, I recall having our cover blown."

Kyle shook his head. "They think we've got a slave for the auction."

That stilled Daniel. It was a horribly brilliant idea but…

He shook his head. "We can't get a civilian omega involved in this. It's too dangerous."

"She's already involved," Kyle pointed out. "From the sound of it, she's dangling herself in front of scouts as bait, except unlike Felicity, she has no back-up. So when someone *does* snag her, she'll be entirely on her own. Do you really think she wouldn't be better off with at least someone watching her?"

Daniel shifted on the stool, wanting so badly to argue. The idea of getting an omega involved in *this* felt wrong. He hadn't liked the idea of Felicity even, but she'd at least been a trained agent.

Alison? She might know how to fight, but that didn't mean she'd understand the risks.

But what other choice do we have?

"Do you know how to get hold of her?" Daniel asked, refusing to commit to the plan just yet.

Tiffany shook her head. "I asked around a few weeks ago, but she's completely off the map. She was really secretive already, and if she's doing what it sounds like she's doing, she probably didn't want to risk anyone else, thus the no contact."

"So you don't know anything?"

"She hasn't been back to her cabin that I know of—we drove up there a while back and there's no sign of life. Where else she lives or stays, I really don't know. She's always really private."

Daniel thought back to the cabin, the one he'd asked the alphas about on the day he'd gone up there to get Tiffany. It seemed he'd been circling around this Alison for a while without realizing it.

Daniel and Kyle said their goodbyes and thanked Tiffany, Kane, Marshall and Kieran for the hospitality.

"You know what we have to do," Kyle said. He was always the practical one, the one willing to admit to things Daniel didn't like to.

"He's already too involved."

"Yeah, but that's the thing. Those same scouts saw him with us. If we're really going to do this, we need him. Plus, he knows the area. If anyone can figure out where she is, it's Trent."

Daniel tightened his lips into a thin line, hating the entire idea. Trent couldn't be trusted and in Daniel's world, that was a hard limit.

Still, he couldn't come up with a better option.

"Fine," Daniel snarled. "Because dealing with him once wasn't quite frustrating enough, let's go see Trent."

* * * *

Trent couldn't believe his ears. If he hadn't been the sort to avoid drugs and alcohol, he'd have said he had to be high, because there was no way Kyle and Daniel were standing in his gym asking him for a favor.

He crossed his arms, about half-a-second from kicking their asses out. It was what they'd have done if he'd ever showed up at their job.

"You're kidding me, right?"

Kyle snorted, but his smart-ass action didn't hold the same derisive attitude he probably wanted it to, because he flinched when it aggravated his nose.

Serves him right.

After a short moment, as if he had to collect himself, Kyle continued. "It's not my first choice either, but we're out of options."

"This how far you've fallen? All the preaching about good police work and rules, but you're willing to rest an entire case on an untrained civilian woman and me?" Trent whistled low. "That's sad."

Daniel cast his partner a sharp look, but it was one Trent knew just as well. *Shut up and let me handle this.*

Daniel did that a lot, stepping in as if he could clean up the messes of everyone around him. "This is a serious case, Trent."

"You think they're *all* serious. Does that help you sleep at night? Thinking everything you do is for a good cause?"

"What I do *is* for a good cause, but I'm serious on this one."

"Don't need to hear about it." Trent turned his back, ready to shut himself in his office until they left. He'd done this with them before. He'd worked with them before. It had all blown up in his face. "I don't need to go through this bullshit with you two again."

"We're going after the last slavery auction in the area," Kyle said.

That stilled Trent's feet.

Kyle kept going. "If we don't catch them now, we won't. They're packing up, and the next shot we'll have? Who knows when that will be. They've got a lot of omegas going onto the auction block in eight weeks, judging by all those missing in this area, and even if we catch the assholes behind this years from now, those women? They'll be gone forever."

Trent drew his hands into fists, frustration soaking into him. He *wanted* to keep walking. He wanted to tell them to fuck off, that this wasn't his problem.

He remembered the last real time they'd talked, when Trent had broken down and told them he was leaving the FBI, when he'd thrown in the towel. He'd needed them then, but what had happened?

They'd taken the move as some sort of insult and kept right on going with their own lives.

But then he thought about the omegas he'd helped, the ones he'd trained up from nothing, and there had been a few who had tasted the life the omegas in that auction would be subjected to.

"I can tell you where she probably works out, given how she fought, but that's all you're getting from me."

Daniel crossed his arms, the scowl looking odd on the alpha's face. Daniel didn't scowl as a rule, or at least he never had in their long friendship. "You can't just turn your back on this. It's important."

"I told you before, I'm out. I can't do this again. It nearly fucking dragged me under last time, and you want me to jump back in? Just pick up and follow because you tell me to? Where the hell have you two been for the last eight years?" The question escaped before he could censor it. *Fuck.* He sounded like a jaded woman, not a man whose friends had moved on when he didn't fit into their lives anymore.

He didn't take the words back, though.

Kyle answered him. "What did you want us to do? You decide one day to quit, to just uproot your entire life. Did you want us to do it, too? To give up everything we wanted because you decided it was too hard? We were more than friends, damn it, and you were the one who decided to change it all. You can't be pissed when we didn't follow where you decided to go."

Trent tore his gaze away, hating how neither of them was wrong. Trent had changed the rules, but fuck, Kyle and Daniel had damn well disappeared, as if Trent wasn't worth even sticking around for. Years of working together, of living together, of taking women together like some fucking little family and all it had taken was quitting the FBI for them to wash their hands of him?

"It doesn't really matter, does it? Who cares anymore who did what or why or whose damn fault it all was. It's eight years too late for those conversations. You guys decided you didn't need me a long time ago. I see no reason why that should change now." Trent went to walk past them—to where, he didn't know, since it was his gym.

Kyle caught his arm. "Remember that last case we had?"

Of course he did. It haunted Trent like his own personal poltergeist, keeping him up at night, springing out of the darkness when he finally thought he was free. It hit him like it always did, right in the gut as he recalled the body of the omega in the hospital room, the woman he couldn't save. Her blood had seemed so dark against her pale skin. "Yeah, I remember."

"Well we're trying to save a lot of women from that same fate. Are you really going to turn your back on that? Can you live with yourself knowing that they might all die, and all for your pride?"

No doubt Kyle knew the answer before he asked. Trent looked like a fucking monster, but he wasn't one, not by a long shot. "Fine," he growled out. "Tell me what you need." He turned and jammed a finger in their direction. "But let's make this fucking clear. I'm helping for *them,* not for you. I want you gone as soon as possible."

"The feeling's mutual," Kyle said.

Look at that, we can still agree on something.

* * * *

Alison loved her gym.

Okay, so it wasn't *hers,* but she spent so much time there, it felt more like her place than her own apartment.

Only her cabin made her feel better, but she hadn't been back there in over six months.

You know it's too dangerous.

If she ended up targeted by the slavers, she wanted there to be no connection to anyone. It was why she'd cut ties, why she'd made sure no one could trace her back to the people she cared about.

Her feet struck the treadmill as she ran, sweat running down her back, soaking into her sports bra.

Her failure the other night, paired with her reaction to those alphas, had her needing to run herself to exhaustion just to deal with it.

When she did this, when she pushed her body to its limits and forced it to adapt, she didn't feel like such a failure. She didn't feel weak or useless or anything.

Still, today might have been a *bit* more than usual. The owner of the gym had cast her a few concerned looks—probably didn't want her passing out and hitting her head—but she waved off his concern as she guzzled down more water.

The steady thump of her feet against the treadmill belt helped relax her. Music in her headphones drowned out the world around her. It let her sink into the rhythm of her steps, into the simple movements that made her feel free.

At least, it did until her machine stopped. She came forward, catching herself on the console, her eyes flying open. Had she accidently pulled the emergency stop? Had she broken the damned thing?

Nope. Even worse.

The three alphas from the night before stood in front of her.

Chapter Four

Alison crossed her arms and leaned against the large desk in the gym manager's office, which he'd been only too happy to offer for their little talk.

While Alison didn't *want* to talk to the three, she figured it was better to do it there than risk them infiltrating her life any further.

"Cops or not, stalking is illegal," she said.

The one with a busted nose—and didn't *that* cheer her up?—answered. "We aren't cops and we didn't stalk you." He lifted his hand when she went to argue. "That is Daniel, my name is Kyle, and we are FBI agents."

"Same difference. The law is the law," she reminded them.

Alison had no love for law enforcement. Sure, some of them were good, she'd bet. However, she'd seen enough do nothing, had seen them turn a blind eye to horrible things, all because it benefited them to do so. And even if she honestly believed all cops were good, that they were doing their best, they were still helping a corrupt system that constantly shoved omegas into danger and servitude.

"And him?" She nodded at the largest of the three, the one she'd tangled with the most the other night.

"Trent," he said. "Not FBI. Just someone in the wrong place, wrong time."

Well, that she could understand. Wasn't that how she'd gotten there, too? Still, in the light of the office, she was able to get a better look.

Trent was, by far, the most striking. She wouldn't call him handsome so much as powerful. His broad shoulders and height meant he took up far too much space in the small room, and his shaved head didn't soften him at all. He looked every bit the dangerous man he'd proven himself to be the night before.

Or perhaps part of that was how different he seemed from the other two. He and Daniel were opposites, with Daniel being soft in all the ways Trent wasn't. The soft, short, dark hair which Daniel wore offset his brown eyes and his 'you can trust me' face.

And Kyle? He sat in between them, smaller than Trent yet more muscular than Daniel. His hair was pushed backward, and a thin mustache and goatee made him look a bit like a stereotypical bad cop. Still, those blue eyes of his were set off by the darkness of his hair.

"So, you tracked me down. Now what?"

"We aren't going to arrest you," Daniel said.

"Then again, I ask, now what?"

"We had a chance to talk with a friend of yours."

"I doubt it. I don't have friends."

"Tiffany."

The name caused a shot of anxiety to surge through her. "If you did anything to her—"

"We didn't. We were the ones who helped make sure she was safe a few months ago. When we described the omega who did *that* to Kyle's nose, she seemed to know exactly who we were talking about."

"And she told you?" A sickness settled into Alison at the idea of being outed that way. This was why she kept her distance. Being around people was a risk, one she needed to knock off.

"She didn't," Kyle cut in. "Trent figured out your gym based on how you fought. Only so many places in town you could have gone to learn that. Kane offered up a bit, but only the basics. Said you were known for protecting omegas, and that you'd fallen off the radar for a while. You've been worrying your friends."

"Again, I don't have friends."

"Funny, that isn't what *they* say." Kyle lifted an eyebrow as if that were some telling statement.

It wasn't. Other people liked to romanticize relationships, and they loved doing it with her. They probably saw her as some lost puppy needing a pack, so even if they weren't actually close, other people liked to pretend there were connections that didn't exist.

"Your point? I'm getting bored."

Trent's lips curled up at that, but he still didn't speak.

Daniel kept going. "We know you were going after the slavery ring."

That got her attention.

"What do you know about it?"

"More than we can share right now. But it seems like we're after the same people."

She pressed her lips together as she worked that bit of information into what she already knew. "So you were there doing recon?" She groaned a moment later.

"That dark-haired omega, she was your plant, wasn't she?"

Alison should have felt bad for thinking unkindly, but she'd seen that omega a mile off. The woman had been entirely uncomfortable and stuck out. She'd assumed the woman had been playing some 'sexy strangers' game, or perhaps had gone there on a first date. Realizing she was bait for the scouts made it even sadder, though.

"She shouldn't be anywhere near undercover work. I spotted her the second she walked in."

"Do you think you could do better?"

"I *did* do better, and if you three hadn't tried to play hero, I'd be exactly where I wanted to be."

"At the hands of scouts?" Kyle asked, his tone dry.

"On my way to getting the information for the auction. Only scouts and buyers are given it. So if I'm with a scout, I get into the auction."

The simultaneous looks of something between annoyance and horror were nearly comical. It seemed none of the alphas were thrilled with her perfectly laid-out strategy.

Well, it would have been perfect if they hadn't gotten involved.

"Getting yourself in the hands of people who sell omegas like cattle maybe wasn't your best plan," Trent said. "Or hell, maybe it was, and you just have really shitty decision making. Do you have any idea what those people do to the woman they catch?"

Alison's mind drifted back to a long time before, to when she'd been more personally acquainted with exactly what slavery looked like. *No. I won't let that grab me.* She refused to sink back there, to remember it all. Instead, she squared her shoulders and met Trent's gaze. "Yes, I know *exactly* what happens to women in that position."

Trent pulled back, as though the knowledge sat in her expression and he didn't much care for it.

Before it could morph into pity, before he could ask—because she damn well wouldn't tell them anything—she continued, "However, unlike you, I've actually done my research. Every scout team has an area and a specialty. That bar is handled by a few people who always bring wild omegas. Their buyers want omegas who can be broken. That means they don't hurt, rape or otherwise mistreat their *products*, or else it dims some of that fight."

And there it is. Surprise.

I hate being underestimated.

It had always been true, that because of her pretty face and youthful looks, people thought her dumb. They never realized how clever she was until she outwitted them.

"How exactly did you get all that information?"

"The FBI isn't the only one with sources, and mine are just a lot better."

Daniel shook his head. "It was still a dangerous game to play."

"Well, we're running out of time. The auction is in eight weeks, and if I'm not there—" She cut herself off before she said the rest.

The hell? She normally excelled at being tight-lipped, yet, somehow, she was ready to spill her secrets to these three. What caused that? She'd been attracted to plenty of people before, so she couldn't believe it was just that she'd gotten off to fantasies about them. Could it be that she didn't deal with alphas like this—not even one, let alone three—and that created the pull? Whatever it was, she didn't care for it.

"What happens if you're not there?" Kyle pushed.

"Nothing that's any concern of yours. Are we done?"

"Not yet. We have a proposition for you."

Alison let out a short, harsh laugh. "Yeah, buddy, you're barking up the wrong tree. I am not an omega you want to proposition."

Daniel stepped in. "Not like that. The other scouts saw us grab you. Our plant was obviously useless. Now that we've been noticed, we can't keep hoping to find scouts to track. It leaves us with one more option."

Alison's stomach sank as she realized exactly where this *option* was going. It felt like a car crash, when everything slowed down, when she could see the other car heading for her but couldn't do a thing to stop it.

And just like that car, Daniel kept going. "We want to go undercover and pose as scouts looking to sell at the auction."

Which, since the other scouts had seen them pick her up, was believable.

"And me?" She didn't need to ask. She knew exactly where she fitted into the plan. Still, something inside her wouldn't make that jump on her own.

"You'll pose as the slave we're selling."

* * * *

"I hate this place," Trent said as he walked into the living room of the sprawling home, scowling as though it had personally offended him.

"You hate everything," Daniel pointed out.

It was one of those quirks he'd been used to when they'd spent more time together. Daniel was the levelheaded one, Kyle the jokester and Trent the cynic.

"How can you hate this?" Kyle asked. "It's basically a mansion."

Trent curled his lips, darting his gaze around the room. "It's too big."

"Big is good," Daniel pointed out. "Big says we're wealthy and assholes. Besides, Gregory assured us this will sell the story."

Gregory. Daniel tried to repress the shudder from even saying the man's name. He'd learned early in his career that to take down criminals, sometimes he'd have to work with people who seemed just as bad.

Gregory was one such man.

He'd been stalking an omega, using his connections to make her life hell, going so far as to abduct her at the end. That wasn't what had made him useful, though. Instead, it was his involvement with the slavery ring.

He was more of a silent partner—the type who put money in and handled details but never actually attended, saw, bought or sold the girls. That had meant that when he'd been caught, he'd been quick to offer up information in exchange for a lighter sentence.

In this case, it meant helping to sell the story about the three alphas being scouts from out of town. That included this house with a paper trail that would sell their story of being associates of slavers in the eastern parts of the country.

"Do you think she'll show?" Kyle asked.

"She will," Trent said from where he stood, staring out of the window.

"How can you be so sure?"

"Because I know that look in her eye."

"She looked scared to me," Kyle said, his voice softening. Then again, did any of them enjoy scaring women?

Maybe in some situations, but only when it's consensual.

"The idea of her being scared of us after what she did *to* us doesn't make a lot of sense," Daniel pointed out.

Trent shook his head. "You two don't get it. You've been dealing with the problem instead of the person for too long, and it's always made you miss things. That girl is stubborn as fuck. She's afraid, sure, but that sort of steel? She'll be here."

Daniel ran his fingers through his hair before broaching the topic *none* of them really wanted to address. "We haven't done this in a long time."

"We've never gone undercover as slavers," Trent said, purposely missing the point.

Daniel used his best 'I'm trying to be delicate, you idiot' voice. "We haven't co-topped anyone in a long time."

At that, Trent turned, his expression pinched tight as if he were trying to hide whatever was going on there. "We aren't co-topping shit. We are pretending to train a slave. That's it."

"And in pretending, we need to look like we're doing what we did together for a long fucking time," Kyle chimed in. He didn't sound happy about it, but were any of them?

It brought back memories—a lot of really good ones—of back when the three of them *had* been together, when they'd shared omegas, when they'd worked together to take apart a willing female. It had been a good life, no matter how it had ended.

And here they were, sharing one again. Sure, it was all make-believe, but that didn't change that the action would be the same. They'd still need to play the part, and that part was way too close to home.

Trent turned toward Daniel. "I can keep it professional. It isn't like we are *actually* going to be fucking her."

Daniel nodded. Sex wasn't needed for what they had going on. They'd need to deal with getting comfortable, with getting her comfortable, with how she needed to behave, but that didn't mean they actually had to indulge in what had once been such a large part of all of their lives.

Which made Daniel think back to the last time, just for a moment, before it had all gone bad.

The woman had been a beta—they tended to like betas since they were less complicated—and she'd had long red hair. It had curled at the ends, and the dim lights had brought out the freckles on her face. Her flush had looked lovely against the collar around her throat.

Daniel shook his head, trying to push back the thought. That had been a different time, when they'd been different. That had been back when they'd trusted one another, when they'd thought they *could* trust each other.

They'd grown since then, changed, learned the truth. Even though Kyle and Daniel had still taken women together, they hadn't indulged in the same sort of play.

It hadn't seemed right with just the two of them, as though something important were missing.

A knock on the door made Daniel stop and turn his head. It had to be her.

A small part of him that recalled the old life seemed as if it stretched and woke, a thrill for things he'd missed, that he'd denied himself.

It's all pretend, he reminded himself.

If only his damn cock would believe that.

Alison shifted her weight from foot to foot, trying not to look nervous.

Not that anyone could blame her. Who wouldn't be nervous about going to live with three alphas she didn't know, to pretend to be their slave?

She'd gotten no real information from them, just an address and an assurance of her safety.

No one can ensure anyone's safety. Besides, that was why she'd become as tough as she was, so she could make herself safe.

Still, she'd stood on the doorstep for at least two full minutes before knocking. Only fear that they knew she was there, that they knew she was fighting with her nerves, made her knock at all.

The only thing worse than being a coward was for others to know she was one.

I can do this. She'd seen slaves for years, had grown up watching them, knew how one should act.

It won't be that difficult to pretend, will it?

The door opened and Alison's stomach plummeted. Somehow, seeing Daniel there was the worst. Trent, Kyle, they both had a bit of that rough edge. Kyle might mask it with humor, but there was a bite to his words. Trent didn't hide his aggression beneath anything.

Those two she understood, could deal with.

Daniel, though? Already he seemed to look at her with those honest 'I really want to help you' eyes.

She curled her hands into fists, her duffel bag over her shoulder. It dug in, heavy, but she'd packed what she needed.

Daniel smiled—which made her feel all the worse—before he stepped backward so he didn't crowd the doorway.

The house, even from the street, had loomed, standing out like something that didn't belong. Even with the other expensive properties surrounding it, this one seemed to be on its own level. The large white double doors at the front would open wide, making for an impressive entrance. The driveway was cobblestone and prefect, winding up a short hill from a gated road. The house itself was classic, without the big modern windows. Instead, it reminded her of the old southern style, a wide balcony on the upper floor.

Inside, a huge entryway stood, showing off a spiraling staircase that screamed *money*. Alison had never been in a place like this, at least never when invited.

"I wasn't sure you'd show." Kyle had his arms crossed, and the light streaming in from the high windows highlighted how dark the bruising on his face was. It started at the center, where he had a bandage covering the bridge, then spanned out like starbursts around his eyes. He eyes narrowed. "You're smirking. Don't think I really like that look when you're staring at what you did to my face."

The little exchange helped Alison settle. Somehow the reminder that she *wasn't* weak lightened the burden for her. She'd made the choice to be here. She wasn't actually a slave, wasn't putting herself in the hands of strangers.

I'm playing a part. Nothing more.

"Where should I put my things?" Alison let Kyle's comment stand, not wanting to address it. If he was expecting an apology, he was going to be disappointed. *If he doesn't want girls to break his nose, he should try not abducting them.*

"Up the stairs. Second door on the left," Daniel said. "But that should wait."

"For what?"

"We should sit down, have a talk."

Alison straightened her back. "What is there to talk about?"

None of the three alphas answered, but the looks on their faces said it all.

They were getting ready to play a rather dangerous game, one that would require a lot of trust.

Trust was one thing they wouldn't get from her, though.

Alison shifted and shook her head. "I don't think anything really needs to be said. We know the job, we know what we're supposed to do. We don't need to do"—she waved her hands between them all—"this."

Still, no one seemed to give in. There was no slumping of shoulders, no softening of expressions.

"That isn't how this works."

She blew out a long, slow breath. *Not five minutes in this house and they're already treating me like a slave.*

The reasons it was a horrible idea were mounting.

Her gaze roamed toward the front door, toward her escape route. She could turn around. She could tell them to fuck off with their stupid idea.

I already found out more than they have.

Except, what had her way gotten her? Some information, sure, but also a lot of wasted time and a few situations more dangerous than they'd needed to be.

Besides, Anne couldn't wait for her to fumble around. She was running out of time.

"Why don't you go set down your things in your room and take an hour or so to settle in."

Alison turned to meet Trent's gaze, his words helping her to pull in a full breath. A moment to rebalance herself, to remind herself why she was doing it, would make everything better. Not to mention, just to *hear* the alphas listen to her, to give her an out, helped remind her that she wasn't a slave and they weren't her masters and, more importantly, they knew it, too.

Maybe Trent wasn't so bad.

"After that, however, we *will* talk," he tacked on.

So much for liking him…

Chapter Five

Sitting around the dining table felt disingenuous. Trent avoided the situation by standing and occasionally pacing.

He'd already gotten an earful from both Daniel and Kyle about how they had to have this talk. Granted, Trent had never cared for deep conversations, for the type that risked emotions and exposing of one's feelings. He still knew they were necessary sometimes.

This is definitely a time one is needed.

However, the alphas had been working at a distance for too long. They had clearly forgotten exactly how to handle skittish omegas.

Alison might have proven herself strong and capable, but that didn't change that she was as skittish as far as they were concerned. The difference? Others would run, but she'd bare her teeth. If Daniel had pushed her much further, she'd have turned around and stormed out. The armor going up was easy to spot if someone was looking for it.

So she'd needed a bit of time to settle her nerves.

The next conversation wasn't going to be an easy one, not for her and not for them.

Which was a damn pity, because negotiations were *supposed* to be fun. Nerve-wracking, sure, like a first date, but they were meant to be an exploration, a chance to glimpse another person in a new way.

Instead, this would be uncomfortable and clinical.

The pad of her footsteps was so soft he nearly didn't catch it. It was her scent that came down first, something soft and sweeter than he'd have figured for a woman as tough as she was.

She wore the same outfit. Pants rolled up to just below her mid-calf and a loose black shirt paired with black sneakers. Her hair still held those curls, and her full lips gave her that youthful look that was so deceiving.

Alison brought her gaze up, meeting Trent's. *Shit. Caught staring not five seconds in. Great job, idiot.* He tore his eyes away, as if that would undo it. He didn't blame himself for his reaction—if anyone understood basic biological reactions, if was him—but he tried not to unnerve her any more than he had to.

A chair scraped against the tile floor, and he turned back to find that she'd taken a seat at the table as far away from the other two seated alphas as she could.

Kyle spoke first. "How's your room?"

"Fine." Her short, sharp response didn't bode well for a nice friendly chat.

Kyle leaned back as if giving up.

Daniel took over. "Look, we're not trying to make you uncomfortable here. We have to figure out how this will work. For undercover work, people typically have a lot of training before trying it. The last thing I want is to end up upsetting you or making you feel uncomfortable."

Alison crossed her arms and set her elbows on the table. "Let's get one thing straight, all right? I spoke with Tiffany—I know you all handle this slavery ring taskforce and that before then, you focused on other large-scale omega crimes. I am *not* some broken damsel who needs you to walk carefully around me. I'm not one of your charity cases."

"No one thinks you're weak," Daniel went on. "If we did, we'd never have agreed to this. There have been former slaves who have offered to help, to play the part you're going to play, but we turned them down because it wouldn't have been right to put them in that position. Trust me, if we thought you were broken, you wouldn't be here."

Her eyes narrowed, but Alison didn't say anything back. Did she believe them or did she think they were bullshitting her?

The desire to figure her out, to learn her tells, ate at Trent and he filed it all away for later. Even if this were all make-believe, he still needed to deal with her, and the more he learned about her, the more he realized he'd need his best game to do so.

"Even if you're totally solid," Kyle added in, "that doesn't change that we need to agree on what's expected. Going into this blind isn't going to help anyone."

"I've spent six months on this job. I'm not going anywhere blind. We'll have someone from the association come and do two visits to ensure you do have a slave for sale and to take down all information in order for accurate pricing and pairing. The actual auction is set for just under two months away, but the location won't be told until the day of. During the auction, you'll be allowed to stay with me until payment had been remitted from a buyer. There are usually about thirty omegas in an auction. How am I doing on understanding?" She spoke quickly, as if rushing out all the information.

Trent rubbed his thumb across his jaw. He'd bet that usually worked. She'd toss out facts rapidly, unsettling those around her, making herself sound arrogant enough that no one challenged her.

Too bad it was a ploy. He saw the uncertainty in her pretty green eyes. She *was* tough and committed, but that didn't erase her worries.

A crease appeared in Daniel's cheek. "Yeah, you've got the basics. None of that addresses that we'll have to go through those meetings, that you'll have to play a part, that we *all* will have to play one. That means we've got to be clear about how that'll go and what limits there are."

"Limits." She huffed a mocking sound out. "Slaves don't get limits."

"You aren't a slave, though, and the last thing I want is to risk stumbling over some trigger you have. We might not actually be your Doms, but we're going to be stepping into that role for a while. That means honesty."

And there is was, the widening of her eyes, the quickening of her breath. *So, she's not a fan of honesty, huh?*

Kyle went next. "I promise that we won't lie to you, Alison. We won't do anything you tell us is off limits."

His reassurance should have helped, but her body only seemed to grow more tense. "I don't need kid gloves. We have a job to do and anything we need to do to find the fucking auction is fine with me."

Kyle pressed his lips together.

Which meant it was Trent's turn. He pulled a chair out directly next to her, one that made her lean away slightly when he sat. "Have you ever been in any consensual power exchange situation?"

She shook her head.

"Do you have a history of abuse or sexual assault? Anything we should know about that could cause you to freeze or panic?"

Again, she shook her head.

The fact that she answered surprised no one more than Trent, but he'd guess that using her own no-nonsense tone had helped. He didn't play the 'I'm so worried about you' card, but rather spoke as if filling out forms at a doctor's office. Being seen as weak seemed to be a hot button for Alison.

"Why are you so nervous around us, then?"

That question shook her loose from her open and honest moment, though. Her eyes narrowed and she curled her hands into fists. "Maybe because I don't care for arrogant alphas who think they have a right to pry around inside my head. I'm here to do a job and, to be quite honest, you need me more than I need you."

Lie. They needed one another, from what he could see.

Still, he let her keep the lie this time. "In order to pose as someone who had been our slave for weeks—especially since our cover is a trio who sells extremely high-dollar slaves with training—you're going to need to *learn*. There isn't any way to do that other than to actually train you."

She blinked, slowly, followed by a loud swallow. Even still, her voice kept its almost bored and more than a little hostile tone. "If you just want a slave, I'm sure there are plenty of omegas willing to play your sick little games."

Trent snorted. "We've had plenty of omegas who enjoyed our little games, and I'm going to bet you'd be more trouble than all of them put together, but no, this isn't some game. How the hell do you expect to play a part you've never experienced? You'll need to get comfortable with us around you. You'll need to look like you've spent the last few weeks being trained by us and the only way for that to happen is to actually train you." When she opened her mouth, he held a hand up so he could finish. "With limitations and safe words, of course. *That* is the point of good communication, so you can say 'don't pull my hair,' and we'll know to never do that. Without, we could stumble on a hard limit for you we were never aware of."

She shifted in her chair, most of her attitude dissipating.

It made Trent wonder...*what's beneath all that attitude?* If she actually let her guard down, if she stopped fighting just to fight, what would he find beneath it? Someone shy? Someone who loved praise? A person who got off on humiliation?

He normally loved this time, when he was able to find out the secrets that every female kept close, to see how she was unique, to discover all the beautiful things she hid.

Except then he reminded himself—that wasn't the point with Alison. They would only discover what they needed to in order to complete their task.

Daniel leaned in, his elbows on the table and his normal good-guy expression in place. "Don't think you're the only one uncomfortable in this, Alison. This is new territory for us, too. We've established that you don't have any experience with this sort of relationship, no large traumas involving men or alphas, so why don't we give you your homework, then you can go on to bed?"

"Homework?" Her look went past disrespectful to downright mean. "I haven't done homework since I was in high school, and honestly? I didn't do it then, either."

Daniel laughed and pushed a stapled pack of papers across the table to her. Trent knew what was in them—they all did. They'd written those up years ago, and just seeing a glimpse of them reminded him far too much of their old lives.

She flipped through the first few pages, her cheeks going pink at what she found. "You have got to be kidding me."

"Not at all," Daniel said. "Fill that out—thoroughly and honestly—and you won't even have to discuss it with us."

Trent could see it all in his head—the questions about her medical history, her personal history, about her hard limits and experience. They were the same packets they'd go over with potential subs back when they'd *played* more seriously. The thought of Alison filling it out made him uncomfortably turned on, and he struggled to keep it from showing.

This was proving to be far more interesting than it had any right to. She seemed to awaken things in him he'd thought were gone, a part of him that wanted to really take her, to watch her come undone, to taste each little shocked moan when he pulled passions from her she had no idea were there.

That can't happen, though. He sighed as he shook his head, trying to drive home the most important part. *This is just a game, and that makes her off limits.*

* * * *

Kyle chuckled as he read over Alison's paperwork. She'd left it on the kitchen table as though that was the end of it. *Girl has no idea.*

She'd answered all of nothing. A few questions had smart-ass remarks—after the anal sex question she'd put 'only if I can shove something up your ass first'—and the rest were blank. Saying she'd half-assed it would be giving the girl *way* too much credit.

"She's going to have a rough two months," Trent said as they got ready to go have a talk with her.

"Funny thing is, I don't think she's even all that opposed to some of this. I think she just likes to be difficult," Kyle responded. "It's like she fights with herself and decides she should argue, so she does."

Daniel offered a grin as he picked up the water bottles they'd pulled from the fridge. "I don't mind a brat one bit."

"You will when it isn't one you get to have fun with," Kyle pointed out.

Daniel's smile fell, as though someone had just dashed his hopes. After another moment, the smirk came back. "Hell, I'll take a little emotional torture, and you know she isn't going to be happy about redoing this."

Kyle chuckled, ready for the wild omega to have herself a world-class hissy fit over being forced to not only actually answer the questions but do so with them there. Then again, since giving her space hadn't convinced her to be forthright, he didn't mind changing up tactics.

She was lying out by the large indoor pool, and Kyle damn near lost his balance when he saw her. She'd been stunning in those tight pants she'd worn the first night, but they were nothing compared to *this*. She wore a bikini that showed off her amazing figure. It wasn't the sort of body a woman got from not eating, but instead one honed by hard work. The black of it stood out against her pale skin, and the large sunglasses on her face only made her look even more like some doe.

He caught himself before he face-planted into the concrete floor and spilled all the food on the plate. Still, the action caused enough noise that she lifted her head to look in their direction.

And *damn*, he'd had no idea a person could feel an eye roll, but there it was.

She suddenly looked like a sulking teenager annoyed by her parents' presence. "Yes?"

"Need to have a talk," Daniel said.

"Haven't we talked enough?"

"Sure, if you actually said anything. However, since you decided to phone in the questionnaire, we'll need to try it again."

She sat up, then pushed up her glasses so they rested on her head. "I told you everything you're going to get out of me."

The screeching of the patio chairs against the concrete grated on Kyle's senses, but the slowness of it helped to send the message. They were in no hurry and she couldn't maneuver or manipulate them. Once the chairs were moved over—three, since they left her on the ground—Kyle handed over a fresh packet of papers and a pen.

She narrowed her eyes. "No. You don't *need* to know any of this."

Kyle offered her the same stubborn look back. "Actually, we do, and this isn't negotiable. It's about the only thing that isn't, sugar."

She snorted at the nickname. "What are you going to do? Refuse to work with me?"

Playing hardball? Kyle wasn't sure if that was her just being difficult or if she was truly that uncomfortable with the idea of sharing her past with them.

He leaned back in his chair as if it didn't matter to him a bit. "Yeah, we will."

That got to her. She sat up tall. "You're bluffing. You need me for this."

"Yeah, we do need you, but we won't hesitate to call it off if we need to. We won't do this the wrong way, won't put you or us in danger by going into it when you won't even fill out a simple form. I mean, Alison, if you couldn't trust us to even tell you some of our history, would you ever want to put your life in our hands? Would you think we could handle a case like this then?"

She shifted to her knees, the action seeming almost instinctual in a way that Kyle tried to ignore. "You didn't fill one out," she argued.

"That's where you're wrong, sweet." Daniel held up the three packets the alphas had filled out. "This isn't a one-way street. We aren't asking anything from you that we won't do. In case you didn't know, my safe word is red and I am not into pegging."

Her eyebrows inched toward one another.

Daniel's laugh was downright pleased. "Oh, you are too much fun. Doesn't really matter what pegging is right now. My point is, this all goes both ways. You want to know about us? It's here. Now, are you going to be a good girl and fill that out?"

She blew out a hard breath but nodded. She might not like it, but apparently, she'd damn well do it.

And Kyle had to admit, he couldn't wait to hear her answers.

I wonder how much trouble I'd get in for rebreaking Kyle's nose…

Probably quite a bit. If they threatened to pull the plug on the case over paperwork, she suspected broken bones was one of those hard limits they'd talked about.

She held her hands out for the paper.

"Uh-huh, pet," Trent said. "You had your chance. I want to make sure each answer is satisfactory, so we'll ask, you'll answer, and I'll write it down. Don't like it? Then next time, do as you're asked the first time."

Alison's mouth hung open. She'd never been spoken to like that, at least not since she'd become an adult.

And yet all the indignation in the world didn't change what needed to happen. "Fine," she muttered and crossed her arms. Only after a too-long stare by Kyle did she realize the action made her breasts press together and gave her a hell of a lot of cleavage. She stopped immediately and ignored his chuckle.

The first questions were easy. Medical history—only a tricky shoulder that acted up from time to time—and personal history. That one she was vague about.

Trent's lifted eyebrow meant he'd caught it, but they let it go. Her childhood wasn't relevant, and she had no desire to put it on the table for them to dissect.

"Virgin?" Kyle asked.

She offered up her best deadpan stare. "I'm thirty. Of course I'm not a virgin."

"Have you ever slept with an alpha?"

Her sputtering likely answered that one for her. "I really think that is going too far."

Daniel answered in that voice that seemed to have endless patience and amusement. "These questions are here for a reason. If you've never slept with an alpha, you don't know what it feels like to be knotted. That matters. If you don't know what it's like to be around alphas, you've got no idea the sort of pull they can have."

"That's sex. We aren't having sex, so why do you need any of this?"

Trent sighed, setting the pen on the paper before giving her a look that seemed to lock her gaze to his. "Because this is the exact paperwork we would have done if you really were a slave. If we were really training you, we'd know all this. What happens if during a meeting, the person there asks about deep throating? I say you're good at it for short periods of time, but you say you hate it. We're playing the part of people who actually train and know about the omega we're selling, and there's no other way to do that than to actually take the steps. I don't want to argue with you every step of the way, Alison, so you need to decide if you want to do this or not. If not, you're free to walk out."

That got her attention. Where Kyle had made a similar threat, Trent meant it. She had no idea what sat there in the shadows of his eyes, but this seemed personal. He would let her walk out if she kept pushing.

She took a deep breath, then released it slowly. "No, I've never slept with an alpha."

Trent nodded and sat back, writing down the answer.

Daniel asked the next questions. "For the next ones, I need you to answer first if you've tried it or not, then a one, two or three for interest. One means yes, two means maybe and three means it is a hard limit."

Her body heated as she knew what was coming. Of course, she'd looked through the list, even if she hadn't answered most of it. So many things on there that she hadn't even been aware people did, let alone enjoyed.

She'd thought herself sexually free, since she'd screwed men in bars and motel rooms plenty of times, yet just half a page into their little packet, she'd felt like an old lady who had no idea what the kids got up to anymore. At least it made most of the answers easy. She'd done little of what they'd mentioned, though it was her answers of two that surprised her the most. She hadn't tried them, but the moment her brain got going on those pictures, she'd known they were maybes.

I'm the least experienced whore ever.

She found herself really regretting her little act of rebellion right about the time Trent's deep, rough voice started rumbling out all those things like items at an all-you-can-eat buffet. She felt like checking them all off. *Yes, I'll take an order of bondage with a side of spanking and maybe a little double penetration to finish off the meal.*

"Pet." Trent's voice forced her gaze up to his intense dark eyes.

It took a moment for her to realize he hadn't been asking her a question, but rather using *pet* as a name to get her attention. She blinked, waiting for the outrage to hit and finding none. She chalked that up to being so horribly turned on she couldn't think straight.

"I asked if you had a safe word you wanted to use."

Oh. "Um, stop?"

His smile was simply unfair. A man who looked as intimidating as he did shouldn't also have a killer grin. "Usually we'd use red, but I want something you can say even if we're being watched. How about 'master?' Call any of us master, and we'll know you need to stop whatever is going on. If we're alone, it will be an immediate end and check-in. If we have someone from the slavery ring here, we'll ease off whatever is happening and try to fix the issue."

Alison swallowed hard, the word *master* feeling heavy in her mouth. She reached for a joke, unsure how else to deal with the issue. "I figured every man's dream is for a girl to call them master."

Kyle huffed out a laugh that made her impossibly wetter. "Ah, sugar, I much prefer being called 'sir'. By the time girls are saying that, one-syllable words are a benefit. They can't remember much beyond that."

His words were a whisper that went straight to her cunt, but the thing that really got her? The thing that made her again doubt whether this was such a good idea?

He winked at her, as if he knew exactly what those words did to her.

This might have been a horrible mistake…

* * * *

Why did I open my stupid mouth?

Alison cursed herself again as she paced her room.

She hadn't even *realized* what she was saying until it had already come flying out of her mouth.

She eyed the window. A lock rested on it, making it impossible to climb out. Which was a stupid thought, because she could damn well walk out of that front door. As much as she disliked the alphas, she knew they wouldn't keep her there against her will.

And yet admitting to them that she might bail seemed too far.

A knock on the door had her wishing she could turn the thing to ash with only a glare. When it didn't even smolder, she sighed. "Come in."

She expected Daniel. He tended to be the 'let's smooth everything over' one. Instead, Trent walked in.

"What's that?" She nodded toward the black items clutched in his hand.

Trent took one and lifted it on a finger.

A collar.

Heat simmered in her lower stomach, her skin growing hot. How could something both excite and frighten her?

He reached out, and Alison offered her wrists without thinking. Her hands were so small against his palms, and he set all the items on the small dresser before pulling just the cuffs out.

Alison waited for them to hurt. She imagined rough leather that would chafe, that would sit tight enough to scrape her raw.

Instead, something soft stroked her skin. Trent worked quickly, efficiently. After sizing them, he ran his finger between the cuff and her skin, the touch feeling far more intimate than it should have.

"Are they too tight?" Despite checking himself, he still asked.

Alison shook her head, the weight of the cuffs surprising. They weren't that heavy, she'd guess. It was a mental thing, as though they seemed to weigh a thousand pounds, as if she could focus on nothing but the way they tugged at her.

They were padded and lined with a soft cotton, yet her entire world had shrunk to where they touched her.

"Breathe," he told her.

Alison sucked in a breath at the command, cold air rushing into her lungs. *Guess that's why my chest hurts. Breathing is important.*

He studied her quietly for a moment before moving on. "The collar now."

How he could tell she was ready, that she'd regained her courage, she wasn't sure. The press of the same fabric against her throat felt as shocking as if someone had choked her. It didn't fasten tightly, didn't impede her breathing at all, and yet the clicking of the metal buckle, the brush of his fingers—it all made it feel too real.

He performed the same check he had with the cuffs, slipping his finger between the collar and her neck, sliding it around to test how tight it was.

He touched the collar, his fingers sliding over the front. "You look nice in this."

Her mouth had gone dry, as if she'd never drunk a drop in her entire life.

His lips curved into a half smile. "You're supposed to say, 'Thank you, sir.'"

The words tumbled from her lips, soft and unsure and yet she didn't have to think about them at all. "Thank you, sir."

The rush of wetness between her thighs surprised her more than it would have anyone else, she'd bet. She fidgeted, pressing her thighs together to try to keep him from noticing.

He breathed in, and a darkness in his gaze told her he knew.

"If you have trouble sleeping in the cuffs or the collar, just come let one of us know. If they pinch or feel uncomfortable, we'll fix them." He slid his large hand to the side of her neck, the touch solid and showing just how much bigger he was than her.

She expected him to use that grip to pull her against him, to take her lips in a kiss she was *sure* would melt her. Hell, she had no doubts that if he tried—even a little—he'd not only get a kiss but have her on her back in a heartbeat. Somehow, all those nerves, all the things she'd been nervous about, all transformed into pure lust.

Except he didn't.

He dragged his thumb along her jawline before releasing her. "Goodnight."

Alison didn't get the chance to even respond before he left the room. Her gaze floated past the full-length mirror on the door, and something that dangled at the front of the collar caught her attention. She went closer, catching the silver—a heart-shaped padlock that hung from a loop—and twisted it to read the engraving.

Ali

It had been made for her, with her name. She clutched the heart between her fingers, the collar still warm from Trent's grip.

The entire list of things she'd filled out ran through her head as she recalled Trent's large hand against her neck, the way he'd checked the fit of each item, and she let out a broken moan at how badly she suddenly wanted to try out that list with him.

Which meant she was in trouble, and not just from the slavery ring.

* * * *

Trent groaned as he stroked his cock. He'd heard Alison moan when he'd shut her door. He'd breathed in her delicious scent, knew she'd been drenched when he'd put that collar on her.

It had been years since he'd collared a woman, and he'd forgotten how damn pleasing it was to do.

And he wasn't made of stone, damn it, which left him in the shower, his hand around his dick, his other arm against the wall, the water streaming over him.

That omega is a menace. Something about her strange dichotomy got him. She was tough as nails, had gone head to head with him that first night, but then she'd turned naive and innocent a heartbeat later. It wasn't fair, damn it. No one could resist that.

And he didn't *have* to resist in his own head. He pictured holding that collar as he fucked her from behind. He pictured putting clips on her nipples, blowing cool air over the peaked tips.

"Fuck," he growled out, moving his hand faster.

When he came, it was with something far too close to a roar for his comfort. He was left panting and tired and far too fucking confused about what had come over him.

He hadn't ever wanted a female like this. Why was it the one female he couldn't possibly have?

How the hell was he supposed to act like her Dom, train her, treat her like a slave while also keeping her at a distance? He tried to picture running his hands along her skin, teaching her what positions to stand in, how to kneel and not giving in to even the slightest kiss.

Impossible.

And yet he had to find the strength. He had to build up his defenses to her charms because he had a job to do. He couldn't ignore what needed to happen for what he wanted.

He'd given up so much before to do what was right, and he'd give up what he wanted this time, too.

He had to.

Chapter Six

Kyle always woke first, something he'd grown used to. Daniel didn't sleep in, but he preferred to take a long shower, to go through an entire routine to get his day started right.

Kyle's morning needed a big cup of coffee. Nothing much mattered before that.

He all but stumbled into the kitchen, half-awake, expecting to find the room empty.

Instead, he nearly ran into Alison, who stood there staring at the fridge.

He stopped short, just before actually touching her, his brain catching up despite his lack of caffeine. It seemed like spotting her was as good as a coffee for waking him up.

The black collar stood out at her throat, and he admitted…it had been the right choice. It looked marvelous against her light skin, sitting right at the level where her hair fell.

Then he got a better look at her. She wasn't moving, seemingly frozen in her spot. Whatever ran through her head showed on her face, and it was nothing good. She wrung her hands together, the action making the metal loops of the cuffs clink together.

What's got her so nervous?

"Hey there, sugar. You okay?"

She blinked slowly, as though waking up. Still, when she spoke, her voice seemed quiet and distant. "I didn't know if I was supposed to..."

He frowned, trying to work through what she didn't really say. Finally, it hit him. He slid around her to put himself between her and the fridge.

She lifted her gaze to his, the immediate response more pleasing than it probably should have been.

"You worried about what we expect from you?"

She nodded.

Kyle backed her up a few steps before he grasped her around the waist and lifted her.

The little gasp she let out was gratifying, but not as good as the fact that she clutched his shoulders as he set her on the kitchen counter.

Kyle moved forward between her knees, so he could look at her and she had nowhere else to look but him. "I'm not expecting you to get up early and cook us breakfast, darling."

She didn't react to his closeness, and that said everything about how unsettled she was. "I thought..."

Kyle ran his fingers over the leather of her cuffs, teasing the skin around it. "You thought what? That we'd have you be our servant?" Her expression said that, yeah, that was exactly what she'd thought.

Well, no wonder she'd been so nervous walking into the place if she thought she was going to have no safety net, if she truly expected to be treated as a slave.

But that wasn't it. She didn't think it out of nowhere, not with the shadows in her eyes. She'd concluded it because of something she'd seen before, something she knew.

"What had you thinking that?" He continued to stoke her soft skin, trying to ease her, rewarded by her heart not racing as it had been.

He tugged softly at the restraints on her wrists, a way to try to focus her on his question.

"I'm not stupid," she said, her voice low. "I know exactly what a slave does, what's expected of one."

"When have you seen slaves, darling?"

She blinked slowly, as if waking up. *Well, she said more than I thought she would.*

After a moment, she drew her eyebrows toward one another. She pulled her wrists, and he released her.

Part of being dominant was knowing how far to push someone, and he'd pushed her plenty.

Even though he let her go, though, he didn't move away. It kept her on the counter and temptingly close. "You'll tell me the truth," he assured her.

"Good luck with that."

Ah, there it was, that hard look in her eyes that dared him to challenge her. It drew him in, especially after seeing the softer side of her, after seeing her for that one vulnerable moment before she'd put on her armor again.

Kyle stroked his thumb across her pouty bottom lip, mesmerized by how it gave beneath his finger. "You will. Now, as the one in charge, I say you should sit right there and keep me company while I cook. Do you eat eggs?"

He pulled back and grabbed a fry pan from the hanging rack above them. When she didn't answer, he twisted toward her and raised an eyebrow.

Pink spanned her cheeks, but she nodded.

Fuck, I like when I win with her.

What the hell was I thinking?

Alison couldn't figure it out, no matter how much she thought about it. She'd stood in that kitchen, feeling like she was staring at her past.

She'd remembered the way her mother walked through the large kitchen of her childhood home, effortlessly, as though drawn by routine.

It had been routine, though. Her mother, Sasha, had known exactly what she was supposed to do, what was expected of her. Alison's father had always made his expectations clear—to everyone.

Alison recalled the way he'd grasped her chin and cleaned a smudge from her cheek when she was six, his lips pulled down in disappointment.

Nothing in his world was ever out of its place, and he'd had the same hard attitude with Alison.

And worse than her little walk down memory lane? The way Kyle had witnessed it.

She'd all but blurted out the truth to him, drawn somehow by the way he'd moved her, the way he'd seemed solid when she couldn't tell past from present.

Thank god I didn't say it all.

At least Kyle hadn't pushed. He'd cooked food, moving around the kitchen while Alison had remained on the counter. She'd thought about getting off it—

mostly because he'd told her to stay—but she'd lacked the energy for that.

Instead, she'd watched him.

Kyle was odd. He worked as though he didn't care about anything, as if he moved to his own music. He'd toss glances at her, as though making sure she was okay, but otherwise? He seemed unaffected by anything else, as though the world didn't touch him.

He'd cooked scrambled eggs—hers mixed with veggies and everyone else's with ham—and sliced fresh fruit. By the time he'd finished, movement in the rest of the house implied the other two had woken.

Daniel came into the kitchen, dressed in a pair of slacks and a button-up shirt. "Smells good."

Kyle grabbed one of the plates he'd made and handed it off to Daniel, who pulled a stool into the kitchen.

Trent came in next, wearing only a pair of jeans, his feet and chest bare.

And holy shit…the man was built.

His skin was darkly tan, as though he spent a lot of time outside without a shirt. Then again, if someone had a body like that, why not?

Kyle took a plate of his own and hopped onto the counter, handing one off to Alison and balancing the other on his lap.

Trent pressed his lips together for a moment before he got a plate from the cabinet and served his own food. He piled on the fresh fruit, then came over to lean against the counter on Alison's other side.

It left her between the two alphas, with Daniel across the way.

It was nearly as unsettling as it had been every other time. It wouldn't be so bad if they weren't so large, but it was as though there was no room for her in the kitchen, not with them there.

Trent shifted and offered her a piece of pineapple clutched between his fingers.

"I can feed myself," Alison snapped.

"But I like doing it. Stop arguing, pet." When he lifted his eyebrow, Alison reminded herself to fall into her role. *You've only got so long to get used to it, so stop being difficult.* She took the piece of fruit from his fingers, careful not to actually touch him. It was tart and juicy, and Alison nearly moaned at the taste.

Trent went back to talking as if he hadn't done that, as though it weren't weird as hell. "Gregory is putting in our information today. Any idea when to expect a visit?"

Daniel shook his head as he ate, finishing his bite before speaking. "Probably pretty soon."

Kyle shrugged as he balanced his plate in his lap. "I bet you anything they'll have someone come check us out before then. I don't care how good Gregory's rec is, no one as careful as this slavery ring is going to just accept some no-name trio from out of town."

"They'll accept us," Alison said after swallowing another bite that Trent offered. "They need us. With the problems they've had here, they'd love some more scouts. This is going to be the last chance to make any good money, so if they think you've got something worth selling, they'll risk it."

Which brought her back to Anne, again, back to the reality that she was missing and Alison was still no closer.

Is she even alive?

A bump to her shoulder had her turning to find Trent staring at her. Being watched so carefully, having people who saw so much of her feelings, unnerved her.

She only offered a quick shake of her head, so he shrugged and picked up another piece of fruit—cantaloupe, this time—and offered it.

Alison took the piece, but it had become so normal already that she wasn't quite as careful. Her lips slid against Trent's warm fingers, tasting the juice from his skin.

Which heated her up in far too many places.

Not that he mentioned it. Did he even notice it?

He continued to feed her pieces, always giving her the best of the fruit on his plate, while her own food in her lap became forgotten.

Trent discussed the case with Daniel while Kyle ate—rather loudly—and chimed in from time to time. None of it required Alison's advice. Not being the direct topic of conversation or focus for once felt nice. It seemed as though every moment spent with the three alphas made her the center, and she'd grown tired of it.

Other than the show she'd put on in the bars to tempt the scouts, Alison was far more of a 'work from the shadows' sort of woman. She didn't care to be looked at, to be noticed.

Being noticed doesn't tend to go well, in my experience.

So when they spoke amongst themselves, when she was able to just listen, to absorb it, she felt normal for the first time.

Besides the fact that she continued to eat the food Trent supplied. He'd steal a bite for himself now and again, but only of the things she wouldn't eat. He didn't mention it as he did it, as though it were nothing out of the ordinary. Stranger still, he seemed pleased by doing it.

She tried to think back to her childhood. Had her father ever treated her mother this way?

No. Mom did all the work. If anything, she'd be the one feeding him…

The thought did what it always did—made her tense. She recalled being in that house, always doing everything wrong, never living up to who she was supposed to be. What would he think if he saw her now?

He'd be happy to see me collared…

Fingers caught her chin the way her father used to and tugged until she met Kyle's blue eyes.

The touch was the worst part of it. She was playing a stupid part, and she couldn't even do that right. The way Kyle's fingers gripped her chin—not hard enough to hurt, but then again, her father had never hurt her physically either—took her back to being that same kid.

"Whoa there, pet," Trent said before taking the plate from her lap. She'd forgotten all about it and had nearly toppled it to the tiled floor.

Kyle held her chin, studying her expression. It was only then she realized how shallow her breathing had become.

She wanted to yank backward. She wanted to shove his hand away and tell him to never grasp her chin like that again, but the words wouldn't come.

Be a good girl. Her father's voice repeated in her head like an echo of a life she'd thought she'd killed and buried.

Telling Kyle to stop would mean admitting she couldn't handle it, giving in, proving she wasn't up to the task.

And the part of her that strove for perfection wouldn't allow her to do it.

He let her go after another moment, and Alison curled forward, closing her eyes to slow her breathing. *In. Out. Nice and slow.*

None of the alphas rushed her. They didn't tell her to get over it, didn't even ask what *it* was. They only stayed there, like solid, unmoving presences, giving her the time to get her shit back in line.

When she finally shuddered, the last of that panicky energy slipping from her, Trent held up another piece of food. "Still hungry?"

Alison shook her head, not trusting her voice.

He set the food on the plate and placed it all beside him, then turned his focus on Daniel, whose gaze seemed locked solidly on Alison. "I'm thinking lasagne for dinner. We should make a list, because whoever stocked this place didn't know shit about feeding people."

The warmth of Kyle's arm, the way Trent had shifted to talking about mundane things, all helped her regain her footing.

And wonder exactly how far she'd be able to take this.

* * * *

"Fuck," Kyle muttered as he paced the length of the pool.

Trent sat back and let him storm about. That was Kyle's way. Daniel was the sort to see a problem and try to fix it immediately. Kyle liked to talk it through until he all but killed it. Trent? He preferred to sit back and examine it until he had what he saw as a great idea.

So after Alison had gone upstairs after breakfast, ready to shower and get prepared for the day, the three of them had gone to the indoor pool.

Best place to talk without being overheard.

"She's clearly lying about a past," Kyle said.

"Maybe." Daniel sat in one of the lounge chairs, at the foot so he was still upright. "Maybe it's just a reaction to being around alphas for the first time?"

Kyle gave Daniel the sort of look that said he thought he was an idiot. "No. Nerves, those are one thing. I know what nerves look like. Her? That's fucking panic." He ran his fingers through his hair, pushing it back.

Kyle so often looked like the go-with-the-flow sort of person, and he was in a lot of ways, but give that man something he couldn't fix, and he lost his shit.

"I walked into that kitchen and she was totally frozen, thinking we were expecting her to wake up early and cook us all breakfast."

Trent snorted softly. When the other two turned their gazes to him, he continued. "She's fucking difficult. She doesn't want to talk, but look what happens she doesn't know what she's supposed to do. Girl has herself a panic attack. Clearly we fucked up and need to actually give her our expectations."

Daniel rubbed his hands against each other, staring at them as though they'd make the whole situation easier. "I'm going to be honest here and say… I'm not feeling entirely professional about her."

I sure as hell get that.

Kyle huffed. "Who could? Girl looks way too tempting in a collar and cuffs."

"We're talking about giving her expectations, but that feels way too much like getting close to a line I'm not sure we can walk."

"So what? We throw in the towel?" Kyle crossed his arms, pausing only long enough to send Daniel a withering look.

"No. We just need to be aware of it. Treat her like we would a sub we were watching for someone else."

Sure, in a perfect world that would work. If she had a Dom of her own, if they were only supposed to be taking care of her, they'd have clear boundaries. In reality, he didn't lie to himself well, and he knew she didn't belong to anyone. *I want her to belong to me.*

Which was exactly the wrong thought to have.

"Ground rules for us," Daniel said, listing them while lifting a finger for each, counting them off. "No kissing. Nothing sexual. Even if she offers, we don't take her up on it."

"Do you really think you'll be able to say no if that girl offers anything?" Kyle asked.

Daniel pressed his lips together, then sighed. "I'm trying to keep us all from getting fucked over here. You've seen her react already. Do you really think she's going to be in any state of mind to decide anything in the moment?"

Trent wanted to argue that point, but it was fair.

Subs who got a taste of something they liked, who had never experienced it before, often craved it. Normally that wasn't a bad thing. Hell, how many had he shared with Daniel and Kyle over the years? Women who had begged for a little more, ones who Trent had been able to watch as they experienced it for the first time?

Too many to count.

Still, Daniel wasn't wrong.

When Alison had her pupils blown wide, when she smelled like delectable arousal, that wasn't the time for her to make any decisions.

"Anything sexual has to be agreed on by us all," Trent offered as a compromise. At their looks, he shrugged. "I'm not an idiot. If that girl decides she actually wants any of us, we aren't going to be able to just turn her down forever. But if we all agree beforehand, it gives her time to rethink it and makes sure it's all on the up and up. Fuck, maybe dealing with all three of us will help her stay on good behavior, too."

Daniel and Kyle exchanged looks, the closeness of the two grating on Trent's nerves. Hell, it pissed him off. After everything, he was the outsider. He was the one cut off from the trio they'd been.

He pushed that hurt from his mind—now wasn't the time to deal with it—as he waited for them to make up their minds.

Finally, both other alphas nodded.

"Sounds like as good a plan as any other," Kyle said.

Even as they agreed, as Trent's idea seemed to please everyone, he winced as he thought about just how appealing the stubborn, surprisingly fragile omega was turning out to be. If she *did* want to try anything with them, if they explored that together, how the fuck would they walk away at the end of the case?

He only had to hope she had more sense than it seemed he did, because he doubted there was any fucking way he could resist her.

* * * *

Daniel went over the list with the other two alphas a few times until they'd all agreed, which wasn't something that was always easy for alphas.

They tended to like to get their own way, and even when they were a group, even when they didn't get jealous, when they were closer than brothers, they still wanted to win.

However, after some push and pull, they'd come up with a general idea of expectations for Alison.

They'd decided to give it to Daniel to deliver.

Probably because I look the least threatening.

Which was funny, because anyone who got to know him realized that wasn't an entirely accurate description. After spending some time with him, most women realized he was the one to be the most nervous around.

Alison was on the swing in the small outside area, the one hidden from prying eyes. Her hair was still damp, and it made it seem longer and darker, the curls lengthening beneath the weight of the water. She wore a pair of leggings and a long-sleeved shirt—both black. If that wasn't a 'stay away' statement, he had no idea what was.

He closed the door louder than needed to signal his arrival without startling her.

Sure enough, her eyes popped open, and the look she gave him was chilling. Well, it was probably supposed to be, but his body warmed beneath the unhappy glare.

"If you're here to talk about earlier—"

"I'm not. Not exactly, at least." He pulled a chair from the table over toward the swing, then sat in it so he was facing her and their knees brushed. He could have picked the seat beside her, but he wanted her to look at him, and he needed to read her expression.

She was a difficult woman to pin down.

Don't think about pinning her down.

"I had a talk with the others, and we figured you struggled this morning because you don't have clear expectations. You don't know what we want, and you don't care for doing things blind."

She sat up straighter but didn't respond. A tightening in her jaw was set off by relief in her eyes.

This was why he wanted to be in front of her. The girl was a constant contradiction. She didn't want to admit she needed boundaries, yet she did need them.

Difficult omega.

Still, Daniel kept on, figuring they didn't need to call her out for each little tell of hers. "I printed up a list for you, so you know exactly what we want. Anything on that list you don't agree with, speak up and we'll discuss it." He handed a paper to her, then tapped at the first line. "Which brings us to the first one. Honesty."

And *that* didn't go over to well. The paper crinkled slightly in her hands even though she didn't voice a complaint.

Daniel kept going. "You don't have to tell us everything, but if you're bothered by something, upset, uncomfortable, you speak up. If you're not feeling well one day, you tell us. If your knees are hurting, and we want you to kneel, you tell us you're in pain."

She opened her mouth, those full pink lips forcing him to focus on the topic and not how pretty they'd look stretched around his cock. As quickly as she was going to say something, though, she closed them again, as though she'd thought better of it.

He let it stand. They had a list to go over, and perhaps as they worked through it, she'd feel better about voicing her concerns.

He went through it, one item at a time. They'd included things they expected of her and things they didn't.

She didn't need to use any special address for them, didn't need to wait until they spoke to speak, didn't need to kneel unless requested.

They weren't difficult, didn't want high protocol. The only real chores they insisted on were all self-care-based. He didn't need a housekeeper, after all.

One of the items further down hit a sore spot, and Daniel took a moment to address it. "You don't care for losing your room?"

She gave him a withering look. "I don't see why I need to sleep in any of your beds."

"Because it'll help you get comfortable. Not a lot of things create that sort of comfort more than spending eight hours asleep beside someone."

"And how do I know you aren't just trying to see what you can get out of this? Maybe you're just enjoying however far you can push this? 'Yeah, sweet, you need to take your pants off so we can really sell the ruse.'"

Daniel grinned at her tone, at her attempts to pull him in to some sort of argument.

She could rile Trent up, even Kyle, but not Daniel. He was too level-headed. "Don't rush me, sweet. If you keep looking, we address sex and nudity further down."

That got her to snap her lips shut with a loud pop. She scanned down, and he could tell when she reached it. "You've got to be kidding me," she muttered.

"Not at all. What are you opposed to?"

"How about you taking my clothes?"

He offered her a smile—probably patronizing, but she was being purposely difficult. "Read it again. I'm not expecting you to be naked. However, again, when we have the visit, when we show up at the auction, you have to be convincing as a woman who has been living with us, being trained as a slave by us. How exactly will you do that if you're so nervous about the tiniest bit of contact? How will we sell that if you don't carry any of our scent?"

Alison's gaze lifted at that, and damn if it didn't spring up his own ideas.

Omegas could carry an alpha's scent in a few ways. Being around one could cause it to cling to the omega the way smoke would, but it was a shallow scent that dissipated with ease. Contact—the sort Daniel had already mentioned—would make it hang on to the omega more readily, but it would also sit only skin-deep.

The *real* scenting, however, the way to truly claim an omega, would be with an exchange of fluids. Kisses could do it and so could oral sex, but the deepest sort, the kind that caused an omega to carry the scent of her alphas no matter what, was sex.

And that made him think about how it would feel to bury his nose in her throat and breathe her in, to smell that way their scents integrated and become something new.

A flame in her eyes, the reddish hue on her cheeks, all said her mind had gone to the same place, and that she liked it.

She's never been with an alpha. She's never carried one's scent before.

His groan was deep and he had no hope of holding it in.

She took her bottom lip between her teeth, pressing into that plumpness there, making Daniel want to do it, too. He wanted to nip at her, to draw out a whimper and leave a mark.

Alison inhaled sharply, then dropped her gaze back to the page.

"So how little clothing are we talking?" Was that a quiver in her voice?

"We'll go slowly. How about we start with not having every inch of you covered? The point is not to hide." He nodded down at the list. "Anything else strike you as unacceptable?"

She shook her head, even as her gaze stayed locked on a single point.

Daniel could guess where it was even without her admitting it. "Really? Because you look pretty worried about something."

She let out a hard breath, blown out slowly before narrowing her eyes at him. "If you know what I'm looking at, why do you ask?"

"Because you need to get better at asking for things. You don't like to do it, you know? Even when it's gnawing at you, you don't like to admit you need something." He didn't bother to ask her why—she wouldn't answer, and it wasn't the time to press his luck—so he just left that statement and waited for her.

Finally, she huffed and sat backward, the paper resting on her thighs. "You know what it is. The last one."

Daniel curled his lip into a smile. He'd known that one would stick. "Punishment?"

She gave him one curt nod. Ah, but there those shadows were again in her green eyes, ones that hinted at a past that wasn't so far away to her.

Daniel reached out and set a hand on her knee. He wished he understood what she had going on in her head, that he could figure out what it was that haunted her. "Breathe, sweet."

She did as he said, the beautiful way she obeyed as though out of instinct something to be treasured. Sure, the moment she realized she'd done as he said, her face hardened, but he only shrugged.

That first instinct always tells me the most.

"We're not going to hurt you. I don't care what you do, what rule you break, you will always be safe with us, and you always have your safe word."

"Then why do we have to do all this? Why do we have to have rules and punishments?"

Daniel kept his hand on her knee. "Because even if this is all a ploy, what happens if the person evaluating us comes and asks a question—one any actual slave and trainer would know—but we haven't worked this out? We haven't been living like this? They'll see right through it."

"But somehow you think having safe words and rewards and punishments makes sense? You are naive."

Daniel chuckled, his thumb rubbing along her knee, through the leggings. "I can't say I've ever been called that before."

"Slaves don't have those things. They're told what to do, and they do it or they pay the price, and let me tell you, the price isn't some pre-arranged and worked out thing they agree to."

Again, proof that she'd seen slavery up close and personal before.

"You're so sure you know everything, but you never stop to think maybe, just maybe, we have some information. Trust me—"

"Why? Why would I trust you? I don't know you."

"And you haven't tried to get to know me, either."

She sat straight at the admonishment. *She can't argue with me on that one, can she?*

"Do you want me to sign in blood?" The curt questions dripped sarcasm and Daniel's cock perked up. Why was it that he loved sassy women? Women who enjoyed being brats were always a bit of fun, always pushing the limits, always letting him push back.

Trent had preferred tough women, yet he'd always wanted to spoil them rotten. He loved to praise them, to experience how sweet they could be, how they could melt. Kyle? He'd been the one to enjoy naturally submissive women, as if the way they gave in pleased him.

Which, Daniel wondered, might be one of the reasons they'd never found a woman for the long term. Finding one who fitted the wants of three such different alphas was a tall order.

We aren't looking for that now, either. Trent isn't part of the equation anymore and Kyle and I don't need that.

Even as he told himself it didn't matter, that they didn't need or want a submissive, his gaze locked on where Alison took the pen and signed her name at the bottom of the list of rules.

It sure feels like it matters…

Chapter Seven

Alison could feel *nothing* beyond the heat of the alphas.

She couldn't even quite tell where one was versus another. It was all just alpha pheromones and heat and impossibly large bodies.

Which was annoying, since they weren't doing anything that intimate.

At least, not physically.

Kyle had brought a board game she'd never heard of, and the plastic wrap on the pieces inside the box said he'd never played it. *Tell Me More* appeared to be a get-to-know-one-another game for dinner parties.

And she'd dreaded it the moment she'd seen it in Kyle's hands.

It felt like yet another piece of her they wanted to tug free of her grasp, like another thing she hadn't been expecting to give up during the case.

Daniel sat to her left, Trent to her right and Kyle across from her. They all were on the floor around a coffee table, the game board out and set up.

Trent had picked out the kitten piece to represent Alison without even asking her, and her glare wasn't just because the way he'd called her *pet* rang in her ears.

It was also for the way it heated her.

Kyle handed her the dice, their fingers brushing at the exchange. Alison rolled, a six coming up. She moved forward on the board, tapping her piece along the squares until she stopped at six, a purple square.

Kyle picked up a card from the purple pile as he explained. "Each card has three questions worth one, two or three points. The more points, the more personal the question. The color you landed on gives bonuses based on what type of question it is. What do you want?"

Alison pressed her lips together. Who cared about losing a game? "One."

Kyle chuckled as though he wasn't shocked. "Favorite type of pizza."

"Pepperoni."

"Coward," Trent muttered as Kyle put the card in the discard pile and added Alison's one to her score.

The next was Daniel, who rolled a two, and picked a three pointer on a yellow card.

As the game went on, Alison picked up the rules. There were three card colors. Purple were 'favorites' questions, yellow were history and red were risqué. Thankfully, she missed all the reds. She could pass on a question, but then she got no points.

Though, she did pick up some details she hadn't expected along the way.

Like Trent's hobby of collecting shiny rocks when on walks, or that Daniel had a longer daily skincare routine than she did, or how Kyle had once stolen his parents' car when he was fifteen in order to impress a girl.

They all took the top-level questions, whereas Alison picked the least risky option.

She had to play—skirting rules was something she excelled at—but she didn't have to care about it.

Trent groaned when he landed on red but muttered a three as Kyle pulled the card.

Kyle let out a harsh bark of laughter. "Wildest place you've ever had sex."

Trent shifted, as though the floor weren't the most comfortable place he'd ever sat all of a sudden. He blew out a slow breath, then shrugged. "That cliff, out in Texas?"

Daniel snorted. "That wasn't a cliff."

"Seemed like a cliff," Trent shot back.

"You think that was wilder than the storage room in that museum? Remember the docent knocking on the door, yelling at us in French?"

Trent let out a soft laugh. "I'll take an angry docent over a twenty-foot drop any day."

"Were you guys sleeping with each other?" Alison asked, as if everything made more sense and less. The strange connection between the three, the closeness, that all fit. Though, with how they'd looked at her…she felt as if she'd confused it.

Kyle was the one to answer, his voice gentle as if he were amused but trying not to show it. "No, sugar. We have a history of fucking women together."

And if that didn't make the temperature of the room shoot up a good twenty degrees…

Without being able to help it, Alison pictured it. She thought about how they overwhelmed her already, but realizing they had a history of doing this, of taking women together, of working together, made her body react as if it was begging.

She wished she could sit her body down and have a long heart-to-heart, remind it why that wasn't going to happen. Not that it would listen.

Vaginas were hussies that did what they wanted.

"Your turn," Trent said, his lip curled into a smirk that said she'd already missed his first statement.

Bastards.

She rolled the dice, getting a red. *Fuck.* "Pass," she said quickly.

"You didn't even hear the question. You aren't trying," Daniel said.

"So? You said I had to play. You didn't say anything about me having to win."

Trent snorted. "Never figured you for a brat. Fine. Let's up the stakes."

"You can't, not after I'm already behind! That's not fair."

"Sure it is," he said. "Rules say you give up your bed tonight, right? So, how about winner gets to pick what bed you sleep in? That means if you win, you get your own bed tonight, and if you lose, well, it isn't any different than if we hadn't played at all."

Alison's mouth fell open before she leaned forward to find the score card in front of Kyle. She had three points, Kyle had eight, Daniel seven, and Trent was leading with ten, since he'd gotten two red cards, which were worth more.

That was a large distance to make up, but she *needed* to win. The thought of ending up in one of their beds for the night had already bothered her, but now she'd found a hail-Mary that would save her—at least for a night.

"Three," she said quickly.

"Well, well, isn't she in the game now?" Daniel said, his voice all amusement.

Kyle lifted the red card to read it. "First kiss."

Alison frowned as she thought back. The question could have been far worse—she figured she ought to be thankful. "I was thirteen," she said, recalling the freckle-faced neighbor boy who had stolen her heart.

Which was funny, because it wasn't as though she'd been naive before then. Her father had sheltered her, but that hadn't stopped her from knowing things. It just meant she hadn't been exposed to many people, so when she'd finally gotten out from beneath that cloak, she'd gone a bit crazy.

"For three points? I need more," Kyle pushed.

"He was a year younger and had red hair. He hit my lip with his tooth, and I thought for a while after that I was a lesbian, because it really sucked."

Kyle stared at her until she fidgeted. Finally, he responded. "Well, my first kiss was with also with a red-headed boy, and it for sure put me off men, so I get that."

A heartbeat later, Trent broke the silence with a loud laugh. Daniel joined in, with Kyle only grinning at Alison.

And, despite her best attempt, she cracked a smile and released a soft chuckle at the absurdity of his statement.

That was possibly even more dangerous than anything else he'd done.

An hour later, Alison clutched the dice, ready to try to blow on it just to get a good roll. Funny that she'd gone from unwilling to answer her favorite food to answering everything happily.

Anything if it meant she got to sleep in her own bed.

She was points behind, mostly because the alphas had *no* shame. They would tell her any part of their past as if it didn't matter. Then again, the three knew each other well enough that none of their stories seemed to be a surprise.

And they didn't mind telling her about their sexual history, which she tried to ignore as best she could.

Which was *not* easy, especially when Daniel started talking about his favorite part on a woman—turned out he was an ass man—and Alison felt suddenly aware of her own body.

Worse, Daniel had danced his fingers along her back, the touch soft and coaxing. She'd worn a spaghetti strap tank top, so he stroked over the bare skin above it, then below it.

"You can't increase your odds by procrastinating," Kyle told her, enjoying her struggle far too much.

Trent was ahead, meaning either she rolled a red card, or she lost.

So it would be her own bed or Trent's.

If I ever needed mental powers, it's now. She shut her eyes and rolled once more, a silent prayer.

A dark chuckle made her heart sink before she even opened her eyes. It was far too amused for her to have won.

She cracked her eyes to find a two, and a quick look at the board put her on a yellow.

Which meant she'd lost.

Trent's smile was shameless as he set his elbow on the table. "Looks like you're spending the night in my bed, pet."

Trent tried to ignore how good it felt to get his bed ready for someone else. How long had it been since he'd slept beside someone?

Six years? Hell, he couldn't even be sure.

Of course, he hadn't planned to have that person be an omega who was only pretending to want to be there.

The look on her face when she'd realized she'd lost the game, when she had to come to terms with sleeping in his bed—he didn't much enjoy that.

Daniel probably did. The bastard loved to push boundaries, enjoyed that edge of unease.

Trent much preferred trust.

She doesn't know you. How can she trust you?

He sighed as he set a bottle of water and a glass on the side of the bed she'd sleep on. He planned to take the one near the door—*old habits die hard*—so she'd have to deal with the other side.

A soft knock made him smile. That first night, when she'd out-maneuvered him, he'd expected her to be brash, unstoppable. Instead, she'd proven time and time again to have more uncertainty than he'd have ever guessed.

She had confidence, sure, and she'd proven herself a capable fighter. None of it changed that when it came to him, when it came to Daniel and Kyle, she was in over her head and knew it.

"Come on in," Trent called, not wanting to crowd her at the door.

The hinges squeaked as she entered, and after a moment of hesitation, she closed the door behind her.

She wore a pair of tight shorts that showed off the muscular curves of her pale legs. A tight tank top covered her torso, and it either had one of those included bras or she'd gone without, because she had no bra straps. It made her look impossibly casual in a way he liked *far* too much.

Sometimes she seemed out of reach, like something to be seen but not touched. Ready for bed, though, she looked perfect.

"Got water for you," he said, pointed. "Also put vitamins next to it."

"I don't take vitamins," she argued.

"You do now."

Lines appeared in her forehead, but she didn't complain any more. *Good girl. She learns fast.*

Trent didn't much abide arguments. It was one of the things he liked about being in charge. He'd listen, of course, to real feedback or concerns.

If Alison had said pills made her sick, he'd help her find a type that didn't. If she'd said she had her blood tested and didn't require some of them, they'd locate brands that only had those things she was deficient in.

However, he suspected Alison's knee-jerk reaction was to argue. It had nothing to do with real problems with whatever was offered but done out of her desire for independence.

Though…as he watched her, he wondered how real that need was.

The way her pupils would dilate, the flush on her cheeks when he'd hand-fed her, those things all implied that she had a desire for someone to take those reins even if she didn't know how to accept it.

What happened to make her this nervous?

"You don't need to stare at me," she snapped.

Trent blinked slowly, as though woken. "Sorry. I was thinking. Why does it bother you when I do, though?"

She wrapped her arms around herself, not venturing any further into the room. "I don't like it. It feels like you're trying to figure me out."

"Would that be so bad?"

"Yes."

He huffed out a soft laugh at her insolence and pouting before he gestured at the open door inside his room. "Bathroom is through there if you need it during the night. You were up early this morning—do you always wake up that early or was that special?"

"I couldn't sleep," she said, her gaze on the bed. "I figured there wasn't any reason to stay in bed if I can't sleep."

He nodded, recalling nights like that. Sometimes the best thing a person could do was get the hell out of bed when sleep wouldn't come. The more he'd lain there, the more frustrated he'd gotten and it had been less likely sleep would actually happen. "You always sleep poorly?"

"I'm a light sleeper. Please tell me you don't snore."

"I don't think I do, but I haven't slept beside someone in a long damn time, so who knows. If I do, just kick me and I'll roll over and stop."

"What's a long time? Gone a week without one of your crazy exploits you like to talk about from the red cards?"

He laughed as he caught the bottom hem of his shirt and pulled it off. He'd already showered, but he'd be damned if he was sleeping in anything more than he had to. "I never mentioned sleeping in any of those, did I?"

She didn't quip back, which surprised the fuck out of him. At least, it did until he got his shirt over his head and saw the way her gaze was pinned to his chest.

Well, it seemed there was *something* she liked about him.

Not that Trent understood that in the least. He was partial to women, to their softness, to the gentle sloping curves of their bodies. He'd seen plenty of naked men in his life—hell, he knew Daniel and Kyle's bodies almost as well as he did his own, since they'd taken women together often enough—and they never stirred a thing in him.

The soft scent that left Alison, though, said it stirred something inside her.

"Get into bed, pet, and I'll turn off the lights."

He gave her the privacy to collect herself as he went into the bathroom to escape her scent for a moment.

An entire night in bed with her? What a fucking beautiful disaster.

Still, sleep came slowly.

Wonderful heat surrounded Trent's dick later, though how much later, he had no idea. Fuck, how he'd missed that feeling, the way the scent of a woman would cloud his judgment and make his cock impossibly harder.

He rocked his hips forward, enjoying the friction and the moans and the stuttering little gasps. It was all a dream—the way everything moved, that weightless quality of it, all said it wasn't real. He didn't give a damn, though.

Alison. He knew it on some deep level, recognized her scent already, her body. Sweet curves and sinful heat—that was what she was.

He could see her in that moment, her full, pouty lips letting out soft whimpers as he spread her thighs and slid into her hot wet cunt.

He growled low in his throat at the possessive need that swamped him, at the desire to fuck her until she begged, until she fully submitted to him. He'd never felt such a powerful need before, as though each thump of his heart happened only to get him closer to that goal.

And her? She gave. The girl who could take, the girl who was capable of resisting anything, clung to him. Her scent surrounded him, rich and sweet and full of fire. He dug his fingers into her, holding her tight, wanting to grasp her because she seemed so distant the rest of the time.

A bite of pain from nails in his back drew a deep groan. It was primal and made him feel needed.

Tension pulled through him, dragging him toward a staggering release. It had been so long since he'd felt this, since he'd *needed* to come the way he felt. He buried his nose in her throat, inhaling her. It sent him over that edge.

The next thing happened out of instinct. He closed his teeth over her shoulder just as his release rushed through him.

And just as it happened, when his back tightened, when that moment of bliss hit him, his eyes snapped open.

He caught sight of a startled and obviously just woken Alison, her cheeks flushed, her full lips in a surprised *O*.

And yet that didn't stop the oncoming train of his orgasm—like anything could stop that once it had left the station—and Trent couldn't help the low groan as he came.

Chapter Eight

Alison shivered from the orgasm that had rushed through her on the heels of waking. Something warm and sticky was between her thighs, and she was pretty sure it wasn't all from her…

Her knuckles ached and her shoulder burned, and it took another moment to realize the reasons—she'd dug her nails into Trent's back, and he'd bitten her shoulder.

A claiming bite. Hell, many bonded mates never did that, and yet now she had a wound on her shoulder from it. The mark would heal, but it would never go away entirely. There would always be a scar from it, as though her body knew to hold on to it, to cherish it.

Trent released her shoulder, the action drawing a whimper from her and another rolling wave of need that coursed through her. "Fuck," he said, his rough voice deeper than usual. He drew back, and the action caused her to look down and realize the rest.

He'd worn boxers to bed, but at some point during the long hours, she and Trent had ended up tangled together. His cock, which was hot and softening, was tucked between her legs, and that warm stickiness?

His cum sat on her thighs, which filled in the rest of the story.

Her faceless lover from her dream? The mind-blowing orgasm she'd had while asleep? Trent had rutted against her until they'd both gotten off.

"You going to freak out?" he asked.

Alison ran her tongue along her bottom lip, and the soreness there told her she'd chewed on it in her sleep. "I don't freak out."

"I didn't plan this." He extracted himself from the bed with a wince, as though the wetness from his cum was unpleasant.

Try having it all over your thighs.

Alison rolled over and put her feet to the floor, his scent clouding her head. Worse, each movement made another shiver run through her sensitive body. She stared down at the white on her thighs, her chest uneasy. It was so much alpha around her, and worse, she'd already reacted to it.

The wound on her shoulder burned, and she refused to look at it. It felt like a chain, like a tighter binding than the collar or cuffs.

A towel hit her lap, startling her back to the moment.

Trent nodded, then turned to look at the bed, as if deciding if he needed to change the sheets. It drew her attention to the scratches on his back. Scratches Alison had put there, a need that had terrified her resulting in them.

She wiped her thighs, though she didn't do a thorough job. Just enough to get the obvious streaks. As soon as she'd done it, she got to her feet, needing to get out of the room. It smelled like sex, and she hadn't even *had* sex.

"You're supposed to sleep here," he said, though his words lacked firmness.

"I feel like we've sort of wrapped up the sleeping thing."

He twisted his hand to peer at his watch. "It's three-twenty. You aren't ready to get up."

"If it means I don't have to get back in that bed? Sure, I'll get up now."

He offered a low growl, as though backed into a corner. "At least let me look at your shoulder." When he reached for her, Alison jerked backward. He froze, his hand dangling in the air before lowering slowly. "Right." The word was full of a lot, but Alison was too close to the edge to decipher any of it. "You're not sleeping alone. Daniel or Kyle. Your choice."

Alison wanted to argue, but more than that, she wanted to leave. The choice wasn't a hard one, really. Daniel was sweet, but Kyle kept things nice and surface level.

"Kyle's."

Trent nodded back, but didn't come closer, didn't move, when he let Alison flee. She didn't go to Kyle's room right away, first going to the restroom. It gave her a moment to collect herself.

This was a stupid plan. Did I really think I could resist three alphas? This is why I'm never around them.

She went to Kyle's door afterward, but as she lifted her hand to knock, it opened. Kyle stood there, his hair messy from sleep, the same smirk he always had on his lips. It tightened when his gaze landed on her shoulder, but didn't slip away.

He probably thought she didn't realize.

"Come on in." He made space for her, and past him she spotted the bed, unmade and all together inviting.

On the nightstand sat an open first-aid kit, which meant Trent had already spoken to Kyle. At least she wouldn't need to repeat the story.

Kyle set a hand on her lower back, leading her to the bed. When she sat, he picked up a packet from the kit. He tore it open, then pulled the small cloth out. A grip on her chin set off those old feelings, and she yanked back.

"Easy, sugar," he whispered and released her. "Tilt your head for me, would you?"

Alison shuddered out a breath but did as he asked. She hissed at the first pass of the alcohol pad.

"Sorry, but we should clean this," he explained. "The less of his saliva in the wound, the less it will scar."

"Well then, scrub it raw," she whispered.

He huffed a soft laugh, though there was still an edge to it. He covered the wound with gauze, then took a wipe from the packet beside the kit.

It was then she looked at her thighs and heat covered her cheeks. She hadn't cleaned up that well, and it was obvious from the stickiness still there. Getting into a man's bed with another man's cum on her thighs wasn't the sort of thing she'd done before, and certainly didn't make her feel all that good.

She expected Kyle to hand her the wipe, but instead, he worked to clean her himself. He was thorough and careful, not showing a bit of disgust or discomfort. He slid the cold wipe along her skin, catching each tacky area, even spreading her legs and dropping to his knees to clean her inner thighs.

How the hell can this turn me on again? Wasn't earlier enough?

Yet, there she was, as though she hadn't learned her lesson from the last time.

Worse, Kyle inhaled once, released a low groan—one that sounded as though he wanted things and was disappointed to not get to have them—before he finished and took the kit and trash into the bathroom, leaving her alone.

Alison's collar and cuffs seemed awfully heavy at that moment, the gauze made her shoulder itch and she had no idea how to recalibrate her body.

She could have been truly mad if Trent had pushed a boundary on purpose, if he'd forced her into something. Instead, as proven by her own orgasm, she'd been a willing participant in their little dream-session.

What the hell am I supposed to do with that?

"Stop thinking so much and lie down." Kyle's voice came a second before the light in the room clicked off. He left the bathroom one on, as though he knew she might need it. The bed dipped beneath his weight as he settled in, and Alison did the same, her back to him and the large distance between them evidence of just how little she trusted him.

Him? What a joke. Clearly, I can't trust myself, either.

* * * *

Daniel let out a low growl as he stared at Trent. The man wouldn't even *look* at him.

Alison was up in the shower, which meant Daniel hadn't gotten to see her shoulder, but Kyle had explained it well enough.

"You *marked* her?"

Trent's shoulders went rigid, as though the very words bothered him.

Good. He should feel guilty.

"Not on purpose." Trent stirred his coffee, not facing Daniel.

"What the hell does that mean? You agreed to the rules! Hell, you made them."

Trent finally turned, leaning his back against the kitchen counter. "To be fair, I didn't kiss her." His deadpan delivery only drove Daniel's temper more.

"Don't play that game with me. What the hell were you thinking?"

Finally, Trent sighed, his shoulders falling. "I wasn't thinking, okay? I was fucking asleep. So was she. Neither of us made some big plan about this. As it turns out, when you're horny and have an omega in your bed, sometimes shit happens."

Daniel snorted, crossing his arms. "*Shit* didn't happen. We aren't talking about a wet dream here. You bit her. You have *never* done that before to any woman."

"I know, and I don't know what you're expecting me to say. I didn't plan it, I don't know why it fucking happened, and I never wanted to bite her in the first place. Yell at me all you fucking want, I've already been kicking my own ass over it all morning."

The misery on Trent's face was the only reason Daniel managed to wrangle his frustration at all. Trent looked about as happy about it as Daniel felt. A claiming bite…something rare that only happened between mates, and often not even then. It was some holdover from a more primal side of alphas, something most alphas had even shed over the millennia of evolution they'd gone through.

Why did it surprise him that if any of them had that drive still, it would be Trent?

"This is exactly why you aren't with the FBI anymore," Daniel snapped.

Trent narrowed his eyes at that. "Are you really going there? Don't try and turn this into some proof of shit." Trent's voice was low, a warning there that Daniel didn't mind trampling over.

"Isn't it? Alison has a claiming bite on her. Forget how fucked up that is for her, how complicated it makes any of us working together, but how the hell do we explain that to the person who is supposed to come and examine her? Lot harder to pass her off as merchandise when *your* claiming bite is on her, isn't it?"

Trent's jaw popped, and for a minute, Daniel thought the other alpha might sail across the kitchen.

It wouldn't be the first time he and Trent had gone head-to-head. Neither of them were hotheads, yet they seemed to be the only ones to end up fighting. Maybe they were too different—or too alike—but it was *always* them.

"Always worried only about the job, aren't you? Somethings never do change." Trent shook his head and left the kitchen, coffee in hand, steps angry and loud.

"Look at that, we're back to normal." Kyle's voice was breezy as he came in, letting Daniel know the bastard had listened to everything.

Which wasn't shocking, because Kyle was nosy.

"You can't tell me you're okay with what happened. You were the one to bandage her."

Kyle hopped onto the counter, his hair still damp from his own shower that morning. "Am I thrilled? No, but shit happens when you house alphas and omegas together. "

"None of that deals with the fact that Alison didn't agree to that."

Kyle waved off the concern. "Alison isn't the fragile thing you think. Exhibit A?" Kyle waved at his face, at the bruising still there.

"Yeah, and all you were trying to do was help her when she did that. I'm pretty sure leaving a permanent claim on someone's skin is a little different."

"I took care of her afterward. The girl was freaked out, but it wasn't by *him*. The second I started cleaning her, she was trembling and wet again. Her reaction shook her more than what Trent did."

Daniel had no real argument back to that, though it did derail his thoughts as he considered how nicely Alison heated up, the way that scent of hers would fill the space around her like a lure—one he wanted to go for no matter the risks.

"Besides," Kyle continued. "It's easy to get high and mighty when you're not sleeping next to her, when you aren't the one breathing in that smell all night, when she isn't that close to you. Trust me, your tune might change when you have to try and sleep while your cock keeps giving you much better ideas of what to do with the hours till morning."

Creaking drew Daniel's attention over to them to find the omega in question coming down the steps, her hair dark from the shower. She didn't walk like a woman who was fearful, like one being pushed into anything she didn't want.

Even with the gauze on her shoulder, she walked with her back straight, with her chin high, as though she wasn't afraid of a damned thing.

And right then Daniel felt a spark of fear, because no matter how much he focused on the job, on what needed to be done, when she walked like *that*, he wasn't sure he could follow through on keeping it all about the case.

* * * *

Alison smacked Kyle's hand when he straightened her collar.

"You are the most unruly slave I've ever dealt with," he muttered, though his lip remained curled into a half-smirk. "I feel like I'd have to give you an *F* when it came to slave training. "

"I'm pretty sure a bad slave means a bad master."

He chuckled before checking her cuffs, running his finger beneath them to test the tightness. She'd found that the alphas did that a few times a day, always checking to see if they rubbed against her, if they had chafed, if they were too tight. The concern was something she never knew quite how to deal with.

"When is he supposed to get here?"

Kyle stilled as he checked the second cuff, as though the question weren't a welcome one. "Tomorrow. The call said about nine, but I can't say I expect these sorts of people to be very punctual." He released her wrists but didn't step backward. "You nervous?"

Alison snorted softly. "Me? I'm never nervous. Have you forgotten I was the one using myself as actual bait?"

Kyle tugged her down and into his lap as he sat on the couch.

Alison had thought, after the difficult night, they'd lighten up on her. She'd thought getting bitten would give her a get-out-of-jail-free card for at least a day where they backed off.

No such luck. They'd continued to press her boundaries, always careful, as if that hadn't happened.

Well, everyone except Trent.

Trent didn't even look her way.

Being pulled into Kyle's lap made her uneasy, a closeness she wasn't accustomed to, but she took a deep breath and tried to submit to it. While she wasn't being watched, she needed to practice, to school herself into behaving as she should.

"Yeah, but you were still in control then."

"In control while being held to be sold into slavery?" She cocked an eyebrow.

"Don't look at me like I'm stupid." Kyle pressed a finger to her eyebrow until she lowered it. "You thought you'd be playing your own game, all on your own. It's easy to fool someone else who doesn't know what you're playing at. You in that bar? You were playing your part by yourself. If you had to play that with someone else who knew, though?" He left it open.

And it hit home. There was some truth. Pretending on her own was one thing. Pretending with someone else was personal, and Alison did not like anything personal.

"So, sugar, are you nervous?"

She blew out a slow breath. Was she? Why didn't she even know if she was nervous?

Kyle slid his arm around her to draw her closer to him, so she leaned against him. "You are a stubborn, difficult woman, you know that?"

The soft chiding made her wince. In her head, she heard her father's voice. *You are a difficult child. If you are an omega, you are going to have a very hard life learning to fit in.*

"Look at me." Kyle's voice beckoned her back, and Alison followed it, away from her father's flat and disappointed words, to find Kyle staring at her, his hand rubbing over her back.

Why the hell do I keep doing that?

"Where do you go when you zone out?"

She swallowed hard, wanting to make a joke, to insult him, to do something to bypass the conversation.

He shook his head before she could. "I'm serious, Alison. There is a huge tripwire here we keep getting caught on, and I don't know what it is. I don't need you to pour your heart out—I'm not going to try and force you to give anything you don't have to—but I need to understand where that line is so I stop falling flat on my face over it."

Alison said nothing at first. She let the stroking of his hand over her back take away some of the anxiety inside her.

Finally, she answered, choosing her words carefully. *Tell him only as much as he needs to know.*

"My father," she said softly. "He wasn't very approving of me."

A soft rumble came from Kyle's chest, one that eased her further. "Parents sure can fuck us up, can't they? What was his problem? I can't imagine being all that disappointed in a kick-ass daughter like you."

That praise, small as it was, took up space inside her, space that had always been dark and heavy and full of all the ways she didn't live up to expectations. It drew more of the story from her. "He thought women should be silent, meek, *obedient*. I tried to do what he wanted, I really did, but I never could follow the rules enough. I never was quiet enough."

Kyle let out a low sound, something that implied that he was listening but didn't want to interrupt.

"He always said I was difficult, that I was stubborn."

"Is he still alive?"

She imagined his harsh features, the dark eyes, the way he stood straight and could unnerve anyone with a silent stare. "I have no idea."

Kyle rubbed his forehead against hers, a sweet nuzzle she had to stop herself from leaning in to, from returning. "Is that why you don't like when we touch your chin?"

That question hurt. Her stomach rolled and she closed her eyes, the answer slipping from her without her even having to think about it. "He never hit me—he believed if you had to hit a woman, you'd already failed as a man. He'd grab my chin, though, and stare down at me with this level of disgust, like I was the lowest thing he'd seen." The words came from her like shards of glass, as if they sliced and tore at her on the way out.

Kyle did that low rumble again—a purr?—and wrapped his arm tighter around her. "That's enough, sugar. I'm sorry he did that, and now that I understand, I'll make sure we're more cautious about that. Shh, just relax for a minute."

Alison wanted to snap, to tell him she didn't need to relax, that she was fine.

Except, she realized she was shivering. She wasn't cold, yet her body trembled as though she were naked and wet and freezing. The warmth of Kyle's body, the strength in his arms and that wonderfully relaxing vibration from his chest all called to her.

So Alison let herself have something she'd *never* allowed herself before.

She rested against Kyle and shut her eyes, surrendering for real, just for right then.

* * * *

Daniel chuckled at the way Alison fidgeted. For the first time, they'd bound her. With the meeting tomorrow, they needed to move forward with pressing her, and he had to admit—he enjoyed her reaction.

He wouldn't have liked fear.

Real fear was sour, acidic and altogether unpleasant. Unease, though? That edge of worry? *That* he found irresistible, and it filled Alison.

She knelt on the floor, a pillow beneath her knees to take the strain off, her wrists cuffed behind her. It made her chest push forward, and it would have been impossible to not notice how lovely her figure was.

Even if he wasn't supposed to notice, the way her tank top hugged her curves was a thing of beauty. Her chest wasn't that large, but it also meant that when she wore no bra—or something thin without much support—her breasts were still high on her chest and stunning. Her bare skin was flushed, and her shorts showed off the expanse of her toned legs.

Kyle had sat down with Trent and Daniel earlier, had explained what Alison had told him.

While Daniel was grateful for an understanding of the girl who was so tight-lipped that—despite how close he'd gotten to her—she still seemed like a stranger, he'd had to grapple with his own frustration about her family.

He wouldn't deny he enjoyed some humiliation. He liked to force a woman to blush when he pointed out things that embarrassed her, things that *shouldn't* embarrass her but did.

However, he only liked that when the woman did, and clearly that was off limits with Alison.

Daniel checked her cuffs behind her, catching a tremble that ran through her when he moved out of her line of sight. "Everything feeling okay?"

"Why do you ask such a stupid question? Who on earth finds being tied up comfortable?"

Daniel wrapped his fingers in her hair and tugged, a gentle pull to remind her not to mouth off. "A lot of people, if it's done correctly. And a little discomfort isn't necessarily bad, but we want to make sure nothing is too tight, that your left shoulder doesn't hurt at this angle."

She froze, as if he'd said something entirely unexpected.

Daniel lifted his gaze to Kyle. *Did we misread her history? She said it was her left shoulder.*

Kyle shrugged.

Alison's gulp—a tell-tale giveaway that she was nervous—came before a surprisingly direct answer. "It doesn't hurt."

Sometimes dealing with her felt like wandering a minefield, like he was traipsing around and had no idea when the next step would blow him up.

But they were pushing her enough this afternoon. There was no need to make it more uncomfortable, so he let it go.

"Good. If that changes, let us know. Right now, you can just tell us. If it's when we need to be entirely in character, use your safe word, and I'll try to figure out the issue. Do you remember your safe word?"

"Master." The word was whispered like a vile curse, and Daniel had to admit, he didn't care for it, either.

He'd never been in for the twenty-four-seven thing. He loved a willing submissive, and yeah, he'd slip into that mode quite often, but he didn't want a slave.

"Good girl," Kyle said, seated on the couch in front of her. He reached out and dragged his fingers over her cheek. "Now, when they're here, we'll have you bound just like this. Blindfolded, headphones on. It'll help reduce you having to play along too much. Don't worry, we'll turn the noise canceling off on the headphones so you can still hear us."

Tension left her shoulders, as though that was what she'd needed to hear. "So how long do I have to be like this?"

Daniel huffed a chuckle at her annoyance. If it was *only* annoyance, it would have been easier to ignore. However, the moment she'd gone to her knees, when Kyle had pushed her shoulders to guide her down, that delectable scent had blossomed in the room.

She didn't *want* to like this, but she did. It made Daniel want to press his lips to her exposed skin, to taste her.

She hasn't asked for that, though.

"You've got to look like someone who has been bound and played with enough that it isn't surprising anymore," Trent said.

He'd stood back, still seemingly unnerved by the entire bite thing.

"Played with?" Alison furrowed her eyebrows and took that plump bottom lip between her teeth.

How could she be as dangerous as she was, as tough as she was, and still somehow look so innocent?

Daniel took his seat behind her, in a chair he'd pulled in from the kitchen. It meant she was kneeling surrounded by all three of them. "I'm sure you know exactly what we mean by that. You aren't a virgin."

"No, I'm not, but I'm also not someone stupid enough to let people tie me up."

Of course not. Bondage required some real trust, and Alison didn't trust herself, let alone anyone else. No way would the girl let someone tie her up and have fun, no matter how much her reaction showed she would love it.

She was close enough that Kyle cupped her cheek and rested her head against his thigh. It put her very close to him, but that was why they were doing this.

Alison had to look as if she'd done this, that they'd spent the last few weeks in such close contact. There was no way to fake that level of comfort, especially with a girl as guarded as Alison.

Tension ran through her muscles, and she seemed a moment from bolting—or at least trying to, since her bindings would hold her.

"Yes, playing," Kyle said as he toyed with her hair. "Even though we aren't planning on actually fucking you, you need to seem like we have been. If we'd spent the last few weeks actually training you, you sure as hell would be comfortable kneeling for us, or accepting our touch. So, that's what we're doing now."

"Or you're just trying to justify why you can touch me," she pointed out. "What's next, you're going to say that to really sell the story, you need to actually have sex with me?"

"Well, if you're offering..." Kyle had a full grin on his face.

She offered him a hell of a glare.

"Sex doesn't need to happen," Trent broke in, leaning back in his chair. "But you can't act like a prude, either."

"I am not a prude."

Daniel snorted at that. She *was* a prude. It was impossible not to be one when she wouldn't let her guard down, ever. How exactly was someone supposed to get into sex, to really enjoy it, if they were constantly on guard?

She moved off Kyle's thigh and twisted to glare at Daniel. The look was so much less intimidating when she was bound like that. "I'm not. You act like I'm some naive, virginal teenager."

"Never said that, but having sex doesn't mean you've got much experience."

"You don't know anything."

"Oh yeah?" Daniel fed off her attitude, desperate to see her ruffled. "Because I remember our little getting-to-know-one-another game. You answered those red cards, but you sure as hell didn't have much in the way of wild stories to tell. You ever have sex outside of a bed?"

"Of course I have." The red on her cheeks was all frustration at that moment, but damn, it was pretty. "Quickies in bar bathrooms are a thing, you know?"

And why didn't that surprise him? Because her level of prudishness wasn't about not having sex, it was about not actually giving herself in to it. "Not a shocker," Kyle said, picking up the conversation. "Hell, I bet it's been all backrooms and motel rooms with you. You ever have a guy back to your place?"

Silence.

Kyle kept going. "You ever let one hold you down?"

"Maybe I like holding *them* down."

That got a bark of laughter from Daniel. He loved that she kept him on his toes. "Well, you did leave some marks on poor Trent. Man won't be able to go to a pool for at least a couple weeks without people asking what wild animal got a hold of him."

She shifted, and he *knew* it was because she'd grown wet from their conversation. "Just because I'm not into kinky sex doesn't make me a prude."

"Not into and never tried are two different things. You know, sweet, your problem is that you want shit you're afraid to ask for. You'd rather pretend you don't want it, that you aren't interested, instead of risking anything. I bet you if we tied you up, for real, you'd enjoy it."

"This feels pretty real to me." She tugged at the cuffs to make her point, the metal jingling as she did.

Daniel slid his fingers over the edge of her shirt, then traced her spine up to her collar. "This isn't real. Real would have you naked, and we'd be allowed to touch."

"You *are* touching."

"Not really, not the places we'd both like a lot better."

The conversation had gone so far off the rails, but Daniel didn't care to yank it back on track. The job, the case, all stopped being an issue.

Suddenly they were three interested, dominant alphas with a beautiful, drenched omega on her knees.

"Like where?" She asked the question in a whisper, the sort that said she probably hadn't even meant to ask.

"Everywhere, pet." Trent answered. "You're already carrying some of my scent, but you'd have theirs by the end of the night."

"So why haven't you done that? Why keep trying to act like this is all professional?"

Daniel wrapped his fingers in her hair again, drawing his hand into a fist and forcing her to look up and back at him. Her pupils grew, telling him she damn well liked that sting in her scalp.

"Because this *is* professional. What we're doing, it's what the case needs. The rest? Those things aren't needed, so we don't act on them."

"And if I wanted to?"

Daniel smiled and traced his finger over her lip. "You'd have to ask *very* nicely."

When she darted her tongue out and the warm wetness of it touched his thumb, he groaned.

Please, let her ask…

Chapter Nine

Daniel's words kept repeating in Alison's head. She couldn't help it. She wanted…

Something.

She didn't even know what exactly. All she knew for sure was that everything they did teased some deep part of her that had never awoken before.

It terrified her and excited her and made her want to both hide and drop to her knees and beg.

Still, after Daniel's statement, they'd released her. No one had mentioned it again while they ate. Trent had hand-fed her again, and though she had her own plate, she'd found herself eating what he offered instead.

Why the hell do I like that?

Now, after night had fallen and she should have been sleeping, she stared at the ceiling.

Daniel had his e-book reader out, his back against the wall in the bed. The backlit reader meant he'd turned the lights off for her, but it seemed he hadn't been quite ready to turn in.

He confused her most of all. He could seem so sweet and easygoing, and yet there was a darkness in his gaze when he looked at her some of the time. How he'd pulled her hair and told her she'd need to ask *nicely* showed a different side to him, one she hadn't expected.

One she really liked.

Why not ask?

The thought surprised her as much as his statement had. Alison didn't ask for anything, let alone for someone to do...well, whatever they wanted to do to her.

She thought back to her sex life. She'd thought herself some liberated, modern woman, sleeping with men in backrooms or motel rooms or wherever sparked her fancy.

She'd thought herself experienced, yet suddenly she wasn't so sure. The way they'd looked at her, the things they hinted at, she didn't understand them. How could she be naive?

And yet, she *wanted* to know them.

She wanted to have experienced them, at least so she could look back and say, *"I tried it and I hated it."*

You're such a liar. You won't hate it.

She considered the end of the case, when she'd walk away and go back to her own life. She'd never considered such things before—even if she'd known enough to think she wanted them—because she didn't care for messy entanglements.

This wasn't messy, though.

It was temporary. It was a job. At the end of it, they'd all go back to their own lives no worse for wear.

Which made it perfect.

What if she gave in? What if she surrendered? She could pretend it was for the case, that it was to get into character—as if that might help her not feel so strange about it—and once she'd experienced it, she could walk away.

Alison rolled toward Daniel, looking up at his face, which was lit by the glow of his reader. He had on a pair of glasses—he only wore them when reading—his attention on the book.

She risked it, reaching over and setting her hand on his bare stomach, just above where the sheet covered his waist.

His stomach tightened in response, but he didn't stop what he was doing, didn't acknowledge it.

Alison took the chance to stroke her fingers over his warm skin. He wasn't as lean as the other two, with a more relaxed physique. She could feel the muscles beneath the skin, beneath the layer of fat, so she'd never think of him as weak. Dark hair ran from his navel down below the sheet, and more covered his chest. She teased that trail of hair to where the fabric stopped her.

"You're supposed to be sleeping," he said, his voice deep.

Alison scooted closer until she pressed against him, seated lower in the bed so her face was near his ribs. She followed the trail back up, past his navel, so she could trace over his chest. She circled his flat nipples and stoked along the dark, coarse hair.

His body was so different from hers. How had she never realized that before?

Well, she had, in a clinical way, but when she'd slept with men before, it had always been quick. It hadn't meant anything, and she'd been only too happy to finish as quickly as possible. She hadn't wanted to explore, to spend any time on their body beyond what was necessary to get to business.

This time, however, she wanted to touch, to feel the bumpy skin on the outside edge of his nipples, to feel his breath catch when she raked her nails over his pecs.

Daniel set his reader aside, as though he'd given up trying to pretend he didn't care or notice exactly what she was doing.

He rolled over her, moving her with such ease that she released a gasp. She'd fought hand to hand enough, been trained enough that she understood how to counter nearly any move, but she didn't *want* to counter this.

Daniel pinned her wrists above her head in a single large hand of his, his warm body over and against hers.

The way she spread her legs to give him a cradle to fall into, to keep him close, was so quick she was embarrassed by it.

"I don't hear you asking," he said.

"Isn't it obvious?"

He smiled at her snark. "Yeah, but I need to hear you say it."

"Do you get off on women begging or something?" Even as she asked, the very thought made her temperature rise a few degrees.

Does she mean to shame or embarrass me? She has a lot to learn, doesn't she?

"Yeah, I do," he said. "But this is more about making sure *you* know you want this. The last thing I'm about to do is trick or push you into anything. So if you can't ask, if you can't even tell me what you want, well, you must not want it bad enough."

His lips sat a whisper from hers, and the need to lower his head, to take that kiss, swamped him. He wanted so badly to taste her, to know how soft they really were, to feel her writhing under him as he drove her crazy.

"I'm curious," she answered.

"Curious? Hell of a way to put it."

She twisted her hands, and he got the sense she wanted to shove him away. Not because she wanted him gone, but because she wanted to keep him at a distance so she could lie to herself.

He held her still. She could always safeword or even tell him to stop, but the girl needed to learn to use her words.

"I just thought..."

"Thought what?"

The look she gave him would have sent a lot of men running. "We're doing this until the case is over. You're right—I've never done any of those things you mentioned. "

"But you want to?"

"I want to try. It isn't something I have in my regular life."

"Why not?"

"I can't trust people enough, haven't ever wanted to trust them enough. This might be my only chance."

The longing in her voice killed him. She deserved so much, but as time went on, he realized self-denial seemed to be her motto in life.

"But you trust me? Us?"

She shook her head. "No, but we're here, going halfway with this nonsense. Why not try something here? I can walk away afterward knowing what it's like."

He stifled the growl at 'walk away'. Why the hell that set him off, he wasn't sure, but he knew he didn't care for it at all. He wanted her to *want* to stay. He wanted her desperate for another touch from him, begging for another kiss, not putting timelines on it as if he were nothing more than a sex toy to try out and discard.

And, yes, he realized how stupid that thought was, but it didn't stop him from having it.

"So what do you want? Make it clear." He kept his voice low, not bothering to hide the slight growl to it.

She opened her mouth, but before she could say it, she closed it.

"Not that hard. You want us to touch you? To fuck you?" He didn't curse much, but damn if that hadn't rolled right off his tongue. There wasn't another way to describe what he wanted to do to her.

She swallowed hard but didn't answer with anything but a nod.

"Say it."

Still nothing.

Daniel sighed and rolled off her. "You don't want it yet, not bad enough, not if you can't even say it. Let me know when you change your mind."

He picked up his e-book reader and ignored the way his cock *pulsed* inside his pajama bottoms. It would be so easy to roll back over, spread her thighs and slide into her. She wanted it, he wanted it, why wait?

Because she'll damn well be begging before I give her anything.

And judging from the frustrated groan as she rolled away, he doubted that would be all that long.

* * * *

Kyle laughed as he stood in the small outside porch. Daniel had already told him about the night before, and now Kyle couldn't stop thinking about it.

Damn, he knew how delicious Alison could smell, but would he have been able to pull away like Daniel did?

"You are a sadist," Kyle chuckled.

Daniel sat on the swing, leaning back, looking as though he hadn't gotten nearly enough sleep the night before.

Then again, sleeping with a hard-on and an all-too-willing omega beside him wouldn't do much for any alpha's sleep.

"A bit, but really, we all agreed that she needs to ask for anything she wants."

"I'm pretty sure I'd take a lingering glance as her asking right about now," Kyle admitted. "I don't think I've ever wanted a female this much. What the hell is it with her?"

"You just want to screw the girl who broke your nose. You're worse than the rest of us."

Kyle grinned, unable to deny it. Something about a girl who could best him was an unbelievable turn-on. The more he discovered about her, the deeper it went, though.

The way she'd sat in his lap as she'd admitted her past, how she'd talked about her father—it had chiseled away any of his resistance. She'd been...almost sweet.

The girl was never helpless, but she had cracks that ran through her, the same as anyone, and Kyle getting a look at them made her feel all the more like *theirs.*

The slider opened and drew both Kyle's and Daniel's gazes to it.

If Daniel looked as though he hadn't slept, Alison was worse. Dark circles rested beneath her eyes, and he'd watched her down two large cups of coffee, drinking them as if the meaning of life were at the bottom.

It seemed the girl didn't sleep well when horny, either.

"Late night?" Kyle made sure to pair the quip with a smirk.

Alison offered a half-hearted glare in return.

"That's it? Wow, you really aren't up to snuff, are you?"

She shut the slider behind her, the light that streamed in between the vines covering the outer patio lighting up her pale complexion. She looked like some goddess, and with how she'd turned his world upside down?

He wasn't sure that was an altogether wrong description.

"I didn't sleep well," she admitted, her gaze on the ground.

"And whose fault was that?" Daniel didn't look all that sorry. If anything, he seemed to enjoy that he'd done that to her.

"Yours." Her tone came out sharp.

He clicked his tongue. "All I said was that you needed to tell me what you wanted, clearly. That's how this works, all of it. If you want something, you need to say it. We're happy to give you what you want—within reason—but you've got to learn to ask."

She stood beside Kyle, one hand picking at the nails of her other.

He thought back to what she'd said to him, about her father, to the bastard who had taught her she wasn't good enough.

He doubted she'd had the chance to ask for much of anything in her life. She seemed like the *pull yourself up by your bootstraps* sort of woman, the kind who would rather go without than just ask. *Obviously, she is. She went without last night because she just didn't want to voice it.*

He was glad Trent wasn't out there. Trent was always the softy, the one who would give in. He'd have taken her in his arms and told her he'd take care of it all.

Soft-hearted idiot. Trent might like rules, but he also bent over backward to take care of those around him.

Kyle, however, could be hard if it was in her best interests, and this was.

Alison drew her hands into fists and squared her shoulders. *Ah, there's that steel will.*

"I don't want to have sex with you."

Kyle nearly grumbled at that, because it wasn't at all what he'd hoped she'd say. *Force her to talk and that's what she comes up with?*

Before he could say anything or show his disappointment, she kept going, as if she needed to get it all out at once. "Not yet, at least. But I'm carrying Trent's scent already. I don't know what I want to do, not exactly, but I want to…try."

Not specific, but a hell of a lot better than before.

Kyle glanced Daniel's way, wanting to get a consensus on whether that was clear enough for him.

The curl of Daniel's lips said he had no issues with the request, and thank fuck for that. Kyle wasn't sure he could have just turned around and left if Alison's begging wasn't good enough.

Still, he wanted to check on things. "If this is just about scent, I think you know we could remedy that with something less *intimate*. Not that hard to get you to wear our scent."

And...*fuck*...even that made Kyle wish he'd been sitting. He considered all the ways he could have her wear his scent without actually touching her. It made him picture her down on her knees, as she had been the night before, and he'd stroke himself until he came. She wouldn't even touch him, but he wanted to rub that into her skin, to make sure she wore his scent while he told her what a good girl she was.

"I know," she answered, and her side-eye toward Kyle said she'd picked up his arousal, his reaction to their conversation. "What I said last night, I meant. I've never had the chance to experience this, and clearly you know what you're doing. I want to try."

Kyle gave up being passive. She'd made her wants clear, and he *needed* to touch her. He grasped her collar, tugging it until she was in front of him—careful not to grasp her chin—until she looked up at him. "We won't fuck you, not yet. Any other lines you don't want crossed?" He leaned in, her breath sweet and hot against his lips.

"Don't kiss me," she said.

He hid his disappointment. Limits were limits and he'd obey hers, even if it was hard to imagine not taking her lips. "Okay, sugar."

"Okay? I thought you'd argue more," she whispered back.

"Why would I do that? There are plenty of other places on your little body to enjoy, and I plan to explore each and every fucking one of them."

Chapter Ten

Alison couldn't breathe. What was she supposed to say back to *that*? Each time she thought she could handle the alphas, they'd prove again why she couldn't.

She'd shored up her courage to approach them, to ask, feeling confident and sexy, like some vixen. She'd expected to walk up, in control, and tell them exactly what she wanted.

And yet a few words from Kyle had her breathless and needy.

Which wasn't fair at all.

And yet, even when she couldn't seem to gain ground, she didn't feel unsafe. *Uneasy? Unprepared? Out of control? Absolutely.*

But she still felt safe, especially as Kyle drew back from her lips, respecting the stupid boundary she'd chosen.

Why a kiss? Why does that matter?

Because it feels personal. She didn't kiss the men she slept with, either. After that first disastrous red-headed boy had kissed her, when she'd decided she hated it, she'd stopped. Someone fucking her, well that was simple mechanics. A kiss?

It felt like more. *Like too much.*

She didn't need that complication.

Somehow, Kyle could look attractive even with the discoloration of the bruises on his face. It seemed altogether unfair. Even though Alison never focused on her beauty, she knew damn well that the times she'd ended up bruised, when she'd been hurt, she hadn't looked even better.

It wasn't fair, especially when everything else these alphas did was already sexy.

It seemed that everything was stacked against her. There hadn't been a chance at not succumbing to this, had there?

She expected Kyle to pull her up to his room—or Daniel's—but instead, he brushed his fingers over the curve of her breast, then palmed her through the thin fabric of her top. The heat soaked through the shirt, and she gasped at the feeling.

"Out here?"

Kyle's smirk never seemed to fade, only widening when he found amusement in something she'd done or said. "You shy?"

"Someone could see."

"No one can see, and even if they could, this only helps to sell our story, right?"

The thought of being watched turned into another stroke against her as she imagined eyes staring at her, watching her being taken by these men. She'd had people stare at her before plenty of times, and normally she *loathed* the experience.

Her beauty had always felt like a tool at best, an annoying lie the rest of the time. However, with *them* there, people wouldn't be looking at her as something to own.

Heat simmered through her.

Kyle chuckled before dragging his fingertips across her chest and over her other already-pebbled nipple. "You like that? Oh, sugar, how I want to show you off. I know a little club, the sort where people have some freedom, where they get to explore things that aren't allowed in most places. You'd look pretty like this—only wearing a lot less, like just the collar and cuffs. I'd put you down on your knees so you could suck my cock while others watch, then pull you into my lap to fuck. *Everyone* would stare, because you are quite the sight."

A whine so thin that she felt it more than heard it escaped her lips. Her entire body felt electrified in a way it had never been before.

How could a few words do that to her? How could she fall this deep into want with nothing but some dirty talk and an almost innocent touch?

He grasped the hem of her shirt, then tugged it up and off.

The air that touched her bare breasts made Alison wish she'd worn a bra. She didn't often, choosing tank tops with just enough support to keep everything in place, but perhaps around the alpha, something with more steps was needed.

Kyle knelt, moving as if he were doing any task, with efficiency rather than crazed passion.

It unnerved her.

Not that he noticed—or perhaps he did but just didn't feel the need to comment.

He grasped her leggings at the waist and tugged them down, leaving her simple black panties in place. His fingers skimmed her as he went, the brushes of skin to skin like teases. He lifted one leg, then the other, to work the pants off, not asking, trusting her to keep her balance.

Of course, he went slowly and carefully enough that she didn't even worry about falling.

He rose, then moved backward, looking at her as if studying something.

She shifted her weight from foot to foot, unsure how to proceed, how to react.

Was she supposed to try to pose? She thought back to when she'd been trying to draw the attention of scouts at the bar. Should she act like that?

No. It didn't feel right to…pretend, not right then.

"Lovely," Kyle said, voice breathy. His hot gaze traced over her breasts, down her flat stomach, over where the black cotton gave her her only cover, then over her legs. Everywhere he looked so intently, goosebumps rose.

Even though he'd called her lovely, his stare remained oddly impersonal, like he was examining something he wanted to buy. Had she *ever* been looked at so thoroughly?

And why did it make her cunt pulse the way it did?

Kyle came up, and again, she expected him to take—to rip off her last layer of defense and do whatever he wanted to her. That was how men were—wild and without patience.

Except he didn't. Instead, he grasped her wrists and forced her backward. Her calves hit something, and she nearly fell. Large, warm hands grasped her hips, helped guide her, and only when she felt the hot, unmistakable male behind her did she even remember Daniel was there, too.

His hard cock pressed against her ass, separated only by the thinnest of cotton, and for one foolish moment she wished she hadn't said the whole *no sex* thing.

Kyle pulled her wrists up, slowly, as he stared at her face. A click, and Alison glanced up.

He'd hooked her cuffs to a longer piece of tie that wrapped around the top of the swing. It kept her hands up, made her stretch out in Daniel's lap.

She tugged at the restraint, her heart speeding at the sudden sensation of being trapped.

They'd tied her up once, but it had only been her hands behind her. *This* was different. She felt Daniel's body behind her, Kyle's looming presence in front of her, and she couldn't get away.

"Eyes on me," Kyle snapped.

She lifted her gaze to find his eyes. Everything floated away but the blue there, but the humor he wore like a piece of armor. It helped her breathe, reminded her that she'd asked for this, that she *wanted* this.

When she did, a shiver ran through her at how…good it felt. The anxiety mixed with desire, each feeding off the other and growing.

Daniel pressed his soft lips to her shoulder, offering the kisses she'd refused. Meanwhile, Kyle reached into his pocket to pull out two more pieces of black that matched the leash hooked to the swing.

"What's that?" Nerves dried up Alison's mouth.

"Doms are always prepared, sugar. Never know when we want to tie up a wild sub," Kyle explained as he came over and wrapped one of the black items around her ankle. Silver at the end—a clip—jingled as it hit the metal of the swing beside the cushion.

The ankle cuffs weren't as soft as the ones she wore all day—not leather, either. These were just a black fabric, lined in something softer that rested against her skin. He bent her leg at the knee, then hooked the small silver clip to the metal frame of the swing.

He worked quickly to repeat the process on her other leg, offering a soft kiss to her ankle as he hooked that one in place as well.

It left her in Daniel's lap, but her feet on the outside of his thighs and her arms stretched out above her.

She was *entirely* on display. She couldn't hide, couldn't try to shrink or keep anything secret. The black panties were all that covered her, especially with her legs so lewdly spread wide.

Daniel slipped his hands forward from her hips, first tracing the line of her underwear then up and over her ribs.

She was used to men fumbling, to them touching her with hesitation. Even when passion consumed them, they always touched her with some mixture of worry she'd turn them down and a lack of care whether she liked it.

Daniel was different.

He cupped her breasts as if he'd done it for years, as though he had no concerns about doing so at all. Alison's head dropped back to his shoulder when his callused palms rubbed against her hard and aching nipples.

She let the feeling wash through her.

Each time she shifted, when the cuffs prevented her from really moving, from doing anything but submitting and accepting what they chose to do, she whimpered. Her cunt was drenched, and each little adjustment made her damp panties drag against her already swollen clit.

Kyle undid his pants, his movements slow as ever. He dragged down the zipper, then shifted them so they were low on his hips. He wore nothing beneath, which meant she was met first with his dark pubic hair. *Finally* he reached into the pants and grasped his cock, pulling it free.

Alison had never before truly lusted after a person. She'd been horny—something that was entirely about her—and slaked that on any other person. She'd never wanted someone in particular, though.

Until right then.

As she stared at Kyle's long, thick cock, she salivated with the need to taste him. Her cuffs jingled as she tried to reach—without thought—and the metal hit against the other cuff.

Kyle curled his lip. "Well, don't you look pretty?" He walked forward, but stayed just out of range. She couldn't reach him, couldn't *get* what she was suddenly desperate for.

Meanwhile, Daniel reached down her body with one hand, feathering two of his fingers over her covered slit so lightly, it felt like torture.

His cock was still tucked between their bodies, trapped between his lower stomach and her ass. Small rocks forward with his hips said he enjoyed the friction.

And Alison? She bit her lip to stop herself from begging for him.

Hell, she was ready to plead with them to fuck her.

Kyle stroked his cock, his gaze lingering over her body. He leaned in and stroked the tip of his cock over one nipple, then the other, leaving glistening pre-cum on her breasts. "You have the prettiest tits," he rumbled out, the words surprisingly sweet given his language and subject. "I bet I could get you off with just these, couldn't I? We'll have to try it. I'll put you spread eagle, tied wrist and ankle to the corners of your bed, and tease you until I make you come just from these." He repeated the motion, this time pressing roughly against her sensitive and hard nipples.

Daniel took that moment to rub more solidly at her clit, zeroing in in a way that told her he knew a woman's body *very* well. There was no fumbling, none of the searching around that often happened. Instead, Daniel acted as if there were a homing beacon right to that erect bundle of nerves, and stroked it with two fingers, so it fit in the groove between them.

Alison straightened more, her hands curling around the tie on her cuffs, so she had *something* to cling to. She cried out, but they didn't stop.

If anything, they went harder, as if the reaction were exactly what they'd wanted. Kyle teased her nipples—and it *was* a tease, because all she could think about was wanting to actually taste him—and Daniel stroked her clit with sure and strong movements.

She twisted. She writhed. She moved as if she could get more or less or both at the same time, but nothing changed when the alphas did.

"You look good when you struggle," Daniel whispered into her ear, that sweet voice he had shifting, taking on a darkness that made her cunt squeeze around nothing. "But struggling doesn't change anything. Best you learn that now. We'll still do exactly what we want. Your body? It's ours now, and I plan to enjoy it for just as long as I please."

His words pushed her the last little bit. Why it did, why she liked that so much, she didn't know. Normally such words would have set her off in a far different way, but when rumbled from him, when he thrust his hips up and rutted against her, when he held her still and toyed with her pussy as he wanted, it was all too much.

She cried out, loud enough that anyone around would have heard. She just didn't *care* right then. Her cunt pulsed uselessly, as if wanting to milk something deep inside her but feeling empty. She arched backward, the bindings keeping her from going too far, and each time she pulled against them, each time she was reminded of how trapped she was, it caused another crashing wave of pleasure.

Daniel slipped his fingers past her underwear, wanting to feel her directly. He pressed two fingers into her cunt, feeling how it pulsed, how it squeezed down.

I wish that was my cock.

Still, he pleased himself with her how he could—and she *did* please him. She was hot, tough and yet beautifully submissive.

Even when she lost her nerve, even when she wanted to snarl, she'd had that look in her eye the moment they'd taken control that said she needed this.

Each stroke of his fingers inside her made her tense and shiver again.

Maybe prolonging her orgasm too much was mean, knowing how sensitive she was, but Daniel didn't mind being a little mean. In fact, he'd long ago accepted that part of himself.

Maybe he didn't look like the typical sadist, what with his happy-go-lucky attitude, but that didn't change that her struggling against her cuffs was one of the hottest things he'd ever seen.

She whined, the sound broken by a gasp when he brushed his palm against her little clit.

"Too much?"

She nodded.

He did it again, harder.

She jolted up as if electrocuted, but she couldn't go far.

Daniel lifted his gaze to Kyle, checking in as they often did. Taking a woman together—especially like this—required communication. They knew each other well enough that a quick glance was all it took.

The smitten look on the other alpha's face? Well, that said he was enjoying it just as much as Daniel was.

Which was...potentially problematic, but having a beautiful, squirming omega rubbing against his cock hardly seemed the time to worry about that.

Kyle rubbed his finger along her bottom lip. "You know, I've always heard about dick-sucking lips, but I don't think I really understood the phrase until I met you."

She shivered, and Daniel took the chance to thrust his fingers inside her again, keeping her on edge and aware of exactly how close they were.

"You have got the fullest, poutiest lips I've ever seen," Kyle continued. He stroked his cock still, even as he stared at her.

And yeah, Daniel had thought the *exact* same thing. Alison had the sort of mouth men fantasized about, and Daniel was no exception.

"Do you want to suck my cock, sugar?"

She squeezed around Daniel's fingers again. He chuckled. "I'd say she does. Her pussy is answering even if her mouth isn't."

"Got to ask for it." Kyle pressed at her bottom lip so she opened her mouth, and he groaned as if he could feel it already.

"Please," she whined when Daniel scissored his fingers inside her. She was tight—*too tight, really.* Even though he wasn't going to be getting inside her today, it felt more like a when rather than an if, and they'd need to get her ready.

"Please what?"

She didn't answer.

Poor girl. She's going to learn to ask, though, because otherwise she won't get a thing.

Kyle slid his fingers into her hair to hold her still, then pulled her down as far as the bindings would allow. He rubbed his cock along those full lips of hers, but when she tried to open her mouth, when she wanted to taste him, he wouldn't allow it. Instead, he released her and moved away enough to keep stroking himself.

A frustrated sound escaped her, and Daniel laughed at the way her cunt betrayed her. Hell, when he wanted to know what she was thinking, all he needed to do was slip his fingers inside her. Even if she was hard to read, her pussy wasn't.

He pulled his fingers from her and held the crotch of her panties aside. The adjustment took only a second before he'd lifted her and moved his cock.

The temptation to slide into her was strong—there was no reason not to admit how badly he wanted to—but Daniel resisted. She'd set a boundary, and he wouldn't cross it. That wasn't how this worked. However, he did tuck his cock against her hot, wet cunt, the underwear wrapping around it. Her angle meant that he rested in the valley of her folds, and the head of his dick teased her clit.

He knew *that* because of the broken whimper she let out.

Perfect.

Daniel grasped her hips and shifted her, forward and back again. It wasn't like it would be inside her cunt, but that didn't matter all that much. It was still better than he thought anything else had ever felt.

Kyle stared down between her spread thighs as though entranced by the sight. He let go of his cock long enough to set his hands on the inside of Alison's knees and spread her obscenely wide. It took away some of the friction for Daniel, but the immediate struggle she let out made up for it.

She didn't care for being exposed, for being on display. Or, at least, she didn't *want* to care for it. When Kyle had mentioned her being watched, she'd been all about that.

Which Daniel figured was a good fucking plan. He didn't see an ability to follow through, since it wasn't as if they could go to that sort of place while on the job, but damn, did he want to. Alison was the sort of girl who deserved to be shown off. He didn't care for sharing with random males—he was an alpha, after all—but he liked the idea of them wanting her.

He'd shared before, never minded watching others take a turn with the woman he was with. Not Trent or Kyle, they didn't count, but friends or acquaintances. However, he had a possessive edge with her that he'd never experienced before.

She was *his*.

The thought forced everything else to screech to a halt, at least for one split second.

When he stopped moving, a roll of Alison's hips—the way that made her grind against his hard, aching cock—brought him back.

He grasped her hips harder and angled her so he'd rub harder against her clit.

She complained, by means of whimpers, but he kept at it.

"Please," she begged.

"Please what?" Kyle asked.

"Please fuck me."

Daniel growled at the offer. He could lift her and drive himself so deep into her in a second.

But…he didn't.

"Sorry," Kyle answered. "You said no sex."

"I was wrong. I need you, please?" she begged beautifully, the plea falling from her lips over and over again.

Kyle pressed a kiss to her thigh, then another, working his way up before repeating it on the other. His shoulder shifted, telling Daniel he still was jacking off. "That isn't how this works. You set a line before we start, that's the line. Once you're more yourself, you can ask again." He nipped the soft flesh there, near the top of her inner thigh.

She yanked at her cuffs and twisted on the seat. If she had her hands free, no doubt she'd be leaving gouges in Kyle's shoulders as she dragged him closer. The girl might be submissive, but she was also an omega, and they weren't ever all that shy when they really *needed*.

A delicious tightness in Daniel's balls said he was close. Each time his cock stroked along her wet slit, when he felt the softness of her cunt, he groaned as he neared the edge.

Kyle stood and leaned close to her, so his voice came out a whisper. "Ask to suck my cock, sugar. You can wrap your hot mouth around me, then. We both know you want it."

She shuddered, and Kyle took her breasts in his palms. He tightened his fingers on her hard nipples—not as rough as Daniel would have been, but enough for her to gasp.

She came again, but neither alpha slowed at all this time. They didn't give her a moment to come down from her high.

Instead, they drove her harder. Daniel started to thrust along with pushing and pulling her to get the friction he craved.

Kyle pinched her nipples, then released them to brush against them, then repeated the process. He tugged at her, ignoring her struggles, her breathless gasping, the way she seemed beyond caring about anything except the sensations they forced on her.

"Beg," he demanded.

"Let me suck your cock, sir, please."

Sir.

That was all it took for Daniel. If they'd demanded she call any of them that, it wouldn't have hit him so hard. Instead, it was like the title had bubbled up from some deep part of her she hadn't even known was there.

He came hard—fuck, harder than he ever had. Even though he hadn't been inside her, it felt like he had just crossed some threshold, like he'd had the best sex he'd ever experienced.

He panted, then reached up and released one wrist. It let him pull both arms down, though he captured them behind her back as he leaned her forward.

Kyle took her hair in his fist again and even though she was still coming, even though she was still gasping and tightening, he plunged his cock into her mouth.

He had to have been close, because less than a minute later, he closed his eyes, head back, and shuddered.

"Swallow it all, pretty girl," he growled out.

Alison gulped, loudly, and she came once. Her tight cunt fluttered weakly against Daniel's cock, which was still nestled against the length of her slit.

Kyle pulled back, then all but collapsed on the swing beside Daniel. They each undid one of the ankle cuffs to finish freeing Alison.

He expected her to pull away. They must have really pushed her limits because instead, once no longer bound, she twisted and rested against the two.

She sat in Daniel's lap, his cum painting her cunt, the underwear keeping it from dripping, as she leaned over so her head was on Kyle's shoulder.

Daniel kissed her temple as she snuggled, that possessive feeling growing even more now that he knew he'd claimed her with his scent.

He was starting to question if he could let her go when it was all over.

Chapter Eleven

Trent dropped the weight with an odd sense of familiarity when it struck the padded ground. He'd been adrift all day, unable to settle. Keeping his distance from Alison hadn't helped at all. He'd thought if he could just stay away from her for a little while, he'd figure shit out. Except the longer he avoided her, the more uneasy he grew.

Is it the bite? Had he somehow created a bond without meaning to? Had he connected them together?

No, a claiming bite didn't work like that. It was a physical sign, nothing else. Nothing mystical. He was just an idiot who wanted a woman he couldn't have.

So, instead of focusing on that, instead of dwelling on it—or at least pretending not to dwell on it—he'd thrown himself into every other task he could think of.

He'd caught up on the news, reorganized the clothing he'd hung in his closet and gone for a swim. Finally, when he'd glanced out the window to find Alison in Daniel's lap, her lips around Kyle's cock, he'd decided there was no option besides lifting the heaviest weights he could.

At least when he was doing that, he wasn't thinking about *her*, or about how badly he'd wanted to go outside and join in.

But he couldn't bring himself to.

The wounds between them ran too deep, created too little foundation. Sure, taking her together would have been like old times, but Trent had said goodbye to that life already. He wasn't a man who liked to lie to himself and he'd accepted that it was over.

"Oh."

Trent turned to find Alison at the doorway to the gym, a towel over her shoulder, frozen in place. A bandage on her shoulder drew his focus, proof of his loss of control the night before.

He turned away, shame crawling along his nerves. "Sorry. I didn't realize you wanted to work out. I'll get going."

He went to pass her, to leave, but Alison's small hand closed on his arm. He had to either stop or try to fight her—and for reasons he didn't understand, he didn't want to fight her.

"You can't avoid me forever," she said.

"I thought you might want some time to yourself." *Meaning without me.*

She sighed but didn't let him go. She probably knew that if she did, he'd keep walking. "I didn't ask for that, did I?"

"No." He turned toward her but kept his gaze on her hands, on her cuffs, anything but her face—or worse, the bandage on her shoulder. "But you ran pretty fast that night."

"You bit me. I am allowed to be a little freaked out."

He blew out a long, slow breath then met her gaze. He expected fear there. After grinding against her in her sleep, coming on her thighs and leaving a permanent bite on her shoulder, why wouldn't she be afraid?

He braced for it, but her green eyes lacked any fear. Instead, he found that same strength he'd spotted the first night, that steel that ran through her.

He'd given her every reason to fear him, but she stood there as though the thought had never crossed her mind.

"I'm sorry I bit you," he said, trying to make his voice as earnest as possible. He *needed* her to understand he hadn't crossed the line on purpose, that he would never do something like that without her permission. "I was asleep, and I had no idea what I was doing."

Alison released him, then nodded. "I know you didn't mean to." She slid her hands over her hips as though to put them in her pockets, then frowned when she realized her pants didn't have any. "We were both asleep. It wasn't either of our faults. I know this isn't the most comfortable situation."

He huffed a sound that was almost a chuckle. Her phrasing was funny—not the situation. "Comfortable, huh? Yeah, I guess that's one way to put it." Even with how easily she spoke of what had happened, he struggled to let it go entirely. "I really am sorry. I'm not anywhere close to perfect, but I'm willing to admit it when I'm wrong. It won't happen again. I need you to know that, to understand that."

She nodded once, a quick jerk of her head. "I know. We're good, okay? I don't think you'll pass as a slaver if you're afraid to even look at me."

Trent lifted his fingers but froze half-way to the bandage. Would she want him to touch her?

Alison didn't move, and that gave him the confidence to touch the soft bandage that covered the only claiming bite he'd ever given in his life. With her that close, it also let him inhale.

She smelled of Daniel and Kyle. That took him back, like an old taste of home.

Maybe that was fucked up, but it didn't stop it from being true. He knew that scent, something he'd lived with, something as reassuring as his own.

"You smell like them," he admitted before his brain could catch up and stop him.

She froze for a moment, then narrowed her eyes. "If you're going to try and embarrass me—"

He shook his head, cutting her off. "Nothing like that. It just surprised me for a minute."

She didn't look away, and her gaze felt far too knowing. "What happened between you three?"

"Nothing that matters anymore."

"With the way you three are acting like scorned lovers? It seems like it matters."

"We had a difference of opinion, had to go in different directions. I'd love to tell you it was some dramatic falling out, but that isn't the case. I couldn't live the life they lived anymore, and with some friendships, you're either close or you aren't. Still, we can work together, don't worry."

She pressed her lips together, the answer no doubt unsatisfying. *Get used to disappointment.*

"The agent will be here tomorrow. Are you ready?"

Trent ignored the pit in his stomach at the thought of facing them, at the idea of sliding into a role he was not comfortable with.

Being a Dom? Sure. He could do that, and even if it had been a while, he *knew* where his priorities were. He knew his line.

But even pretending to be a slaver? Having to act like that? It turned his stomach.

He'd gone to sleep each night with his own little pep talk, telling himself he could do this, that he just had to keep moving forward, that it was for the greater good.

Still, he thought about the omegas they had, the ones who would go through hell if he failed, if Alison, Kyle and Daniel failed, and that made him know there was only one answer.

No matter how badly he didn't want to do this, he didn't have a choice.

"Yeah, I'll be ready."

* * * *

Daniel pulled in a harsh breath when he saw Alison walk down the stairs.

He'd seen her almost entirely naked, but it was *nothing* compared to this.

She wore the black dress they'd picked out for the meeting, a short one that showed off her toned legs and lean waist. It plunged low enough for a hint of cleavage, and the shoulders went down into long sleeves. The back dropped low, so it appeared she showed a lot of skin while keeping herself covered—and the bite safely tucked away.

"Holy shit," Kyle said, the man less capable of keeping in his opinions.

Alison faltered on the last step, as though the praise had thrown her. Her hair was down, the curls adding to her allure, framing her too-perfect face. She smoothed the dress as though she could make some change to it that would make her more comfortable.

"Sorry," Kyle offered. "I just didn't realize you'd be such a knockout in it."

"I'm not really a dress-and-heels sort of girl."

Kyle move in once she stepped off the stairs entirely. He circled her, slowly, his fingers tracing the waist of her dress. "Well, don't worry about that. As soon as we're done, I'm more than willing to strip you out of this."

The pink on Alison's cheeks only made her look even better, especially with how she pulled in a shaky breath.

"How about we focus on the job?" Trent's voice came from the top of the stairs as he passed Alison, not looking at her or saying a word about her attire.

The fact that he was right only annoyed Daniel, especially about *this* topic. "Oh, so you care about completing a job now?"

Trent shook his head and didn't rise to the barb. "We have backup, but they're not close. It means we'll be on our own for the actual meeting. Alison, safe word?"

"Master." She rolled her shoulders, as if trying to release the tension building up there.

Then again, this was likely the first thing she'd done with them that she was in any way comfortable with. Submitting? Trusting? Those things were beyond her expertise, but from what he'd seen, lying and putting herself in danger were par for the course for her.

And why that made Daniel smile, he wasn't sure. Maybe because she'd been so unsettled that he was grateful for the chance at something where she could feel in control.

And a little later, when I pull that dress off her, I can take some of that control from her again.

He'd dreamed of her, thankful that she hadn't been in his bed because he might have just done something they'd both regret later. She hadn't lifted her boundary of no sex or kissing, but Daniel wasn't too disappointed in that. They had time, and as he'd proven to her, there was plenty of fun to be had without his dick ever going into her.

The loud roar of an engine outside had all of them coming to a stop, their gazes moving over.

It was time.

Daniel gestured for Alison to go to the pillow in the living room while Trent went to the front door.

Alison knelt, so much more graceful at it now than she had been that first time. She brought her wrists behind her automatically, and Daniel hooked them. He clipped a leash to the ring at the front of her collar, but left it dangling, hanging down over her cleavage. He slipped the blindfold on next, ignoring the way she licked her lips.

He wanted to kiss her, but he settled for pressing one to her forehead as he held the headphones in his hands. "Try to breathe, sweet. We'll get through this fast, I promise."

With that, he put her headphones on, leaving the noise cancelling off so she could hear the conversation around her.

He pressed one last kiss to her forehead to try to reassure her, then rose.

It was time to get into character.

Trent opened the door when the person knocked.

The man on the front porch didn't look like much.

That had always struck Trent as unfair. He'd dealt with so many monsters over the years, and yet he was still floored by the fact that they rarely *looked* like monsters. They often looked like regular people, like ones he might pass when grocery shopping, or like the same exact ones who would come into his gym.

This one was a perfect example.

He didn't wear a suit, not dressed up the way Daniel, Kyle and Trent were. Instead, he wore a pair of understated black slacks and a white T-shirt, his short hair spiked. He was thirty, at most, though the way he walked and his sports car in the driveway said the man had an ego that made up for his lack of years.

"I'm Galen," he said, not reaching out to shake hands. "I'm here to check on some merchandise."

Merchandise. The word tripped Trent's anger, which was a bad sign.

He'd known the game they were playing, yet somehow a few words in, he struggled with controlling himself.

Maybe this had been a bad idea. He'd hated it from the start, but then he'd accepted it as a necessary evil. Now? Now it wasn't some faceless omega but Alison who was being referred to as property.

Keep yourself under control.

Trent held the door open and gestured for Galen to enter.

The introductions went fast, with the alphas using their fake names, the ones Gregory had used to recommend them.

"Wow," Galen said, then let out a low, lewd whistle. "She *is* a looker. No wonder the other team was so pissed about losing her."

"They were amateurs," Daniel said.

Galen laughed. "Well, they've brought in more product than any other team around, so I'm not so sure I'd call them that. They wanted to take her back, you know that?"

"They're welcome to try." Kyle folded his hands behind his back, standing to the side, his face unreadable. Funny how he could slide into a personality so unlike his real one with such ease.

Kyle had always been good at this sort of thing, though.

"Management already told them to back off. If Gregory is right about you three, we'll make a *far* larger commission off her from you than we would from them. They can stake out another location and pull just anyone." Galen shrugged, then walked closer until he could crouch in front of Alison. "Can she hear us?"

Kyle answered. "No. Our program requires trust building. We only have one meeting where we're from, since we've already established ourselves there. We didn't want to risk upsetting our work by your presence, so we figured her not being able to hear was the least risky way to do it."

Galen reached out, as if to touch Alison.

Trent caught his wrist before he made contact.

The fire in Galen's eyes when he turned his head made it clear he wasn't used to being told no. *Get used to it.*

"No touching," Trent warned, not giving an inch with the steel of his voice. "Like we explained, our training is delicate. I'm not about to risk it so you can play grab ass."

Galen rose to his feet once Trent released him. "I'm used to getting to try out the merchandise."

"We aren't some used car salesmen here," Trent explained. "She isn't a compact entry-level car you can go over to the dealership to test drive for fun. Think of her as a one-of-a-kind, specially made luxury item. We don't let just anyone touch her."

He narrowed his eyes for a moment, then let out a soft snort. "You sure think a lot of yourself."

Daniel gestured toward the couch and chairs in the living room, all situated with Alison in the center.

Galen took the chair opposite her, which allowed Trent to breathe a little easier. He couldn't reach her from there, and while he rarely took his gaze from her, the distance helped. "We don't normally accept new scouts."

"We aren't new. We've been working on the east coast for years."

"So I've heard." Galen took out a cigarette, lighting it without asking if anyone cared. "But that doesn't change that *we* don't know you. What are you doing out here?"

Daniel sat on the couch. "As you know, your organization has taken a few hits lately. There's a chance this will be the last public auction for a while. We thought it worth branching out, finding new clients."

"You don't have enough product for many clients."

"We don't have repeats, though. Just word of mouth. So when we bring her to the auction, only one person can purchase her, but we'll likely have others who want to go on a wait list. It seems like the best way to handle it."

"Any client you find from our auction better end with us getting a cut."

Daniel nodded. "Naturally."

Kyle reached for a set of files on the side table, then held them out for Galen.

"What's this?" Galen opened them, flipping through the pages.

"History. Medical record. Tests. We don't sell anything that isn't healthy. She has been thoroughly examined and found with no defects."

Galen closed the paperwork as if it didn't matter, snorting. "You are crazy, you know that? Our best sellers are the wild omegas, the ones clients want to break. How the fuck do you think having all of this helps? Who would pay a bundle when one hole is as good as another? I mean, yeah, she's pretty, but they don't typically stay pretty that long with our customers."

Trent cracked his knuckles, but when the other two didn't speak up, he jumped in. He had to hold it together. "*Those* aren't the clients we're looking for. Anyone can beat a woman, can break one. That's easy. Why spend money on a slave if you could get the same thing picking up a girl anywhere? We don't just sell omegas."

"So what do you sell?"

"Mates."

Galen snorted. "Who the fuck wants a mate?"

Trent reached over and toyed with Alison's hair, using it as a way to keep himself focused on his goal. "Our training program is second to none. We fetch a high price, but in exchange for that, our clients get a fully trained submissive omega who can be trusted without chains or threats. Our clients can take our products out with them anywhere, and they obey without question. We even file the paperwork to ensure our merchandise is on the delinquent omega registry, which means they have additional legal protections and autonomy when dealing with them. Who wants to spend so much on something they have to keep chained up in a room? That limits the usefulness. Picture an omega who is entirely devoted to you, who will do anything you say at any time. It's all the benefits of a slave without the downsides or risks."

Galen pursed his lips, then stared at Alison as if trying to picture it. "Well, that's new, I'll give you that. I didn't want to let you in, honestly. I don't like new people, and this whole training thing? Not my bag. Management sees things differently."

"Then management understands how lucrative this is. Our products typically start the bidding at five times the next highest at any auction. By the time bidding is over? We often make more than people who sold six or seven different omegas."

"Yeah, well, management has a different idea of what's best than I do. I think he's more interested in seeing your product than he is in the money. Let's just say he's got a similar idea as you."

Trent moved his fingers to the nape of Alison's neck, rubbing over where the collar sat. Tense muscles stood out, and while he doubted he'd be able to relax her, he offered what little reassurance he could. For her, being still was likely the hardest thing.

"So, explain to me the training. How does it work?"

"It isn't that much different from how you train a dog. It isn't about fear—a fearful beast is one that's likely to eventually bite you. Instead, you use positive reinforcement. We don't hit our products, we don't scar them. That gives unreliable results."

"So what do you do?"

"We take everything away from them, break them down with that, then offer them little bits of kindness. They start to rely on us for everything good. This leads them to associating their masters with good things. Eventually, they end up entirely reliant on their masters for everything, and that gives the loyalty and trust people get from our products. It isn't an easy process, but our work speaks for itself."

Galen's expression said he didn't believe it—or, rather, didn't believe it to be worth it. "And they're happy when they go off to someone else?"

"We do the handover, and we're available to come for additional adjustments when needed. However, we also offer complete guarantees. If a product doesn't live up to what we promise, we will replace it."

"How many have you had to replace?"

"Three. Two because of illness we couldn't have anticipated and one because of infertility."

"What did you do with the ones you took back?"

"The ill ones we disposed of."

Galen sat up, surprise on his features. *Could he actually have a heart?* "You could have made good money selling them off cheap."

Nope, no heart.

Kyle chimed in, giving Trent a moment to swallow down the bile that threatened to crawl up his throat. "If we sold sub-par product, it could endanger our reputation. Sometimes there are costs of doing business, and we expect that. It was less risky to just euthanize the ill omegas."

"And the infertile one?"

"That one we did resell. While many of our clients want offspring, not all do. She was perfectly trained, so she went to a gentleman who saw the defect as a benefit."

Galen tapped his finger on the armrest of the chair. "All right. I can see the upside. There's only one more thing."

The way he said it made Trent close his hand into a fist. "And what's that?"

"Omega check."

"You have her medical records."

Galen waved off the response. "Those are easy to fake. We've had people try to pass off betas as omegas before. We don't consider the first check official until I'm sure she's an omega. Normally, that's part of test driving. I know it's an omega when I knot them." He lifted an eyebrow as though waiting.

Not a fucking chance.

Daniel spoke up. "We've already made that clear. If we allowed you to do that, it would erode all the work we've done."

"Fine," Galen said with an exaggerated sigh. "Then there's one other option." He reached into his pocket and withdrew a vial of a clear liquid.

"What's that? I am not about to have our product risked by ingesting something that we have no idea what it is," Daniel said.

"This is a special drug. If an omega smells it, their scent changes slightly. She won't need to drink it, just smell it."

Fuck. Trent had heard of it—most people had. The drug was used to identify omegas, and had been used by a killer a while back who targeted omegas.

Worse? Enough of it could force an omega into a heat...

Still, Trent had no idea how to get out of it. If they didn't prove she was an omega, the entire job was over.

"I understand it also forces them into a heat. That wouldn't be ideal," Kyle said.

"Too much can force a heat, but a quick whiff shouldn't be a problem. This is non-negotiable, gentlemen. Either you prove she is what you say she is, or I walk away and you find your own way to sell her."

Trent pressed his lips together, no other option coming to mind.

Thankfully, he didn't need to answer. He wasn't sure he *could* say yes. Daniel did that, rising to his feet. "Fine."

Alison shifted, and Trent cursed the entire situation.

"She'll need to really breathe it in. It's an odd scent, so they tend to turn their heads away. Usually I'd hold them, but I know how touchy you are." Galen said the words like a joke, as if they were finicky about a prized piece of décor in their house.

Trent was closest, so he helped Alison to her feet. She'd likely feel better that way, rather than on her knees. He took her headphones off but left the blindfold on. "You're going to need to smell something. Do you understand me?"

She gulped, the sound loud. "What is it?"

He slid his fingers into her hair, gripping it tightly. "Nothing harmful. Will you behave?"

She licked her lips, and the nervous energy coursing through her said she didn't care for the idea any more than he did. She tried to nod, but his grip kept her still. "Yes, sir."

Sir. Not master. That meant she hadn't safe worded.

What would I do if she did?

Again, he was reminded that she was far tougher than he was.

Galen came up and popped open the top on the vial. He brought it toward her, and thankfully didn't try to touch her at all.

Trent inhaled a small bit of the scent coming from the vial—something that seemed off, chemically, but he wasn't an omega.

Alison tried to turn her head, her nose wrinkled.

Trent tightened his grip in her hair, his other hand going to the front of her throat, to her collar. He didn't touch her chin, but his hold was enough to keep her from turning away from the vial.

A thin whine left her, and it sounded far too real.

Trent's heart pounded, his stomach rolling and forcing him to swallow to not throw up. His fingers, wrapped in her hair, trembled.

Still, he kept his face clear, swore to himself he wouldn't fail, wouldn't have the deaths of those omegas on his shoulders.

Galen closed the bottle after about thirty seconds, then put it in his pocket again.

He leaned in, still not touching, and inhaled.

His groan was low and lecherous, making it perfectly clear how he felt about whatever the vial had done to her scent. "Omega," he growled out.

"As we said," Daniel answered.

Which Trent was thankful for, because he doubted he could have spoken right then.

"You did. Alright. Expect another call for a meeting in about a week before the auction. We'll make sure you still have her—sometimes the less-controlled scouts can lose an omega or two before the actual date. The day of the auction, you'll get the exact time and location."

Kyle and Daniel walked Galen out, giving Trent the chance to release Alison's hair and pull in a shaky breath.

He couldn't seem to feel his fingers. His feet felt heavy, clumsy. Nothing seemed *right*.

When the door shut, Alison pulled at her cuffs, hands struggling to undo them herself.

Trent unclipped them, and she tore the blindfold off.

She sniffed hard, then blew air from her nose as if she could dislodge the remaining scent of the drug.

Trent watched, stepping backward, his heart racing and his breath short. He couldn't seem to pull in a full breath.

He turned his gaze to Daniel, who nodded, as if he understood and expected the reaction.

Trent fled, like a coward, leaving Alison to Kyle and Daniel.

They could take care of her, because if he didn't get out of there, he'd either throw up or pass out.

Useless.

Alison couldn't remove the wretched scent from her nose, from where it had crept into her sinuses. It burned into her, and no matter how much she rubbed at her nose, she couldn't get rid of it.

"You okay?" Kyle caught her cheeks in his hands, forcing her face to his.

A face that was already so familiar and more calming than it should have been.

"Yeah," she answered, rubbing again at her nose. "That drug just smells wrong. I can't even explain *why* it does, but my brain just keeps telling me it's wrong."

"I know. It should go away in a few minutes."

Alison let the warmth of Kyle's palms sink into her, taking that bit of comfort from him.

Listening to them talk about her had been the worst. She'd *known* people saw omegas like that, but to have to stay still, to hear the vile words, to not be able to react, that had been a more difficult struggle than she'd expected.

She twisted, looking for Trent, only to find him gone.

"He left," Daniel explained.

"Why?" That didn't seem like Trent at all. He was difficult, closed off often, but he also was unfailingly protective. He blamed himself for things he didn't need to. He wouldn't have just walked away before he checked on her.

Hurt settled in her chest even as she told herself it was stupid to feel that way. He didn't owe her anything, yet the fact he'd done that made her question everything about him.

"Don't be like that," Kyle told her.

"Like what?" Alison crossed her arms, going to her go to defensiveness.

Kyle's gaze darted up the stairs toward Trent's room. "He didn't leave until he knew we were here to make sure you were fine."

"Right."

Daniel sighed, then shuffled his foot on the ground. "Trent is a bastard in a lot of ways, but he's also got a few sore spots. I think the conversation with Galen dug into a few of them."

Alison frowned. She'd never considered doing that might have been difficult for them. "Is he okay?"

"He will be. He's tough. I think he just needed to go collect himself. We all honestly need that. For tonight, I'm going to let you make the choice on where you sleep. If you need a night to yourself, you can use your room, or you can pick one of ours if you'd rather," Daniel said.

Alison bit at her bottom lip. Normally she'd have jumped at the chance for her own bed again, but then she recalled the tremble of Trent's fingers in her hair and she knew the answer.

* * * *

Trent's room was dark when Alison entered. She'd gotten out of the dress and into her pajamas, feeling more like herself as soon as she did.

A lingering remnant of the drug remained, a ghost scent she'd pick up from time to time, but otherwise? She'd bounced back.

The truth was that while she didn't want to do that again, it wasn't as bad as she'd imagined. Though, she did plan to kill Galen. No matter what happened, she wanted to gut him for everything she knew he'd done, everything he'd said, all the omegas he'd referenced as though they meant nothing.

Just thinking that helped her not focus on the meeting, to unload the weight of it.

Heaving made her pause. The uncomfortable sound of retching came from the bathroom, followed by a flushing toilet, then water from the sink. *Brushing his teeth?*

A moment later, the door opened, and Trent's form was lit up from the bathroom. He froze as his gaze landed on her.

He didn't speak for a long moment, though after a loud gulp, his hand still on the handle, he asked softly, "You okay?"

Alison nodded, unsure how to deal with this.

She was good at fighting, at taking care of problems, but helping people?

That wasn't something she knew much about.

Yet, despite that, she *needed* to help. Something inside her wouldn't let her walk away, wouldn't let her forget about him.

"You left," she explained, cringing as her words wounded almost like an admonishment.

"Yeah, sorry about that." Trent left the bathroom light on and sat on his bed, his back to her. "I needed a bit of space. Figured you'd be fine with Daniel and Kyle."

"I *am* fine," she assured him.

He leaned forward, his elbows going to his knees and a violent shudder running through him. "You're tougher than I am. Already knew that, but here's the proof."

Alison came over to stand before him. He didn't look at her, didn't move, just stayed in that position, looking as though a weight on his shoulders had crushed him.

She wasn't sure how to help, but slid to her knees before him. It let him lift his gaze just a hair to find hers.

"What can I do?"

His lip curled into a sad smile, one that held no humor. "I didn't care for talking about you like that, for playing that part."

Alison slid her fingers around his calves "It wasn't you—I know that. We all had a part to play."

"I guess I didn't realize just how much I'd hate to play it. I don't think it would have bothered me so much if I didn't know damn well there were people out there who really think that, people who believed that.

Felt like I let one of them crawl inside me, like I've got this slime clinging to my insides now."

She slid forward and rested her cheek against his knee, nuzzling softly. "You're not like that."

He lifted one hand and ran it through her hair, the touch so much gentler than it had been when he'd held it earlier, as though trying to make up for that with sweetness now. "Do you know why I left the FBI? It was a final-straw moment for me. There was this young girl, an omega, who everyone knew was being trafficked. She was taken as a mate to an informant, an important one. I talked to everyone who would listen about helping her, about getting her out of there, but I got nothing but brick walls. No one cared because the informant was helping on big cases. I was ready to step in, ready to give it all up to get her out of there."

A sinking sensation in Alison's stomach preceded her asking, "What happened?"

"We found her body tossed in front of a hospital like trash. I handed in my badge that day. She was dead because my bosses decided the case was more important than the people and I couldn't do it anymore. Danial and Kyle, they didn't get it. They saw the big picture, saw the folks we were helping, but me? I saw her. Today, when I had to say that shit, I saw her again. I remembered doing shit because I thought it was right even though it felt fucking wrong."

Alison wished she had some perfect thing to say. She wanted to be able to tell him it was okay, that it would all work out. Instead, she nuzzled against where he ran his fingers through her hair.

He offered her a strained smile. "You don't need to stay, pet. I'm a big boy. I can take care of myself. I'm sure tonight wasn't easy on you either, and I know for a fact Kyle and Daniel would be more than happy to dote on you all you could want."

Alison heard the out he was giving her, but she didn't have to even consider it. No matter how uncomfortable this was, no matter how out of her element she might be, she wasn't going to leave him.

Hearing the pain in his voice, that loneliness, that struggle to do what was right, it all felt like a glimpse into him, one deeper than anything she'd had before. He wasn't just an alpha right then. He wasn't the jerk who gave her lists of expectations and made her kneel for him. Instead, he was a man with a scarred past, one who so desperately wanted to be a good man no matter how much he felt like he was failing.

So rather than walk out, she straightened up and did the thing she'd sworn she wouldn't, the thing that was so dangerous she wasn't sure how she could be stupid enough to do it.

She brushed her lips to his and kissed him.

The warmth of Alison's kiss thawed the places inside Trent that were frozen from the meeting, the areas where the jagged edges of ice pierced him.

He didn't move, didn't return the kiss, unwilling to participate but unable to stop her, either.

She slid her hands up his chest until she cupped his cheeks. Those full lips he'd imagined far too many times felt better than he could ever have thought. His fantasies had done them no justice, and when her soft, hot tongue brushed his lips, he groaned.

"You said no kissing," he whispered to remind her. "I don't want you doing anything out of pity."

She pulled back far enough to see him but kept her hands on his cheeks. "It's not pity. I'm..." She sighed softly, as though searching for the right words. "I need this. I need you tonight, and I think you need this, too."

Fuck it all, I do.

Right then, the only thing he could think of that might help him get through the night was Alison. It was her scent, her strength, the warmth she had that he needed so badly. He had to reassure himself that he wasn't the person he'd had to pretend to be, that she was safe and not afraid of him.

He grasped her by her nape and pulled her closer. She responded by crawling into his lap, her seeking hands grasping him.

He rolled them so she was in the bed beside him, both on their sides, as he took sweet kiss after sweet kiss. They weren't rushed, weren't frantic. She traced her hand over his side, slipping beneath the fabric of his shirt, feeling his overheated skin.

The kisses tapered off, slowing, until Trent ran his fingers through her hair, staring at her. He'd never felt this way before, and it created a ball of anxiety in his stomach that made a mockery of what he'd felt before.

How many women had he helped get back on their feet? How many had he trained? Built up? And how many had he lost?

He'd seen them torn apart, seen them lose the fight either to the world or themselves, and as he stared at her, as she curled against his chest to fall asleep, he felt a fear he'd never known before.

He wasn't sure if he could survive losing her like that.

Chapter Twelve

Kyle hadn't missed Alison leaving Trent's room early, like some walk of shame she tried to hide.

Her scent hadn't changed, so they hadn't had sex, but they'd still spent the night in there together.

She'd had the choice to pick any room and had chosen his.

Jealousy wasn't what Kyle felt. He didn't tend to get jealous, not even with Trent, who he wasn't exactly close with. Instead, it was interest.

He liked a puzzle, something to figure out, and Alison sure was a puzzle worth spending some time on.

"Morning," he said as she entered the kitchen.

Her jump said she hadn't expected him to already be there, and a petty part of Kyle enjoyed startling her. It was probably the same childish part that wanted to pull her hair until she paid attention to him.

Seems I'm a bit of a brat myself.

After one sharp look, she smoothed her hands over her shirt and tried to pretend she wasn't annoyed—probably because being annoyed made her admit she'd been startled. "Morning."

"Sleep well?"

She went to the coffee pot and poured herself a cup into one of the mugs set out in front of it. "Yeah, I did." Her sharp words created a clear message—*don't ask.*

Too bad Kyle didn't care for boundaries. "Why'd you pick Trent?"

She poured in a splash of cream before turning, holding the mug between her hands. "He seemed like he needed it."

That's what I thought.

Damn, she was more observant, and sweeter, than he'd have expected, especially from the girl who'd broken his nose. "And you thought that made it your job?"

Her shoulders rose in a quick shrug before she brought the coffee to her lips and took a slow sip. Her expression as she savored it was sinful, a soft moan leaving her. Once she'd swallowed it down, she lifted her gaze to him again. "Why's he like that? I have to admit, when he was ordering me around, I didn't expect him to be that fragile."

Kyle considered telling her to ask Trent, but the tight-lipped bastard would never say anything. He liked to put forward his best face, his 'I am an island to myself' persona. "Let's just say he's seen the bad side of what men can do. He's always taken it the hardest. I think playing that part hit him harder than he thought it would."

"I always figured alphas..." She paused, pressing her lips together as if reconsidering. "*Especially* dominant ones, wouldn't want someone to help them."

Kyle huffed a soft laugh, crossing his feet at the ankles while he leaned against the kitchen counter. "That's just what we like to pretend sometimes. The fact is that alphas, and Doms, need help too. We aren't superhuman. We screw up, we get upset, we have days where we just can't deal with shit. Trent, he's steady as they come for the most part, but even he has his triggers, those things that wiggle a blade right into a crack he already has. And you? I figure you're exactly the balm he needed last night to help."

The snort Alison let out was full of disbelief. "I doubt that. I'm just the only one who isn't mad enough at him to go talk to him."

"You really don't get it, do you?"

"Get what?"

Kyle tapped his fingers against his coffee. "You've spent little time around alphas and it shows. You've got this simplified view, where alphas are these hulking laws-unto-themselves and omegas scamper around their feet trying not to get crushed. Is that another lesson your father gave you?"

Her eyes closed and she breathed in the tendrils of steam from her coffee. "Yeah, it was. My mother wasn't my father's mate by choice. She was a slave—bought and paid for—and the only omegas I knew growing up were slaves, too."

Kyle's stomach dropped. Her father had been a piece of work—he knew that—but to think she'd grown up knowing her mother was a slave? That would warp any child, especially one who had to see where she expected her life to end up, too. "What happened to her?"

"She killed herself when I was ten. I used to be angry about it, felt like she abandoned me, but I realized as I got older that she'd been dead long before then. A beta male who had worked as her bodyguard faked my death, setting a fire to help cover it all up."

"He took care of you after that?"

"Somewhat. He set me up in the home of an omega he knew, and he visited me when he could, got me started on training. Eventually he never came back, when I was sixteen. It didn't shock me because that's the world." She let out a hard laugh. "My father used to tell me that omegas were treasures, and just like any treasure, you do what is best for it whether it likes it or not."

Kyle pressed his lips together, wanting to tell her it would be okay but knowing that wouldn't be welcome. "I'm sorry," he tried instead. "That's no life for a kid."

"Maybe not, but it let me see the truth. Trust me, those alphas weren't breaking down while their mates comforted them. It was very much a one-sided thing. After that? When I got out and grew up, I can't say I've seen much better. Do you have any idea how many alphas I've had deal with to get an omega help?" She shook her head, her curly hair shifting around her shadowed face. "Try to tell me all you want how things are different, but I've learned to go by experience, and my experience hasn't been good. I figure, as someone who works specifically on omega crimes, you'd get that."

Kyle fought back the wave of images that threatened to wash over him. He'd seen the worst, things that he had locked away. He wasn't Daniel or Trent, who were haunted by those memories. Instead, he managed to keep them at bay.

"I've seen some bad shit, no doubt. I've made it my life to try and stop it, to do what I can to fix it."

"Don't you reach a point where you realize it isn't just some of the time? Once, twice, sure. I could chalk up all the violence and pain to being a rare occurrence. When it happens enough, though, doesn't it ever become the norm?"

Hadn't Kyle thought the same? He recalled, at the start, when he'd still gone to therapy after especially hard cases. The therapist had spoken of such things, and he'd admitted to worrying about that very thing, to feeling a crushing weight that perhaps alphas were simply bad at their core.

Eventually Kyle had gone the way of most veteran agents and decided therapy didn't help. He'd buried down those feelings beneath his job and a large layer of 'don't fucking think about it'.

"You can't see all that and *not* have it affect you," she pressed.

"It affects me," he admitted, his gaze down. "It affects everyone. Trent? He lost his career and his friends when he walked away, then made it his mission to help battered women. Dan? He let himself keep his hopeless romantic fantasies of finding someone who would fit into our lives and fix it all. Me? Well, I just have a dark sense of humor from it."

Alison stared at him for a long, silent moment, as though digging through the bullshit he'd said and deciding if she believed it.

When she spoke, however, her words were the last thing he'd expected her to say. "I want to put sex back on the table."

"What now?" *Real eloquent.*

She sat up, as though trying to look as in control as possible. "I know I said no kissing and no sex. Well, the kissing thing is already out of the window, and I want to take off the sex limit."

"And why's that? What changed your mind?" Her phrasing said she'd kissed Trent the night before.

"Like you just said—this is all temporary. You guys don't want to settle down with an omega, and I don't want a mate, let alone an alpha, so why leave that limit up? Why not take the chance to actually experience this all?" Her voice quivered the barest amount, as if she was trying everything she had to keep it from shaking.

Maybe Kyle should have reassured her or done something to make her feel better, but he just wasn't that sort of person. Plus, the only time he got the upper hand was when she was tied up or flustered. *Might as well take advantage of it.* "So you're telling me that the next time we get to play, you wouldn't mind taking a cock—or three?"

Ah, there was that beautiful flush on her freckled cheeks, and right on the tail of that? Her scent blossomed, telling him *exactly* what she thought of that the suggestion.

And hell, Kyle figured it sounded like a great plan to him.

* * * *

"So, no idea what crawled up her ass?" Daniel sat outside with Trent and Kyle, all having fled the house to avoid the raging omega inside. Funny how only a tiny female could send the three of them running for cover.

"Not a clue," Kyle said.

Trent snorted softly. "She was happy after she left my room. I'm putting this one in your court."

Daniel lifted an eyebrow to look over at Trent. "I figured it had been so long for you, you didn't remember how to make women happy anymore."

"Like riding a bike, buddy."

The banter came so easily, Daniel stilled for a moment. Falling into old habits, into the old routines, all made it so easy to forget that this was temporary. But did it have to be?

"You know, after this—" Daniel started to say.

The humor in Trent's face slid free. "Don't go there. We both know the answer."

"Come on. You can't tell me you haven't liked being under the same roof, that you don't like doing something important."

"What I'm doing is important, even if it isn't working for the FBI. I don't know when you'll ever figure out that your life doesn't need to revolve around them, that there is more out there than that."

"More? Maybe, but nothing better. Think about it, Trent."

Trent shook his head. "No need to. I'm not going back to the FBI, not ever, and as long as you all work there, I think we all know where our relationship sits."

Up shit creek.

"We could kick each other in the balls down here or we could let Alison have a try. Who wants to face her?" Kyle asked, drawing them back on topic.

"I wouldn't mind paddling her ass for the attitude," Daniel admitted, a grin across his lips as he pictured the way she'd squirm. "But I have a feeling that wouldn't work so well to deal with this. It'd just give her another reason to be pissed at us."

"Like she needs a reason," Trent muttered.

"She should have come and talked to us." Daniel sighed, stretching his leg. "She might be the most difficult woman I've ever known. This could have been dealt with in all of a minute, but instead? Instead she carries on. I feel like that definitely breaks a rule or two. There's the one about talking to us."

"She's wearing a *leather jacket*, with a turtleneck. That's clearly a clothing infraction," Kyle tagged on.

Trent nodded, tucking his thumbs into his pockets. "She's never been punished before. We shouldn't let her rack up too many things before we talk to her."

Trent, forever a pushover.

"You're too soft-hearted," Daniel said. "If keeping her in line was up to you, she'd have a strap-on and you'd be bent over before you knew what was happening."

"Not all of us enjoy women crying as much as you do," Trent snapped back.

Daniel only smiled wider. "I bet her pretty green eyes would glisten nicely."

Trent's narrowed eyes said he wanted to argue, but Kyle stepped in. "We'll go easy-ish, don't worry. I'm thinking maybe dinner tonight could be a more *hands-on* experience."

Daniel wasn't sure what exactly that meant, but as if he'd reject such an offer. Kyle tended to be devious when it came to fun and games, which meant whatever he had in mind, they'd all enjoy it.

Well, Alison might not the entire time—it was a punishment, after all—but by the end of the night?

He was pretty sure they'd all go to sleep satisfied.

* * * *

Alison bit down on the gag Kyle had put in her mouth, pressing her teeth into the black ball there.

Kyle had smiled so nicely while he'd put it in and buckled it behind her head. He'd ignored her glaring and the threats she'd offered up at first. *'You're already in trouble, sugar,'* he'd said as if they were discussing her new shoes rather than her *punishment. 'Maybe you shouldn't add to it by threatening me?'*

That had quieted her down.

Daniel came up to her, and suddenly she felt out of her element. She'd worn a bikini like they'd requested, and when Daniel looked at her like *that,* she felt very underdressed. In fact, when he had that look in his eyes, she figured she could use a full set of plate armor.

Daniel grasped her waist and settled her on the coffee table.

She tried to argue, but the ball gag prevented her from doing anything but making some mumbled noises.

Daniel took her thigh and strapped something around it. She leaned up on her elbows to watch, but Kyle set a hand on the center of her chest and pushed her back down. The chill of the table crept into her bare back.

Daniel strapped the same sort of thing to her right leg. They fit snugly but weren't too constricting. He caught her wrists and after another few clicks, she found she couldn't pull her hands up again. He'd hooked her cuffs to the straps on her thighs, rendering her unable to move beyond a slight writhing.

She lifted her head, but somehow glaring between her knees at Daniel just didn't have the same weight when she was trussed up as she was.

"Not quite done," he said and took a long silver bar out, holding it up.

I don't know what you're planning to do with that but I suggest you don't put it anywhere near me, was what she'd intended to say. Instead, a lot of garbled noise was all that made its way past the gag.

Daniel only chuckled, and how that sound could be both threatening and charming, she had no idea. He hooked the bar between her thighs, which made her spread her knees wide and kept her from closing them.

Kyle had a plate of food which he set on his lap as he took a spot to her right, in one of the chairs he'd pulled closer. Trent did the same to her left, and Dan—the bastard—sat on the bottom edge of the table, meaning he was placed between her spread thighs.

"So, pet." Trent stroked his fingers over her cheek, drawing her focus there. "Do you know why you're in trouble?"

Of course. She shook her head.

He tsk'd softly. "Lying isn't going to make this any better for you. In fact, the gag was my idea so you didn't get yourself in trouble anymore. Do you recall rule one?"

Alison will discuss any concerns or worries with one of the alphas. Of course she recalled it. She nodded once, a quick jerk of her head.

"Very good. You've been storming around and slamming things and making it clear you have something to discuss with us, but you haven't. We gave you all day and evening to fess up, to tell us what you were worried about. Instead of doing that, you decided to be rude, to break other rules like the dress code, and be generally unpleasant."

Because you are a bunch of assholes who talked me into sleeping with you instead of focusing on what's important. If only her look could accurately portray that all.

"She sure has a lot of fire," Kyle said, taking a bite of fruit from his plate. The melon made his fingers glisten. He reached out with that hand and hooked the edge of her bikini top cup with his pinky. A tug exposed her breast, and he stroked the fruit-juice-covered fingers over her nipple. "There's only two ways to deal with fire like that. You can let it burn out or try to douse it." He leaned forward and dragged his tongue across her nipple, licking off the juice he'd left. "I actually like your fire, so I don't want to douse it. Still, it needs to be dealt with. I figure we'll have some fun helping it burn until it's out."

The cool air breezed across her hardened nipple, and she gasped. It wasn't just the touch, but all of it. It was the intense stares, the restraint, the way Kyle spoke. They didn't talk as if they cared for her input. Instead, they simply informed her of what would happen.

As much as she liked that, a flutter of unease ran through her.

Trent moved her bikini, then cupped that breast with his large, warm hand.

"If you need to safe word or stop, tap the table, pet."

That helped, that he'd known her fear without ever having to have her say it.

It let her pull in a breath, but that only pressed her nipple more firmly into Kyle's rough palm.

"Now, we discussed a few ways to deal with this," Kyle continued, though with the two of them toying with her breasts, it was hard to focus on what he said.

"Trent wanted a stern word, Daniel wanted to turn your ass red—"

How quickly she moaned from that terrified her. What the hell? She was an adult woman, one to be feared and respected. She was *not* some silly child who would get spanked.

And yet she couldn't shake the way it turned her on, the way she pictured the sting from Daniel's hand against her ass.

What the hell is wrong with me? It had to be them, something they did to her, because she had *never* been this person.

Daniel let out a groan, low as he stroked his hand up her thigh. "Your reaction says it wouldn't have been a great punishment, but rest assured, sweet, we'll get there." He ran his fingers up her leg and brushed her slit through the suit.

And right then, she really wanted to beg him to go farther. She wanted to feel his thick fingers pressing into her, preparing her for his cock.

"So, why don't you just relax while we talk, since you don't seem to want to offer any input?"

The words made her eyebrows furrow. She'd expected them to talk to her, to force her to answer, to listen to them. What sort of lesson was ignoring her?

Daniel slid his fingers beneath her suit and stroked up to her clit, rubbing with such direct attention that she shifted as if to get away.

Unfortunately, it only reminded her that her wrists were bound to her thighs and a spreader bar kept her knees open.

"Next week I thought we'd rent a couple movies," Kyle said.

The conversation made her give him a look as though to ask him what the fuck he was doing, talking about movies as if she wasn't spread out and almost naked before them.

Kyle didn't even look her way, rolling her nipple between his fingers, as he discussed new movies.

Trent responded, toying with the breast on his side, and when he wasn't speaking, he offered teasing kisses to her chest, her side, and took her hardened nipple into the warmth of his mouth.

Daniel was the worst. He untied the strings at the side of her bikini so the bottom fell off, then he really went to work. He used both hands, pressing two fingers deep into her while his other teased her clit. He was rough and focused, and despite trying to pay attention to their conversation, Alison couldn't keep track.

It floated away, stolen by the stroke of their fingers, their lips. They acted as though she wasn't there, using her body, driving her hard toward a release with impersonal and impassionate touches.

Her back arched as the first rush of sensation ran through her. She cried out against her gag, her eyes shut tight, the tension in her body snapping apart as she came on Daniel's talented fingers.

And when she could pull in a breath, when the ringing in her ears stopped, Daniel's voice came to her. "I heard that movie isn't any good. Let's go for action, instead."

They're still talking about movies?

Her skin burned and a strange shame ran through her that they'd care so little about what was happening to her.

And even more so, they didn't stop. If anything, her first orgasm spurred them on.

It reminded her of being on the swing, where they'd been merciless with pleasing her, as though they got a sick thrill from forcing her to endure each growing release. Of course, that time their focus had been on her.

She whimpered, twisted on the table, but they paid her no mind. She kept her eyes closed this time, and it only made the feelings that much stronger.

Daniel hooked his fingers up, and when he pressed against the front of her pussy, it sent powerful shocks of sensation arcing her.

Lips wrapped around her left nipple and sucked hard before teeth scraped across it. And *still* they talked about nothing.

She was drowning between them, and they couldn't care less. It broke her down as she could do nothing but feel, taking whatever they gave her.

The second orgasm made her hips lift, her toes curling against the table. She couldn't breathe through it, her lungs freezing as everything inside her seized.

This time, she didn't get to catch her breath. Instead, Kyle and Trent worked her nipples harder, pinching them roughly. Kyle slapped at the hard nub, catching it and making her whimper.

She had only a moment to wonder what Daniel was up to when he pulled his fingers from her before warm breath flowed over her cunt. She figured out his plan as his tongue delved deep into her, pointed and insistent. He moved up to circle her clit.

That wasn't it, though. She felt empty, but she couldn't even beg him to put his fingers back into her, not with the gag. Instead, she felt his wet finger against her ass.

He didn't wait, didn't ask, didn't give her a chance to worry before he pressed into her. It was only one finger, she thought, but it felt impossibly thick inside her ass. He sucked her clit, tormenting it with hard draws as he set a hard rhythm with his finger.

"I already saw that," Kyle said as he tugged her nipple, forcing her to arch off the table.

"Well, it isn't all about you," Trent countered.

It all mixed together. Her overstimulated body, the way she felt entirely cut off from the alphas despite the fact that they were touching her so intimately. Daniel nipped her swollen clit, and that shoved her over the edge again.

The orgasm hit her so hard the entire world drifted away.

Daniel knew when she was done. It wasn't hard to tell, not when she broke so beautifully. He'd pushed her hard, wanting her to feel out of control and overwhelmed, and sure enough, she'd shattered with that third orgasm.

Daniel pulled his fingers from her, unhooked the spreader bar, then grabbed her around the waist. A quick lift and he settled her into his lap, her hands still bound to her thighs. Trent undid her gag, and she opened and closed her mouth when he pulled it away.

Trent stayed standing and massaged the joints of her jaw.

Wetness tracked down her cheeks, and she looked downright drugged there, more open than he'd seen her before.

Which was *exactly* what he wanted. "You didn't like that, did you?"

She shook her head.

"You know why we did it?" When she didn't, he continued. "Because that's what you're doing, sweet. You're trying to keep us out, not talking to us, not letting us help you. You need to realize that we *want* to help you, that we need to know what you're thinking, what you want, what bothers you. If you don't tell us, it's no different than being on that table, just like that."

She shivered, and Kyle wrapped a throw blanket around her before he took his spot at Daniel's side.

"Now, what happened today? What got you so upset?" Kyle asked, his voice soft and coaxing.

Still high on her orgasms and reaction, she didn't look into their eyes, but answered in an almost sleepy voice. "This is taking forever."

"What? The case?"

She nodded. "I'm here, playing this stupid game with you, and she's going through fuck only knows what. I can't let her die," she said against his neck.

"Who?"

"Anne."

That made him still. Why hadn't he put it all together sooner? Her chasing the slavers, risking herself? He'd thought it was because they were a danger to the omegas she protected, but that wasn't it. "One of the omegas who was taken by slavers is your friend, right?" No wonder she'd put herself through this hell.

Alison nodded but didn't pull away. That felt like a small miracle, how she only curled tighter against his chest, as though he were her only real comfort.

He looked over her shoulder to meet Kyle's gaze.

Clearly, tomorrow, once she'd come back to her senses, they'd need to have one hell of a conversation.

He was growing tired of her secrets.

Chapter Thirteen

Why was it that every damn time Alison let those alphas get the upper hand, she paid dearly for it?

She groaned softly as she woke, wishing she'd at least gotten those thirty seconds or so to lie there in bed and not realize exactly what had happened. Some ignorance would be amazing right about then.

Instead, she'd remembered it all, every filthy detail, every spilled secret.

Why the hell did I do that?

"Come here," Kyle grumbled and tugged her against his chest. He rubbed his chin on the top of her head as he trapped her against him. "It's too early."

"You're the one who likes to get up early," she pointed out.

"Sure, when I don't have a warm, temping omega in the bed. Turns out that changes everything." His arm was heavy yet reassuring in a way she wasn't comfortable with—*especially* after last night.

She squirmed, unable to relax again.

He let out a long-suffering sigh, as though they'd had this fight a million times and he was used to losing. "All right, let's get up."

Alison slid from the bed, nearly regretting the choice when the blanket stopped keeping the chill away. The bed *was* warm, and Kyle's masculine scent wasn't the worst thing to spend another hour or two cuddled up to.

She winced, memories of the night before coming back. *Nope. Not a chance.*

Kyle, despite agreeing, didn't actually get out of bed. He shifted to sit up, the blanket pulling off him.

Which left him naked. How had she not noticed that before? It wasn't like ignoring his hard cock was all that easy, and it had been pressed against her all morning.

"So, are you over your mood yet? Because if not, I wouldn't mind trying to treat it again."

Alison crossed her arms, ignoring the way it teased her nipples. "You're just looking for another reason to tie me up."

"I don't need a reason."

That got her going, especially when he set his hands behind his head. It stretched him out, reminded her that the man had very little fat on his body. He really was stunning, especially as his nose healed. In fact, he distracted her so well that she forgot all about their bickering, or about the fact she probably didn't want to let him know how much he affected her.

He had to suspect—he could smell her, after all—but letting him know it or have any proof was too far.

Yet...she struggled to draw her focus away. He didn't have the dark hair on his chest that Daniel did, at least not so thick. His was lighter, but it still had that mesmerizing trail down to his groin.

He brought his hand to his cock. "Come on, sugar. Only us up so far. No reason to rush out of bed just yet, is there?"

Alison pressed her lips together, the temptation strong. She'd never really *wanted* to do something like that before, and yet suddenly she could think of nothing else. Before she even realized it, she'd started to move toward the bed. Her knee pressed into the mattress, beside his foot, and, as she crawled up his body, she felt primal in a strange way.

It reminded her of how she felt when she stalked her prey, when she closed in on someone who had been stupid enough to get on her radar. She felt predatory and powerful and now it mixed with her desire. Her gaze remained locked on Kyle's cock, on the way his hand moved over it, stroking in slow, long motions from base to tip.

When she got close enough, he slid his fingers into her hair. The tug against her scalp drew a noisy moan from her as she dragged her tongue up the underside of his cock, then took him past her lips.

Kyle controlled the movement, shifting her forward and backward as though she were a toy. He didn't press in deep and didn't go fast. Instead, it was leisurely, almost relaxing. Alison used her tongue, wrapping it around the thick head of his cock, tasting the pre-cum that escaped and only whetted her appetite for more.

"You're such a good girl," Kyle praised. "You take my cock so well."

His words washed over her, the praise strange yet welcome. She liked being called good, which was a damn odd thing.

She'd lived her life doing what she wanted rather than what she was supposed to do. She'd fought against the stereotypes, against the expectations laid on her, and accepted that she would never live up to what anyone wanted. If she couldn't be what she was supposed to be, then she would be the opposite.

It was easier—and safer—to not care what people wanted.

So why was it that when Kyle looked at her with that pride, when he called her good, when he made it clear she wasn't falling short, it heated up parts of her that had been ignored for her entire life?

Alison gave in to it instead of fighting it. She hollowed her cheeks, tightening her lips around his thick shaft. His groan said he liked the action, and he sped up the rhythm.

"Fuck." His voice dropped lower, into something almost a growl. "I can't wait to knot your sweet cunt, sugar. I bet you're going to feel amazing, all stretched tight around me."

Yes. Alison couldn't even pretend to not want that, all her resistance and worries gone.

Kyle pulled her back so his cock rested just beyond her lips. He let out a deep rumble, his fingers clutching her hair tighter just as his hot cum landed on her tongue.

"Hold it," Kyle snarled, voice rough. His dick jerked as each spurt left him, and after a moment, he withdrew from her mouth.

He tugged her up his body by her hair, then pressed his thumb against her lips. He hooked his finger down when she parted for him and opened her mouth.

His lip curled up even while he panted, breathless. "Look at how well you listen, sugar." He dipped into his pooled cum before pulling away. "Go on, swallow me down."

Alison obeyed as he took her lips in a kiss that stole her breath.

If this was what she'd resisted for so long…

Maybe it wasn't as bad as she'd thought it would be.

* * * *

Trent smiled at Alison. He had to admit, she looked better. She was flushed, but she seemed as though their *lesson* the day before had worked. Some of those defenses of hers hadn't come up again yet.

That and her morning with Kyle. In fact, both she and Kyle had seemed all together better.

They sat at the table, finally ready to address the reality of what Alison hadn't told them before.

Watching how she melted against Daniel, the way she eased when he set his hand on her nape, a mindless touch that soothed them both, made Trent tighten his lips.

He wanted that…

He craved the closeness, the sense of belonging again. Daniel and Kyle had it, had kept their bond after the fallout, and now? Now Alison was settling right into it.

It was petty of him to envy them that, but that didn't stop him from feeling it. What would happen? Would Trent go back to his life while Alison, Kyle and Daniel went off to live some happily ever after?

"Explain, girl," Daniel said.

Alison turned to glare, but Daniel only lifted an eyebrow.

She sighed and leaned forward, setting her forearms on the table. "Her name is Anne."

"How do you know she'll be at the auction? Not to be unkind, but omegas disappear all the time," Trent pointed out.

"Because I know her. She wasn't the type to run off. She mentioned someone was following her just before, and when I looked into it, I found out there's a scouting group that works in her area. I checked hospitals, friends, everything. There just isn't another option."

Trent heard the fear beneath her steady voice. He knew that unease, the worry when someone couldn't do anything but wait.

How many women had gone missing, ones who had just stopped coming into his gym, when he'd had to just wait and see if they ever showed up again?

Most didn't.

"So you dangled yourself as bait so you could find Anne?" Kyle reiterated.

She nodded. "This is the last auction. She *has* to be here, and I'm not going to let her disappear without doing whatever I can."

"And you didn't tell us this because?" Daniel asked.

"Because I thought you might have thought it wasn't a good reason, maybe thought I was too close to the case and, frankly, because it wasn't your business."

Ouch. So it seemed her temper wasn't entirely doused. Then again, Trent doubted it would ever be fully gone. Not that he minded. A wilting flower wouldn't last long in this world.

Kyle didn't look nearly as willing to accept her sharp answer, though. "You need to make sure you stop keeping secrets, sugar. I trust this is the last one?"

She waited a moment too long to nod. Still, Trent knew they only had so far to push.

Besides, no doubt she had secrets of her own, ones she didn't owe them.

"I want you to write down everything you can recall about Anne. Description, history, all the facts. They need to be added to the case files so we can hopefully identify her during the auction raid. We'll find her, pet."

A slow breath blew through Alison's full pink lips. She twisted her hand and squeezed back—an unexpected reaction. "I'm not used to this."

"To what?"

"To having someone on my side."

That got him. He knew exactly how that felt, to always feel as though he had to shoulder everything on his own. Hadn't he just been thinking it? It got old, fast, and Alison had done it her entire life, it sounded like.

"It's new, sure, but new isn't bad. Hell, you might just be surprised by how much you like new," Kyle said.

She pressed her lips together, as if she couldn't quite fathom such a thing, before she nodded.

Trent realized why exactly it bothered him so much to see Kyle and Daniel grow closer to her. She seemed like a stand-in for him, someone getting what he craved, gaining back that sense of family and connection.

He couldn't fault her for it, but damn, he wished he could see a way where he could get that, too.

* * * *

Daniel hated being the one to back down, yet something had nagged him for days.

Each time he looked at Trent, each time they ended up at the same table, when they happened to pass in a hallway, an uneasy gnawing in Daniel's stomach refused to be ignored.

It reminded him of his mother telling him that was his conscience, and that he'd better listen to it before things got worse.

That had brought him out back, where Trent was flipping burgers at the barbecue. *How can someone frustrate me this much but still feel like family?*

If he ever figured out a reason for that, he'd be the smartest man in the world. Family had been pissing one another off forever.

"Let's stop doing this," Daniel blurted out.

Trent looked over his shoulder, his eyebrow lifted, before pointing at the burgers with his spatula. "I mean, they'll burn if I ignore them."

Smart ass. "You know what I'm talking about."

Trent sighed, flipped the burgers, then turned to face him. "We've been over this. I can't come back. I won't."

Daniel fought down the urge to argue, to remind Trent of all the good they used to do together. That fight wasn't one he was winning, so he stayed on track. "I know. Look, let's not bullshit. You're feeling Alison just like us. It doesn't matter if we get pissed, if we fight, clearly we aren't done with one another yet, since we seem to want the same omega."

"Fate does think she's funny," Trent admitted.

"She is hilarious. Alison can't follow us around, right? What if we tried to make this work? You're settled here and so is she. Kyle and I have talked, and we can try to take on less field work, but when we have to go? You'll still be here."

A tic in Trent's jaw said he wanted to like the idea. "You ever think maybe too much time has passed? Like maybe wounds heal and no matter how much we want to go back, we can't?"

"Yeah, I did think that, until I saw how Alison brings us all together. Can you honestly say you're willing to walk away from her? That you're willing to throw this all aside because we had a problem?"

Trent shuffled his foot on the ground, distrust there.

Daniel couldn't blame him, not entirely. What had happened had been horrible. There were times Daniel thought about it—when he didn't think just about his side, but when he actually considered Trent—and he never failed to feel like shit. He and Kyle had walked out on Trent when he'd needed them.

They'd done it hoping he'd come back into the fold, and when he hadn't, the more all of them had pushed, the more hardened in their positions they'd become.

And yet seeing Trent with Alison, Daniel thought for the first time in a very long time there might be a shot. Maybe they could fix this.

"I don't know," Trent admitted.

"Fair enough. Just...think about it, okay?"

Trent nodded, and Daniel left him be, hoping he'd just need time.

They *could* fix this, if only everyone would stop being so fucking stubborn.

* * * *

Waves of nausea rushed through Alison. She huddled in the tub, the water from the shower rushing over her. She'd twisted the dial to cold, but it did nothing to cool her skin.

Her stomach wouldn't settle, rolling and threatening to expel what little she'd eaten that day. *What the hell is wrong with me?*

Her mind moved sluggishly, as though it couldn't quite keep up with whatever she was thinking. All of it frustrated her, had her sliding her fingers through her hair and grasping as though that would make her feel better.

Had she caught a bug? A flu? A cold? Something? It had been days of feeling under the weather.

Whatever it was, she didn't have time to deal with it. She couldn't just go to the store and pick up medication, and the last thing she wanted was to face the alphas and have to ask for anything.

She *hated* to need help, and that was all the worse when it came to failures of her body. Not to mention they'd hover.

Still, taking enough cold medicine to knock her out and sleeping through the worst of whatever this was sounded amazing.

She shivered, as though even with the sweat, even with how it seemed flames were licking over her skin, she was still reacting to the cold of the water.

Something was wrong.

Paranoia got her first, a creeping fear that perhaps the slavery ring had gotten wind of their involvement. Could they have had poisoned food sent there? Maybe the alpha who had come to the meeting had done something to her. The idea of dying from poison before finding Anne haunted her.

Then she stilled, terror filling her.

The vial… The drug…

She recalled the way she'd sniffed, taking in that putrid chemical scent, how it had stuck to her sinuses even as she'd tried to blow it out.

Another rolling wave of pain forced a whine through her gritted teeth.

The answer was so obvious, even if she had tried to ignore it.

The drug had sent her into heat…

Trent glanced at his watch, the food growing cold.

"Is she not going to eat?" Kyle picked at his own meal, stealing bites as though it didn't count if he didn't use his fork. "She barely touched breakfast or lunch."

"She needs to eat," Trent said. The side of him that liked to set rules and boundaries wasn't about to let her skip so many meals, not when he was in charge of her. "I'll go check on her."

Her shower had been running for almost an hour, but the alphas had given her privacy. They were a house full of adults, and even if she was playing the part of their submissive, he understood that need for alone time.

He took the stairs in a quick jog, then knocked on the door to her room. No answer, but if she were in the shower, she probably couldn't hear him.

He pushed open the door, then went to the bathroom. No steam escaped, which had him frowning. He knocked, again, but still nothing.

A tightness in his chest made him knock harder. Fear crept in, slowly, whispering all the reasons she might not be answering.

After waiting another moment, he twisted the handle.

Locked.

"Alison," he called out, raising his voice so she'd hear it above the running water.

Silence.

Heavy steps preceded Daniel's voice. "She had better be in there."

A quick nod from Trent was his only response as he moved away, then leveled one hard kick at the door. The hollow interior door gave way with a loud crack, and sure enough, the bathroom didn't have a bit of heat in it—or Alison.

She'd run.

"Fuck," Daniel muttered.

Trent twisted to find the window open—not large enough for one of the alphas to fit through, but Alison wasn't all that big.

"What the hell was she thinking?" Trent went to the window and peered out, hoping to catch sight of something. Instead, the darkness stretched across the yard and he couldn't spot anything moving.

"Shit," Kyle said as he walked into the room

"Pretty much. The girl bolted. I swear, I'll make good on my threat to paddle her ass over this," Daniel said.

Kyle shook his head, his cheeks pale. "Neither of you smell it?"

"Smell what?" Trent asked.

Kyle offered a hard look, something in his gaze saying he wasn't joking for once.

That was when Trent stopped, forcing him to breathe in, to think, to pay attention.

It hit him fast. Weak—probably why he hadn't picked up on it right away—since she'd been out of the room for at least twenty minutes, but it was there.

Heat.

Suddenly her behavior, her reaction, all made a little more sense.

Alison had gone into heat, and rather than face that with the alphas, she'd run away.

And when Trent's cock hardened, when he let out a feral snarl, he couldn't really blame her a bit.

Daniel's desire to turn Alison's ass red abated some when he finally caught sight of her.

Damn, she looks pathetic.

It seemed her energy hadn't lasted long, or perhaps the cramping pain had grown so quickly, she couldn't run far. She'd made it to the detached garage on the property, the door ajar when they went outside to follow her tracks. She'd gone out through the bathroom window, down the lattice on the side of the wall, then across the yard. A few places showed indents in the dirt—hands and knees—where she'd tumbled.

Each one tugged at him. By the time he actually got a look at her, curled up in the corner of the garage, a soft whimper on her lips, he just didn't have it in him to be angry.

Finding her took the tension down a bit. Whether anything they experienced between them was real or not didn't change that his instincts had recognized he was responsible for her, that all the alphas were. Her going missing had turned the three into snarling, possessive beasts.

"Sweet," Daniel said, keeping his voice gentle as he dropped to his knees beside her. Sweat coated her forehead, and she'd squeezed her eyes shut tight.

She flinched when he brushed her hair from her face. "Fucking drug," she whispered.

Damn it. Heats at the best of times weren't all that fun for an omega, but when spurred by that drug? They tended to hit harder and faster.

Even though a part of him, that primal side that didn't care about right or wrong—the one that thrived off survival—loved the idea of her going into heat, of servicing her, of watching her grow with his child afterward, the logical part knew this wasn't how it was supposed to happen.

"Breathe slowly, pet." Trent sat down beside her, then managed to get her head into his lap, so at least she wasn't entirely lying on the floor. "I want you to try and take a couple of deep breaths."

"And just how many heats have *you* been through, oh great expert?" Even though her words were strong, the tone came out breathless and strained.

"Keep mouthing off," Daniel said. "You might as well get your money's worth out of it right now when we can't punish you for it."

Lines appeared in her face just as she curled in on herself and cried out through gritted teeth.

Trent stroked across her forehead while Daniel rubbed her hand. They weren't much, but right then that was all they could offer.

"We have a sedative, sugar." Kyle crouched, tilting his head as though he could look into her face even though her eyes were shut. "We made sure to have it on hand just in case. It's already pre-measured, so we can knock you out. You don't have to suffer."

Her swallow was loud, and her wince said her throat was already dry. The trembling that racked her entire body showed the strain her heat had already placed on her, and it hadn't been more than an hour. She jerked her head from side to side, a quick, decisive refusal.

"You can't suffer like this," Daniel told her.

"I thought you liked a little pain."

The joke drew a smile from him. "This is not to my taste. Don't be stubborn, not about this. We'll get you into bed and medicate you and you won't have to hurt. We'll watch over you the whole time."

She shifted, nuzzling her cheek against Trent's lap, an oddly affectionate gesture that Daniel was sure she'd never do if she were in her right mind. "I don't want to be drugged."

"I don't like taking meds either, but I can promise you, if my insides were tearing themselves apart like yours are, I'd make an exception," Trent told her.

Again, she shook her head. "I've made it through heats before."

"But never when caused by a drug and never when living with three alphas. Look, pet, even if you could make it through the entire thing without giving in, I'm not so sure we could." The way Trent said it, the tightness in his jaw—it made Daniel ache.

The man worried too much. Daniel had no question that if she wanted to ride the entire thing out without a lick of help—he ignored the way the word 'lick' made his mind go—that Trent and the rest of them could resist.

Another wave hit her, so close to the last that it proved this would not be an easy heat. She dug her fingers into Daniel's thigh, a grip that would leave bruises, and ones he happily accepted. If bruising him helped her, he'd take it with a smile.

Alison shuddered at the end, then slid her hand beneath Daniel's shirt. "I won't take the drug," she said, this time more weight to her words.

"I don't want to see you suffer." Trent sounded defeated and backed against a wall.

"Then don't," she said, crawling into Trent's lap and taking his lips in an aggressive kiss. Her robe opened enough so she was bare to his eyes.

Trent's groan was loud, and he didn't resist, not at first. Instead, his hand went to her hair and he kissed her back.

Daniel rubbed his hand over his face, looking for strength. For what, he didn't know. God, he wanted to give in… He wanted to service Alison through her heat, to knot her over and over again until the insanity of the heat abated for them all, until none of them could move anymore and fell asleep sated and exhausted.

But he owed it to her, to all of them, to be sure.

"Think about this, sweet," he said even though waiting and thinking were the *last* thing he wanted.

She broke the kiss, her eyes glazed over from lust as she looked at Daniel.

"You sure you really want this? Beyond the fact that it means actually having sex, you know the risks. You could end up pregnant."

That made her pause, as though just the word woke her up. She worried her bottom lip with her teeth, her gaze down. "I understand the risk."

"How about you look at me when you say that," Daniel said. "If you can't even look at me, you don't really want this."

She whined, pressing her face to Trent's throat. Through her back, Daniel could feel her muscles go rigid, tensed in pain. After the wave ran through her, after she caught her breath again, she twisted so her forehead rested against Trent's shoulder but she could see Daniel. There was absolute surrender in those eyes.

Of course, whether she'd been worn down by pain or she really wanted them, well, that was impossible to know. It was the risk when dealing with omegas—especially when heats were involved. Was it them or was it biology? "I know the risk," she assured him. "I know you could knock me up. I get it. I'm not some fragile thing that doesn't know how this works. Now, will you stop arguing and fuck me already?"

And *that* was an offer Daniel couldn't ignore.

Chapter Fourteen

"Come on, pet," Trent said, shifting as if he were ready to get up.

The thought of losing the warmth of his body for even a moment was too long. Alison clutched him with one hand, her other reaching for the button of his jeans. "Here."

"I'm not fucking you on a garage floor," he groaned against her kiss.

"Don't care." She bit his bottom lip, undoing his pants to find the hot skin beneath.

"The house isn't that far. We've got bedding there, sweet, and you can make a nest," Daniel said.

The need to make one wasn't there, though. Was it because of the drug? Did that make this unlike a regular heat, so she had no desire to do any of that?

Instead, she could only think about the alphas, about their masculine, heavy scents, their strong hands and hard cocks. She wanted to feel the strength in them, to taste them, and none of that required a bed.

She shook her head and pressed her lips to Trent's throat before delivering a hard bite.

His answering dangerous, wild growl made her whine. The sound didn't fit at all with the alpha she'd come to know, too feral for the sweet man he was.

Maybe that was why it was as hot as it was, why she tugged at his jeans hard, tired of waiting, her body wet and desperate. Someone else stripped her of her robe, and the cool air against her sweat-soaked skin drew a shiver.

Trent lifted his hips, letting her shift his pants and boxers down enough that she wrapped her hand around his hard cock. He was impossibly thick and as soon as she touched him, she was tired of waiting.

She rose up on her knees, her legs straddling his lap.

Her grasp on his cock let her rub him along her drenched sex.

If she wasn't driven so hard by her heat, she'd have taken more time, teased, but right then she wanted nothing more than for him to fill her.

His thick shaft stretched her, and if she hadn't been drenched, no doubt it would have stung. Instead, she let out a thin sound, Trent's hands tightening on her waist as though he wanted to take her in one hard thrust.

Everything inside her lit up, as if her entire body had waited for *this* sensation. She recalled the clawing, painful heats before, the ones where she locked herself away in her cabin miles from anyone and suffered on her own.

This was how it was supposed to be. Even so, even as Trent gave, she moved her hands to his shoulders and dug her nails into him. She wanted to hold him down, to take, to have everything. The need came from something old inside her, something that had grown in the generations of omegas before her.

And Trent seemed fine with that plan. He growled in response to her nails and bucked his hips when she'd taken every inch of his hard cock, as if he needed to make sure there wasn't any space left inside her untouched by him.

He burned her with his touch, seared her so deeply inside that she suspected she'd wear that mark forever, just like his bite.

Her lips met his, though their kisses were surprisingly soft, just a mixing of breath and need.

Alison rose then came down hard, wanting to feel entirely taken by him. Trent kept his hands on her waist, adding power to her moves but following her lead.

It's not even my lead, she realized. Instead, it was pure instinct.

His groan was deep, and he tightened his grip on her. His fingers dug into her sides, into the soft flesh at her hips, as though he needed to clutch her as tightly as he could. He lifted his hips quicker, no longer taking her rhythm. Instead, he thrust into her rapidly, erratic, and she could only hold on and accept the wonderful, punishing sensation.

She didn't have to question when he came, to wonder if it had happened. On the last thrust up and into her, he yanked her down tight against him just as the base of his cock grew. She'd thought he'd been thick before, but it was nothing compared to how his knot stretched her cunt in a way she'd never experienced before.

It triggered a powerful and overwhelming release for her, something snapping inside her as though she'd been waiting forever for *this* feeling, like her body had been on edge, needing this.

She squirmed, everything too much, but Trent—usually the sweet one—didn't let her get away. He hugged her tight to his chest until that knot locked behind her pubic bone.

"Take it," he growled into her ear, his voice nothing like she'd ever heard it before. "This is what you wanted—what you need. You can handle it, pet, you were made for this."

Pet. If that name had revved her up before, it was nothing compared to right then. She cried out against his throat as he forced her body to accept the thickness of his knot, as the warmth of his cum soaked into her, as it tamed the raging need that consumed her.

He kissed her shoulder, the one he'd left the bite mark on, like some reverent act of worship he needed to perform. Each press of his lips made her cunt squeeze around him again. It was impossible to ignore how full she felt, how he stretched her to capacity.

Her mind tripped over thoughts, everything muddled and sluggish. Maybe that was for the best, to prevent her from thinking too much. Anything more complicated than the alpha beneath her—inside her—didn't matter right then.

Warm hands traced up her back, and she arched into the touch. They slipped around her to cup her breasts between her and Trent. When they closed into pinches over her nipples, she whimpered and shifted, the tug of Trent's knot telling her she was still trapped.

"How're you feeling, sugar?" *Kyle.* His voice came from just behind her, his warm breath skirting along her bare skin.

She didn't answer—was there a good answer to that?—but he didn't seem to expect one. He teased her nipples before pulling her back so she leaned against his chest, still tied to Trent.

It felt...*dirty*. She had Trent's hard cock inside her, still had waves of pleasure rushing through her from him, and yet she leaned against Kyle as he touched her. The cool air drifted over her now uncovered front, and the sight of her taken by Trent, with Kyle's hands on her, made her need grow again.

As though he knew that—hell, maybe he did know, maybe that was his plan—Kyle slipped one hand down her flat stomach, He ran his fingers along the lips of her cunt, where she was stretched around Trent. "You've never taken a knot, and now look at you? Do you feel full, sugar? Hmm? Totally fucked open?"

His fingers against her, the way he made her focus on just how thick Trent was, on how her body struggled to accommodate his girth, made her hips twist, but she could do nothing because of Trent's knot.

Kyle chuckled, then brought those torturous fingers to her clit. It made her realize she hadn't actually been touched there. The idea that she'd had an orgasm without anyone touching her clit made her shiver again. She'd *never* experienced that.

And yet the first stroke of his fingers streaked like electricity through her, made her pussy tighten and her back arch.

Too much.

Not enough.

Why couldn't she figure it out?

Not that Kyle seemed inclined to ask her opinion. Instead, he repeated the motion, stroking against her hard clit, driving her mad with the feeling.

"Fuck, that feels good," Trent groaned, his head against the concrete wall of the garage, his eyes hooded as he watched Kyle toy with her.

"Arms around me," Kyle ordered, and without thinking, she reached back and wrapped her arms behind his neck. It spread her out, and Trent stared as though she was a buffet he couldn't wait to start in on.

Kyle didn't get her off, at least not entirely. Her body still had aftershocks from her last orgasm, and she clenched around Trent, waves of pleasure crashing through her, but he kept her teetering on that edge.

It was the sweetest torture, and sweat ran down between her breasts and over her stomach as she was forced to do nothing but *feel*. She was entirely in the moment with them, nothing beyond the walls of that garage existing.

It was such a strange feeling, to not worry, to not think about who she should be or how she should act. Instead, she did what felt natural, and she had no room inside her for doubts.

Kyle wrapped an arm around her, then pulled slightly. Trent's knot tugged at her, but finally slipped free. An empty sensation made her whine, desperate to have that feeling back.

Kyle didn't give her time to worry, though. He stood and twisted her, setting her ass on a workbench beside them. He'd already stripped down, so all that deliciously hot skin was accessible for her.

He spread her legs, hooking one arm below her knee, his gaze trapped at her cunt. Wetness covered her thighs, now both from her own pussy and Trent's cum.

Kyle didn't seem to mind it. If anything, he growled as though he *liked* her being claimed in such a way by Trent.

He rubbed the head of his cock along her drenched slit, teasing her aching clit at the top.

And all Alison wanted right then was *more*. More of everything. More of this moment, of the feelings they made course through her, more of that delicious stretch they forced her body to do. She wanted it to never end, to never stop basking in the impossible feeling, the one she'd never known before.

Before, heats had been suffering, pain and fear, even when she tried to not allow it to grasp her.

There was suffering here, she supposed, as she waited on the precipice of need, but it was the difference between a burn and the sting of spicy food. It made her mouth water and her desire soar.

Kyle nestled the head of his cock against her entrance, then grasped the back of her neck. It trapped her, forced her to look into his blue eyes. It made it more than bodies, and she couldn't think straight enough to wonder why that was.

He surged forward, filling her with a single rough thrust that hilted him, his heavy balls pressing against her.

She opened her mouth to cry out, but he arched over her to steal that sound with a kiss, to take it as though he'd earned it, as if he'd wanted to savor it.

He whispered against her lips. "Fuck, you are tight, and so wet. Nothing better than a needy omega in this entire world. Now, lean back and let me really fuck you, sugar."

He released her neck and hooked both arms beneath her knees. It spread her legs out wide, let him stare down at where they were connected, at how he stretched her as Trent had before. He didn't ease into anything, pulling back then plunging into her with a thrust that made her gasp at the wonderful roughness.

He fucked her as he did everything else. He was sure, confident and relentless. He lifted her ass off the workbench a hair, to let him leverage her against him as well, to make sure he couldn't possibly delve any deeper. He took her as though he were trying to claim every single inch inside her.

And Alison wanted that. She wanted no part of her left untouched after this, nothing that they hadn't taken, devoured, *owned.*

He growled, and when she caught his gaze, his eyes seemed darker, like a beast that she'd let have her, one who would have her entirely.

The need inside her that had been sated for a moment with Trent's cum uncurled and stretched, as though it knew it had more coming soon. Her heat crested over her as she tried to move with Kyle, as she tried to take more.

He leaned over her, using the change in position to fuck into her even harder. If she wasn't drugged on her heat, the roughness might have bothered her. Right then, though?

Nothing bothered her.

He let out a snarl as he bit down on her other shoulder—though not hard enough to draw blood—just as his knot grew. He shifted his hands down to her ass, to yank her against him, to make sure she couldn't escape that growing bulge at the base of his cock, and triggered another breath-stealing orgasm from her.

She shivered against the scrape of his teeth, the way her cunt was already sore yet craving everything he could give her, and the exhaustion knowing they weren't anywhere close to the finish.

Daniel pressed his lips to Alison's head, closing his eyes to breathe in her heat-soaked scent.

He'd stroked himself as he'd watched Trent and Kyle knot the poor girl, as he'd witnessed how her eyes widened and her lips would form a perfect little *o* when she felt how their cocks swelled, when she realized she was entirely trapped.

Why was that as hot as it was? Something deviant inside him enjoyed it, the way when he knotted a girl, she was *his*. For that while, while tied together, she was entirely his.

She was exhausted, but not nearly done. No, she'd have hours left. They should have moved to the house, where snacks and water would be available. While she rested, Trent had dragged himself to the kitchen to grab a few things, but leaving an omega in heat was nearly impossible. They'd have to make do.

She shifted, blinking slowly as Daniel positioned her. They'd spread her robe out, along with their clothing. It wasn't a nest, and it would serve as a shitty bed, but it was better than getting her scraped up on the hard ground.

He shifted her so she was on her knees, her chest to the floor. Trent and Kyle rested with their backs to the wall, putting them beside her. Trent carded his fingers through her hair, a reassuring stroke.

Daniel ran his hands over her hips, then grasped her ass. He spread her cheeks, staring down at her, able to see her puffy, drenched sex along with her ass.

He'd love to have taken her ass right then, but it wasn't in the cards. Her heat required his cum to end up exactly one place.

He leaned down and offered a hard bite to one of her cheeks.

She whined, the sound high and startled. He soothed the spot with a kiss, then bent down more to drag his tongue up her hot, wet slit. Even as he swallowed, her taste took over his senses, narrowed his focus to this one absolutely perfect part of the universe.

He could taste her sweetness, her need, and the musky taste of the alphas as well. Once they'd all had her—many times that night—she'd carry their scent. She'd be *theirs*.

And he was drunk enough on lust and fantasies that he believed that could happen, that he truly thought they might be headed for such an ending.

She squirmed at the feeling, but Daniel took her clit between his lips and sucked hard.

Her cry was music, and he did it once more before relenting, that darkness inside him loving her frantic sounds.

Her cunt seared the head of his dick as he pressed against her, grasping her hips to hold her still. She went wild, writhing, leaning back to take him. *This* he liked. He enjoyed the way she couldn't hide what she wanted. So often she could be hard to read, harder still to understand. In that moment, though, all those defenses were torn free and he saw the passionate, strong omega beneath them.

He tightened his fingers as he slid into her, slow enough to torment her, to force her to feel each inch of him spreading her and stretching her lovely cunt.

Trent ran his fingers through her hair as she rested her cheek against Kyle's thigh. Her chest was to the floor, to protect her shoulder. Even driven as he was by need, he'd never risk hurting her.

She took him as though made for him, like her cunt had been designed to fit him perfectly. Snug, warm, wet. It was perfection, and he allowed himself only a moment to savor it.

Daniel ran his hand up her spine once, focusing on how her back arched, on the lovely curve, the narrow waist, the hips wide enough to hold on to.

He had no idea what he could have possibly done in his life to deserve this, but he wouldn't forsake it, wouldn't risk losing it. He pulled back and thrust into her, taking her harder.

One of his hands remained on her hip, the other spreading her cheeks. He dipped his thumb into the wetness around her cunt, then pressed that against her ass.

She tensed but didn't pull away. "Good girl," he rumbled out. "Let me in."

She shivered, and he took that as his opportunity. He pressed that finger into her, keeping shallow without any real lube, just enough to tease her, to tempt her, to let her know *exactly* what he planned to take next time.

And Alison reacted the way he knew she would. She cried out, her body clutching him as if to never let him go.

Fine by me.

He teased the sensitive ring of muscles as he took her cunt with hard, wild thrusts. "This is how it'll be, sweet, next time. I'll take your ass, and Kyle can have your cunt. Your pretty mouth, well, Trent will fuck that, since he's too nice to you anyway."

She trembled, her body seeming to be in chaos she couldn't control. He stoked those flames inside her, knowing his own end was close. It was only round one of what would be a very long night, so he had nothing to prove, no need to make himself last longer. Truth be told, he'd come in her at least three more times before her heat dissipated, before that need broke and they could rest. This wasn't about showing off, or about trying to make it something it wasn't. No one could do such things when driven so hard by hormones.

Instead, heats were for giving in to what people really were, what they needed. They were for letting go of expectations. So Daniel did that, enjoying the wily omega beneath him, taking what she gave so freely and servicing her in return.

When he came, when his knot swelled so thick that she whimpered and whined, he plunged as deep as possible and locked into place.

She came hard, her cunt squeezing down so tightly it nearly hurt, and he pulled his finger from her. Panting, he leaned forward, offering gentle bites to her back, to her shoulder blades, to the sweat-soaked expanse of skin wherever he could reach.

Reality could stay the hell away. They'd all have to wake up from this spell too soon, and Daniel refused to lose a moment of it to worry.

When he was locked inside her, when she whined softly and trembled against him, he knew something he couldn't ever admit to.

He loved her, and that was going to hurt them all in the end.

Chapter Fifteen

Alison hurt. She'd say she felt as though she had been fucked for hours by three alphas—which was exactly how she felt—but that seemed far too on the nose.

Her clit was sensitive, even after a shower, so the brush of her underwear against it made her let out a pathetic sound that reminded her of the ones she'd made the night before.

The night when I screwed all three of them instead of taking the drugs like a smart woman would have done.

Even thinking about it, she couldn't quite figure out *why* she'd made the choice she had.

Liar.

She sighed, letting the swing move forward and back on the porch. She knew *why*.

This wouldn't last beyond their case. At the end of that, she'd go back to her world and they'd go back to theirs. There was no other way of it working out.

So when the waves of need had hit her, when she'd been faced with the three of them in that garage, she'd wanted a taste of a future that wasn't meant for her. She'd wanted for just one night to know what it would feel like to be someone's mate, to have someone look at her as though they wanted nothing more.

Not just strangers, either, but people who knew her.

For better or worse, these alphas did. Their plan, their time together, had let them glimpse deeper than anyone else had in her entire life.

"Which is yet another reason this can't go on," she said out loud to herself.

The alphas were all still asleep. While her hormones let her bounce back quicker, they'd exhausted themselves satisfying her.

She recalled Trent, after three rounds, groaning when she'd crawled over him, when she'd straddled his waist, needing him another time. She wasn't sure if by that point he'd even enjoyed it, not like he would have regular sex, at least. Still, he'd given to her, without reservation or complaint.

Finally, when she'd all but passed out, they'd brought her back to the main house. They'd ended up in Daniel's room, their bodies entwined with hers in some puzzle that allowed all of them to fit on the bed—barely.

They'd hardly stirred when she'd risen, telling her just how tired they were.

So she'd let them sleep.

It gave her time to herself anyway.

The odds of getting pregnant were low, which was the only reason she wasn't panicked. The thought of having a child—

She couldn't even fathom the idea. That was how foreign it was—she couldn't even come up with a scenario where it was possible.

"Morning." Trent's voice brought her gaze up.

Of course, it was Trent. He was the caretaker. She'd have never figured it on first meeting them, when on that first night he'd looked like some huge brawler.

Yet there he stood, a plate of food in his hand as he set a water bottle on the table beside her.

"Morning."

He lifted her feet, then took a spot there so her legs draped across his lap. The position was intimate, but could she really be upset about that after the night before?

He picked up the fork and got a bite of scrambled eggs on the tines, then offered it.

She wanted to balk—as she always did when he fed her—but instead she took the bite, suppressing the moan at the wonderful taste.

She'd never admit it, but a part of the feeding, the way he hovered, made her happy. She'd never had someone really care about her, not that she could recall.

"How do you feel, pet?"

She swallowed the bit, not surprised that it was good. The alphas all seemed to be adept cooks. "Fine."

Trent's eyebrow lifted in that subtle way that made her stomach drop.

"Sore," she admitted. "But it's not that bad."

He nodded, as though her answer satisfied him this time. He reached into his pocket and pulled out two small red pills. "Ibuprofen. For after you eat, though."

Alison stared at the little pills when he set them on the table in front of the swing, beside the water bottle.

"What are you frowning at like that?" His tone held amusement, as though he wasn't annoyed by her confusion, just entertained.

"I don't like being taken care of."

"Really?" He nodded down at how she'd melted into the position, her legs over his lap, her eyes already on the next bite she wanted from his plate.

Her cheeks heated and she went to pull away.

He caught her foot to keep her exactly where she was. "Wasn't complaining. Believe it or not, I rather like taking care of someone."

"Why? Who wants some overgrown, useless burden around?" She cringed at her own tone, at the way self-loathing dripped from it.

His small huff said he'd caught it. "You sure do have a lot of hang-ups, don't you? You don't like taking care of others, at least not when they can see it, and you don't want anyone taking care of you. Why is that?"

She took another bite from his fork, chewing it as she considered her answer. Once she swallowed, she figured she had nothing to lose by explaining it. Maybe it was still her being off balance from her heat, but the quiet way Trent sat there let her get her story out. "I told you, my mom was a slave. Every female I knew was basically a slave. They spent their lives scurrying around, trying to please some alpha who never really cared."

"So you're afraid you'll be just the same?"

Alison sighed softly. Examining her own thought process wasn't exactly her favorite thing to do. She believed in moving the fuck on, in putting bullshit that didn't matter behind her. "I learned that connecting with people was dangerous. They always screwed you over. It's like..." She lifted her hand, drawing her fingers into a fist. "This is one person, right? Powerful.

It doesn't need anyone or anything. Then, when you open your hand, all those fingers? They're connections. They're people you rely on or who rely on you. Suddenly, you have spots that can be broken, that can be caught. You've opened yourself up to risk, given yourself weaknesses people can exploit."

Trent stared at her hand as though formulating some response. She was ready for it, prepared to hear a long-winded lecture about how risk was a part of life, about how those connections made people human.

She'd heard it before.

Instead, he reached out and clasped her wrist, her hand automatically closing around his, locking together as though he were going to pull her to her feet.

She frowned as she stared, as she tried to figure out his point.

"If I'd done this and your hand was closed, we'd both have been weaker. I won't tell you there aren't risks, but everything has an upside, too." He squeezed once, then pulled away to get her another bite of food.

Alison obediently ate it, not even thinking about it, about him, only about the way his warm hand had wrapped around her, about the strength in that grasp.

It's a nice thought.

Nice thought or not, though, Alison was just too stubborn and set in her ways to change.

She'd lived her life alone, and as soon as they were done here, she'd go back to that.

* * * *

Two weeks had passed, and as Daniel stared at the little omega who took up most of his time, he couldn't help but smile.

It seemed strange, like a life he'd never really pictured yet had slipped into with no trouble, as though it were the life he was always meant to have.

She'd settled in, somewhat.

Somewhat being the reason she was currently tied up on the bed, naked and cursing at him.

"I swear, the second you let me out of here I'll—"

"You'll what? Because from where I'm standing"—he dragged his fingers along her back, then over the curve of her ass—"your threats don't mean much."

She tried to twist to glare, but couldn't manage to move enough. It left her only able to stare at the blank wall on the other side of his bed. He'd thought about blindfolding her, but he'd decided he wanted to be able to see the look in those pretty eyes of hers.

"Why are you here?"

"Because you're a dick?"

He laughed softly. Trent would dislike her mouthing off, since he was a fan of rules even though he was soft-hearted when it came to punishment. Daniel, though?

"You're not supposed to laugh," she snapped, as if his chuckle were more egregious an offense than tying her up or whatever else he had planned. "I thought you were mad."

"Mad? No, sweet, I'm not a mad sort of man. The more you mouth off to me, the more disrespectful you are, the more fun I'll have adding on punishments."

She inhaled sharply. "You can't just add punishments! That's not fair."

"Really? If you get in trouble with the police, and keep breaking the law, they'll keep adding charges."

"You're not the police."

He huffed a soft laugh before sliding his fingers up her drenched cunt. "I'm close enough. Besides, you like this more than you're letting on."

"Don't try to put your perversions on me."

"How about in you?" He pressed two of his fingers into her as he asked, wanting to surprise her, to hear that little catch in her breath when he did something she hadn't expected. Maybe it was because of how skilled he'd come to find her, because she wasn't just anyone, but rather a woman able to hold her own against him. All of that made it sweeter when she gave in, when he overcame her and watched her melt.

She was tight around his fingers, and he was tempted to undo his pants and slip into her wet pussy.

Except he had a better plan already.

"So, what was it again that you did?" He asked the question while he thrust those two fingers into her, rough enough to help keep her off balance.

"I was stupid enough to agree to this with a sadist like you." The end of her little tirade drifted into a lust-drunken moan.

"If you think calling me a sadist is going to hurt my feelings, you're barking up the wrong tree, sweet." He twisted his wrist to stroke against the sensitive front wall of her cunt, making sure to tease her while leaving her clit entirely untouched.

This *was* punishment, after all.

"Come on, I know you can figure out why you're here."

She let out a thin whine and shifted her hips, as though she could get satisfaction from him that way.

She couldn't, of course. He wasn't Trent, who would have given in after the first little whimper she let out.

The sound turned into pure frustration before she blew out a slow breath from her pink lips. "I'm sorry."

"For what?"

He could *feel* her glare.

"For sleeping on the couch."

He smiled softly at her sullen tone. She *hated* to admit to doing anything wrong, at least she hated it in part. The other side of her, that submissive, beautiful creature she tried to hide, reveled in the way he took her to task for each infraction.

Not that he was overly harsh. He only reacted when she did something knowingly. "Now, I remember having this talk with you just yesterday when you did the same thing to Kyle. We agreed that if you wake up and can't stay in bed anymore, you'll let the alpha know, didn't we?" He pulled his fingers from her, then went to the side of the bed she was facing and crouched down, into her line of sight.

She didn't answer, her stubborn little lips pressed tight together.

"Didn't we, sweet?" He traced his finger over her lip, smearing her own wetness over her.

She nodded, some of the fire leaving her.

"So why'd I wake up this morning to an empty bed?"

She opened her mouth, and Daniel slipped the two fingers in before she could answer. Her full lips wrapped around his fingers and licked him clean without him asking. That was the thing—she liked to fight back at times, as if she needed to prove she *could* fight back, but that didn't change the natural instinct inside her that cried out to him to own her.

He pulled his fingers back and resisted the urge to grasp her chin, instead lifting an eyebrow.

It took a moment of confusion before she seemed to recall the question he'd asked. "I couldn't sleep," she said. "I haven't been sleeping well. I just can't get comfortable, and by the time it's four in the morning, I'm miserable and sick of just lying there."

"And you didn't wake me up why? Because either I'd have worn you out so you could sleep or I'd have gotten up with you."

Her pretty green eyes darted away as they always did when she didn't want to answer, when she didn't like the idea of exposing her secrets.

Too bad for her.

He slid his hand into her hair and gripped tightly until she looked at him again.

"I don't like asking for help," she whispered. "I figured you didn't need to lose any sleep over my problems."

And, as it always did, that tiny confession drew up an ache. The girl hated relying on anyone, always so sure they'd turn her away, that they'd only end up letting her down.

He loosened his grip, then leaned in to offer a soft kiss, tasting her own sweet pussy on her lips. "If I didn't want to help you, I wouldn't demand you wake me up. Do you really think I'm the sort of man who does anything I don't want to do?"

She shook her head. *Quiet now, is she? Maybe she's learning.*

He doubted it.

"So am I not going to get a punishment?" Hope flickered in her eyes, a sparkle there saying she'd expected to get off the hook.

"You've spent too much time with Trent spoiling you. No, sweet, you're not getting out of your punishment. However, I want you to tell me your safe words again."

The moment of indecision had his cock hardening more, almost painful against his zipper. That edge of fear, the way a submissive looked at him like they weren't sure they'd love whatever he planned, always did it for him.

"Master and red," she told him with a soft voice.

"And you're welcome to use yellow if you need, too."

"What are you going to do?"

That was the question, wasn't it? He didn't answer right away, savoring the way she squirmed as the more time passed, as he rose and walked behind her and she *still* had no answer.

"Daniel?"

He still didn't speak, letting her stew, letting her own mind get the better of her. Sometimes people could be best affected by the right word, but often times their mind supplied things *far* worse than he could.

Even still, her alluring scent filled the room, telling him that she wasn't scared. Unsure? Nervous? Absolutely. But not afraid.

He disrobed, making sure to set the clothing items beside her so she knew what he was doing. Again, the sight of wetness on her thighs, of how tempting her cunt looked, threatened to goad him into giving in.

He shook his head and grabbed what he'd set on the dresser after he'd tied her up. "Do you remember what I said before, sweet?"

"Not really. I try not to pay attention."

"Well then, let's see if I can remind you." He dripped lube onto his fingers, then used one hand to spread her cheeks. He pressed a finger to her ass, growling softly at the way she tensed against the touch, the way she shifted as though she could get free.

Beautiful. She reminded him of a wild creature, one that didn't easily give in.

"You are out of your fucking mind," she snapped. "If you think I'm going to let you do *that,* you're stupider than I thought."

He continued to rub against her ass, not pushing in yet, teasing and taunting her all at once. "You have a safe word, but nothing else. If you really need to stop, you know what to say. Otherwise? The more you curse and threaten me, the more fun I'll have." He curled his lips into a smile as he pressed into her with just one finger. "You might not have as much, but then again, this is a punishment."

She shuddered through her entire body, as though the sensation were strange and new and overwhelming. Then again, the last time he'd done this, she'd been in heat, which meant he could have probably done *anything* and she'd have enjoyed it.

If she remembered it at all.

"Nothing to say?" He taunted her with his words, and when her chest expanded with a large breath, when he was sure she was about to tell him off, he thrust his finger deeper into her and set a quick rhythm.

Which was more than enough to stop anything she had thought to say. Instead, Alison gasped and dropped into a moan.

God, I want to hear more of that sound.

He grasped her hip to hold her still, not because she was trying to get away but rather because she was pushing back toward him. He'd known she'd enjoy this, that as soon as she let go of her hang-ups—or rather, when he made her let go of them—she'd find it wasn't the terrible activity she'd imagined.

And given that her rule breaking hadn't been *that* horrible, he didn't mind her enjoying her punishment—at least some of it.

He shifted to two fingers, and when she relaxed, he moved to three. At three she whined, a sound that made his cock twitch, the sort of breathless plea that sat somewhere between pain and pleasure.

Which was exactly the thing he'd waited for.

"Okay, sweet, are you ready? Because I've waited a while for this, and I'm tired of waiting."

He pulled his fingers from her, then got onto the bed behind her. He spread her legs slightly, as wide as the bar would let them go, to align them right.

As soon as he pressed against her, when he stared down over her sweat-soaked back, he groaned.

He might want her ass right then, but he was pretty sure that wouldn't be anywhere near the end of it.

Alison pressed her face to the blankets on Daniel's bed to try to muffle the sounds she wanted to make, the ones he pulled from her as he forced her untrained ass to spread around his thick cock.

The sounds were quiet, high-pitched and pathetic. She reminded herself of a prey animal caught in a trap, and she *knew* without question that Daniel would get off to it.

But, even as her mind rejected the entire idea of this, even as she pulled at where her wrists were cuffed to the bar between her ankles, her cunt had never been wetter.

Which was more than a little frustrating, since Daniel had still not touched her clit at all. She'd have been used to that had he been just any man, one she could have given the benefit of the doubt to as just not knowing where exactly a woman's clit was. However, Daniel *knew*. He'd brought her to screaming release more than once already, so he had no issues with knowing exactly how to do it.

Which meant this was on purpose, and a denied orgasm was the sort of thing Alison couldn't just ignore.

All her thinking didn't help distract her from the stretch and sting as Daniel slipped deeper into her, as he took her in a way no one else ever had—a way she'd have sworn weeks before no one else ever *would*.

And for all her complaining, for all the ways she had said no and assured herself she'd hate this, her body responded as though it had been desperate for just this perversion.

Something wrapped in her hair and tugged hard, lifting her face from the blanket.

His searing body pressed against hers when he'd bottomed out, when he'd sunk every last inch of his dick into her. "I want to hear you, sweet," he growled in a tone so low her cunt squeezed around nothing.

Why did that turn her on? Why did she love the sound of his voice like that, when he didn't hold any pity, when he wasn't treating her as though she were fragile? Instead, he might be in charge, but he fucked her as if he knew she couldn't be broken.

Still, she made no sound, unwilling to give that up to him just yet.

"Don't play that game with me," he warned. "Believe me, I can do this longer than you can hold out, and it just makes the prize all that much sweeter. How about this? I'll know you've learned your lesson when you ask me to stop. Asking for things, that's your problem, that's what got you here in the first place, so why don't I just keep going until you ask me to stop?"

The idea was insane, and yet it made her chest grow tight. Alison didn't ask, not for anything, not ever.

"I thought this was about you punishing me. Didn't figure you'd let me off so easy."

"I don't think this will be easy for you at all. In fact, I bet we'll see some pretty tears from those eyes *long* before you give in." Daniel slid back, not far, before plunging into her again. Even with her lips pressed together, the smallest of sounds escaped.

Keep it together.

Even as she lectured herself, as she tried to give herself a pep talk, it seemed to be a losing battle. She hadn't managed to outlast the alphas before—especially Daniel, who only seemed to enjoy her fight all the more—so she couldn't fathom how she'd manage it this time.

Still, she tried to steady her voice. "This isn't so bad," she lied. "I'm pretty sure I can take it."

He laughed, and the deep tenor of it gave her no reassurance. That was a man who was confident. "We'll see, sweet."

Alison gulped at the certainty there, at the way he said it without a speck of doubt.

I am in deep trouble…

Kyle had to admit…Alison was a fucking sight. She was bound, a spreader bar between her ankles, wrists cuffed to it, her cheek against the blanket and her expression pained.

He'd *almost* felt bad about letting Daniel handle the punishment, but from the look of her, maybe it had been the exact right choice.

He'd have let her off easy, since he didn't care much for punishments. At best he'd have put her on her knees and had those pretty lips of hers wrapped around his cock, maybe have watched a show of some sort while she had to just wait. It would have been a good point to make, since her lesson involved leaving. She could have kept his cock nice and warm for him.

"I've got to say, Daniel, it doesn't seem like you've broken her much."

Daniel cast a grin over his shoulder. "We just got started. I told the poor girl I'll stop when she asks me too."

Kyle pulled in a quick breath between his teeth. *That* seemed like a rather hard-ass request.

A good one, but still, not an easy one for Alison.

Hell, he'd almost bet his money on the stubborn omega outlasting Daniel's erection.

Kyle went over to where her face was and leaned down, setting his cheek on his arm as though they were having some sweet conversation between just the two of them, as if she wasn't being fucked in the ass by Daniel. "Hey there, sugar."

Her green eyes were glassy when she opened them, already clouded with lust, yet still with that streak of independence that had her sure she'd resist. "I don't like any of you right now," she said.

Kyle reached out and dragged his thumb along her bottom lip, then pressed into the heat of her welcoming mouth. *Fuck,* he wanted to slip his cock there, to feel that talented little tongue of hers over his shaft, to feel how Daniel's rough thrusts would push her forward, force her to take more of his long cock, maybe make her gag just a bit.

She'll look pretty like that, won't she?

Instead, he pressed down on her tongue, feeling out the inside of her mouth in a way that drove home the important part—*you're ours, and we will do whatever we want with your body.*

The way her pupils dilated more, the way her breath caught, had him groaning.

Kyle looked up to catch Daniel's gaze. "You really think you can outlast her?" His point was clear even if he didn't say it. *Before it becomes actually painful.*

Neither of them wanted to hurt her, just to drive her to a limit she'd actually tell them to stop at. She *needed* that, needed to know that not only would they respect it, but that asking wasn't the end of the world.

Daniel lifted his lip to snarl back, "I'll last plenty long."

"Maybe," Kyle said with a shrug. "But I'm pretty sure with two of us, we could make this far more *uncomfortable.*"

Daniel's lip fell, as though he caught the meaning. A grin afterward said he'd figured it out. "That's not such a bad idea."

Alison's cry when Daniel slid from her, even muffled around Kyle's thumb, was far more exciting than it should have been. He wasn't the sadist Daniel was, but that didn't mean he couldn't enjoy the sounds of a woman who was overstimulated.

And they had just gotten started.

Daniel sat on the bed, his back to the headboard, and dribbled more lube onto his hard, waiting cock. Kyle left her bound—they could work around it, and he wanted her to not have any space, any freedom.

Moving her was easy. Despite her skills and strength, she was still a little thing. He unhooked her wrists from the bar, rewarded by her throwing her bound arms around his neck and taking an aggressive kiss.

She tasted like fire and rainstorms, and he groaned against her lips.

As quickly as it washed over him, though, he woke back up. A glance over her shoulder showed Daniel grinning.

Kyle grasped Alison's waist and shifted her backward. He allowed her to use her grip around him for balance as he situated her. Because of the spreader bar, she couldn't get any ground, forced to rely on the alphas.

Which, he had to admit, he liked.

Daniel grasped his cock as they lined her up, and her whimper said they'd done it well.

She grasped Kyle, trying to keep herself from being lowered onto Daniel's waiting cock, but it was a losing battle. Daniel gripped her around the waist, pulling her down slowly but surely, forcing her to take each inch of him into her ass. Once she had, he unhooked the bar and tossed it aside.

She had her face buried against Kyle's throat, the stubborn woman.

"Remember, all you have to do is ask to stop," Daniel said before taking her knees and spreading her legs wide.

And when Kyle pulled her arms from over his head, he could only grin at the sight.

Her cunt was spread out for him, drenched and open like a welcome sign. He dragged his thumb across his bottom lip, taking longer because she'd opened her eyes and was watching him nervously.

Daniel rocked his hips up, not able to get far, but any movement made her gasp.

Kyle winked once before stretching out on the bed between her legs.

He inhaled deeply, drawing her aroused scent into his lungs. "You're so wet, sugar," Kyle whispered just before he used his tongue to catch a taste. He didn't go near her clit, didn't even try to make it feel good for her. Instead, this was all for him.

His answering growl was ripped from his chest, that same possessive nature that always happened when he got a taste of her taking over him.

He scooted closer so he could get in good and deep, having every intention of driving her crazy with his tongue until she was crying and screaming and begging.

Or at least until she asked them to stop.

He pressed his tongue into her cunt first, stiffening it to get as deep as he could. She clenched around him, especially each time Daniel thrust up.

Kyle brought his fingers to her pussy, spreading her obscenely, wanting nothing to hide any of her from him. "You have a beautiful cunt," he told her as he nibbled at the sensitive folds. "I think we need to take away all your clothing privileges when at home. I want to be able to reach down whenever I want and slip my fingers into you. I want you to have no idea I'm there until suddenly my lips are on your sweet little clit. Hell, maybe we'll just tie you up all spread out again, and just leave you there. It'll be like a piece of interactive art."

She whined, frantic, when Kyle rubbed the tip of his tongue around her clit, under the hood. He teased her with his fingers as he spoke between the licks, between the soft bites.

"I like that idea."

He didn't need to turn to know that voice, the husky tone of Trent from the doorway.

Drawn in by her scent, no doubt. No one could resist a call like that.

Daniel lifted his hips hard, forcing Kyle to adjust his aim, not that he minded. The more she squirmed, the more Daniel jostled her, the more fun Kyle got to have exploring.

"Better yet, let's blindfold her and use the headphones for real," Daniel said.

Trent groaned loudly, closer now. "What do you think, pet? You'd get fucked and have no clue who it was. Never know whose fingers they were, whose tongue, whose cock. You'd be helpless, not even knowing if we were standing around, staring at that tight little cunt, or if we'd walked away."

Alison went wild, shifting more, her erratic motions telling him she was almost there.

Poor girl thinks an orgasm is going to help.

He didn't mind proving her wrong, so he focused his attention on her clit. When he let his gaze move up her body, he found Trent's lips around her nipple, sucking hard enough for her to arch against it.

She snapped, every muscle going rigid inside her. They all stopped moving as she panted. Kyle blew a stream of cool air over her clit but didn't touch, and Daniel kept his cock still.

Her chest rose and fell quickly, and as sated as she looked, she had an air of arrogance.

It only made Kyle grin.

"Seems like that wasn't much of a lesson," she said, her voice breathless. "I mean, not sure what I'll learn from an orgasm. Seems like you did me a favor."

"Did we?" Daniel held her thighs and lifted her, then pulled her back against him, causing his cock to thrust into her hard.

As if a bolt of electricity went through her, she reached out with her hands. Since they were cuffed, she misaimed and would have smacked Trent right in the face on accident.

Thankfully the man was quick, grabbing her hands before she broke another nose. He chuckled and pushed them up, clipping them to the metal work at the top of the headboard. She yanked, the action causing her to rise an inch, but Daniel used his grip to tug her back down and bury himself into her.

"You see," Daniel snarled into her ear, "You get more sensitive each time you come. So me fucking your ass at first? No big deal. But this is after just one little orgasm. You still so certain you don't want to tap out yet?"

And…he really wanted her to last longer. He hadn't had this much fun in…

Hell, he had no idea. It was the first time in so long that he'd gotten to let go. With Trent there, especially, it felt like their old life, and even better, they had Alison. She wasn't someone they had to worry about, that they had to tread softly around.

She had her hang-ups—they all did—but she persevered because she was tough. Playing with a woman who was steel had its advantages.

Doubt crept into her eyes, but she didn't say a word.

Kyle grinned and leaned down, ready to tease her into another orgasm.

So the game continues.

Chapter Sixteen

Trent groaned when Kyle's lips reached Alison's spread pussy, when he dragged his tongue up her drenched sex.

He'd been walking past when he'd scented her, when he'd heard those sounds she made when she was so close to the edge, and he'd been unable to take a single step away.

And now he was damn glad he'd come in.

He captured her nipples between his fingers, closing down on one then the other before tugging softly at both. They'd drawn into hard points beneath his attention, as he rolled them between his fingertips.

"So what did she do to deserve this?"

Daniel huffed a soft sound, as though he didn't need to be punishing her in order to enjoy her. Still, he answered. "Woke up to find her gone this morning. Second morning in a row, and we'd already had a conversation about it."

Not the biggest offense, but he suspected Daniel had been looking for a reason to do this.

Though, of course, Alison had her safe words. She could always stop anything she wanted to.

Which meant she was as invested in this game as they were.

"That wasn't being a good girl."

Her eyebrows furrowed, as if those words *stung*.

That had him almost ready to take them back. A sharp look from Daniel kept him from it, though.

He cupped her breasts in his hands, teasing the nipples with his callused thumbs. "You know better than to ignore us, pet. I *know* you can do better." He used the words to help relieve the sullen expression on her face, to bridge that gap between him, reassuring her, but also keeping the lesson front and center.

He understood, of course. Alison didn't like to listen, not because she wanted to be a brat but because she didn't want to be a burden. She didn't want to wake them if she couldn't sleep. She didn't want to ask them to help her with anything. He'd seen it when her all-of-five-foot self had been balanced precariously on a flimsy stool trying to reach a bowl on a high shelf in the pantry, a shelf any of the alphas could have reached for her with ease.

However, instead of asking them, she'd risked herself. He'd tossed her over her shoulder and pinched her ass before fucking her—not that he expected she'd learned much from it.

This time, however? She wouldn't forget *this*.

She parted those soft lips of hers—no doubt to say something about how it wasn't a big deal—but Kyle delivered a hard lick to her right then, stealing away whatever she'd planned to utter.

He drove her hard, not giving her any chance to resist him. Daniel's hands on her knees kept her spread open, and he shifted his hips up, sinking himself deep into her ass.

She twisted, but there was no way to gain leverage. She was one hundred percent at their mercy, and Trent had to admit, he loved it.

He cupped one of her breasts and brought his lips to it, teasing for only a moment before nipping at the stiff peak, dragging his teeth across it to add yet another element to all they were forcing on her.

Her cry was thin and desperate as she came, that frantic writhing of her body increasing.

And they were only at two. She had a very long time ahead of her if she refused to give in.

They all paused as she caught her breath, that moment her chance to think, to reconsider.

Kyle's gaze ran up her body, his blue eyes intense and locked on her face.

As soon as she opened her eyes, when she'd seemed to come back to herself, he returned to her cunt.

Trent groaned at the shiver that ran through her, and the way she whimpered at Daniel's first thrust made him wished he'd already stripped. He wanted his hand around his cock—something, *anything*.

He contented himself with her perky breasts, with teasing her nipples, with leaving love bites and hickeys across the flawless pale skin. She'd wake tomorrow with the blemishes, like little brands, and she'd think of *him*.

She did every time she saw the bite. As bad as he should still feel about it, he'd shed any real guilt. He *loved* his claiming bite on her shoulder. He'd never grow tired of glimpsing it from beneath the straps of her tops, from the way she'd stroke her fingers over it when she didn't know he was watching her.

Yeah, he refused to feel guilty about one of the few things he'd done in his life that he wanted that much.

"All you've got to do is ask," Daniel growled, his voice deep as he plunged his cock into her harder.

She threw her head back, resting it on Daniel's shoulder, so Trent took the offer and nipped her exposed throat. Something about it felt like so much more, like a submission even deeper than the rest, as though she trusted him to keep her safe when his teeth were so close to her pulse.

The metal on the headboard groaned with her next orgasm, the yanking of her hands showing she was nearing her limit.

They gave her even less time to rest after that one, ramping up the pressure, forcing her to adjust, to accept everything they had to give.

The sounds she made came constantly now, broken only by gasps. Sometimes she moaned, sometimes she whimpered, but every uttered, breathless plea had him ready to come. Hell, at that point he didn't care if he just rubbed himself against the mattress. Anything for a little friction, for some relief.

"Well, I hate to admit it," Daniel said just before he nipped her ear lobe. "But I think I might be outmatched."

Kyle snorted before he flicked her clit with his tongue. "I doubt that. She is fucking *shaking* right now."

And she was. The trembling was so strong it was as though she were frozen, like her body was full of so much energy she couldn't stay still. Each touch from them only made it worse.

Daniel huffed a soft laugh. "I figure one more thing will push her right over. I doubt the stubborn little omega will manage to resist anymore if we get her knotted. Fill her that much and she'll break."

Trent growled, the sound torn from his throat before he thought about it.

A hard bark of laughter came from Kyle. "Pretty sure *that* tells us who wants to help there. Go on, Trent. Something fitting about you, the softy, being the one to force that girl to take two cocks."

Trent didn't need to be offered twice. He all but ripped off his shirt, then stripped out of his pants, leaving it all on the ground before crawling between Alison's spread legs.

Her hair stuck to her forehead, matted by sweat, her eyes shimmering and wetness tracking down her cheeks.

He leaned in, forgoing her lips to kiss over the tears, a tiny act of sweetness to remind her that even when she was being punished, even when she didn't like everything they did, they only did it because they cared.

Whether she got the message or not, he had no idea.

He took his cock in his hand and ran it through her folds. She was beyond drenched, her messy cunt hot and swollen and more than any man could resist. When he rubbed the head of his cock against her clit—*that* got a reaction. She jerked wildly against Daniel's hold and her cuffs.

"Easy," Trent told her.

Daniel snorted before speaking into her ear, just loud enough for Trent to hear as well. "You ready, sweet? He's going to take his cock and plunge it into your sweet little pussy. You think you're full now?

Imagine a thick knot, too. I'm pretty sure you'll be begging us to stop soon."

She opened her mouth, and Trent could *see* the request on her lips. The trembling increased as if the words just wouldn't come, like she was more afraid of them than she was of the alphas, of her reaction.

And that killed him. *Poor girl.* As much as Trent didn't love punishments, he had to admit that if they could make a breakthrough, if she actually learned she could ask them for help, it would all be more than worth it.

He fitted his cock against her and pressed into the tightness of her cunt.

Alison was feral by the time the first inch of Trent's hard, thick cock stretched her. Each inch after was worse, her body so sensitive it shot bolts of pleasure straight through her, and she couldn't do anything to prepare or resist.

Thankfully, Daniel kept still. It was the only blessing, that he didn't further torment her—at least in that moment—because she had no doubt it would happen.

Trent's cock hadn't ever seemed *this* large, and since she doubted he'd grown since the last time she'd had sex with him, it had to be another example of just how far they'd pushed her.

She felt close to breaking, at her limit, and yet the simple words wouldn't come. She couldn't speak them, whisper the easy request.

Why? What the hell was wrong with her?

The cuffs kept her arms stretched up, forced her to endure the feelings the alphas pushed on her without even being able to grasp them, to feel she had any amount of control. Trent's chest vibrated as he growled, the sound so low she wasn't sure she heard it at all rather than just felt it. Still, he forced inch after inch into her until he was fully seated, until he was so deep that she didn't think she had any space inside her at all.

And right then, when she pulled in a shaky breath, when she thought for just a moment that she could handle it, Daniel moved.

He shifted back and plunged in, moving her up just a bit to give him room to really thrust.

Everything inside her broke apart. She squeezed down around them both, her body fighting for some level of control as she came, as she was washed away by their want and their demands and yet felt safer than she ever had before.

How the fuck was that possible? Here she was, pushed past her limits, not even *enjoying* the sensations anymore, at the mercy of three alphas she was pretty sure didn't have any, and yet she had no worries about her safety. She'd never felt more protected, more…cherished?

She wasn't sure she understood that word at all, but the way Trent called her 'pet', the way he fucked her with hard, steady thrusts, the way Daniel slammed into her, his little bites to her shoulder and earlobe, even Kyle's intense stare as he stroked his own cock, they all made her feel important.

Not just a body the three used to slake their lust on, not a stand-in for anyone, not just a pretend slave for a job, but someone they cared about.

Trent bit down on her shoulder—not hard enough to break the skin, but as always, right over the healed mark. His cock swelled, that knot as challenging as it ever was, especially with Daniel inside her.

Meanwhile, Daniel fucked her harder, faster, and when his teeth closed over her shoulder, when his cock jerked hard inside her and she *felt* the heat of his cum searing her, she was helpless against another rolling wave of pleasure that crashed over her.

"Stop," she gasped out, the word ripped from her like a scab over an ill-healed wound. More poured from her. "Stop, please."

Daniel released her shoulder and offered a far-too-gentle kiss to the sore spot before slipping from her. Even *that* was too much. "Good girl," he all but purred into her ear.

Her hands came free, but she was too tired to see if it had been Kyle or Daniel who had released her. *Does it matter?*

The pulsing thickness of Trent's knot pulled another gasp as she shoved at his chest.

He trapped her hands between them, kissing at her panting lips. "You're okay, pet. It's over. I know, but I can't pull out, not yet. Just relax."

Pet. That was what got through to her, what made her take a breath and try to relax, try not to tense against the massive feeling of his swollen knot.

Which seemed impossible right then, when her body was nothing but a collection of overworked nerves.

Lips pressed to hers, and she recognized the kiss without having to open her eyes. *Kyle.* He brushed her hair from her face as he offered the sweetest kisses, soft and full of things none of them dared to say.

And the words ended with the kisses. No one spoke. She got no lectures.

She closed her eyes and snuggled against the warmth and strength of the three, content to let them hold back the rest of the world, at least right then.

* * * *

Kyle lifted his eyebrow at Alison, unsure what to do with her.

They'd fucked her to exhaustion just that morning, yet somehow her panties had ended up twisted so tight someone might think she hadn't been laid in weeks.

He exchanged a look with Daniel, who only shrugged.

Trent didn't seem any more in the know about what the hell had crawled up their little omega's ass in the past few hours.

His phrasing made him chuckle to himself as he recalled how she'd squirmed, how she'd cried out.

Focus.

The sweetness from that was gone, and he had no idea where it had disappeared to. Daniel had taken her into the shower and cleaned her off, since he'd started the whole punishment thing. Even when walking out, though, she'd been happy.

Fuck, she'd been downright glowing.

So what had happened between them and now? Dealing with Alison forever made him question himself. It seemed like a test she was always changing the rules to.

Alison brushed past him as she set the table, refusing to make eye contact, storming around. She didn't break any rules—smart girl—but her little acts of defiance were loud all the same.

Sick of it, Kyle reached out and caught her wrist by the cuff.

She gave him a look that screamed the threats she wanted to make, even if she kept them in. "Yes?" she said through gritted teeth.

He tugged her to the living room and pushed her to her knees on the pillow they'd left there. He lowered himself into the seat in front of her. She took the position without thought, showing why they'd had to slip into these roles twenty-four-seven, so such things became automatic.

"What's wrong, sugar?"

She glared at him, her lips turning white from how hard she pressed them together.

Kyle sighed and slipped his fingers into her hair. He tugged her forward until she pressed her cheek to his thigh, and ran his fingers through her hair, hoping she'd relax. "You can't be mad about the punishment. You sure as hell weren't mad right after, and you can't claim you didn't deserve it."

She lowered her gaze, like she didn't want to look at him. That wasn't uncommon. She seemed to retreat inside herself when she was forced to really think about *why* she did something, as if she'd never put in effort to do so before.

"Talk to me, sugar. I'm not asking for a lot, here. You were happy as fuck afterward, then something changed. What happened?"

She huffed, an angry little sound like that of a dog forced to lie down when it didn't want to. "Why aren't you still mad?"

He tilted his head. "What do you mean?"

"I screwed up. As soon as we finished…you all were over it."

He couldn't help his frown, not when he couldn't seem to understand her point. "Of course. We weren't all that mad to start with, but there was a consequence, and we needed you to learn a lesson. Once you asked us to stop, you'd learned it. Why would we still be mad?"

She shifted, as if the words she wanted to say—the ones she needed to say—were alive inside her and fighting not to come out. "People don't get over things that fast."

Ah. Kyle let out a soft sigh as the pieces came together. He didn't answer right away, trying to soothe her with the stroking of his hand through her hair. Finally, he found the words. "We're talking about your father, aren't we?"

She tensed but didn't answer. She didn't really need to.

He nodded, continuing the gentle touches. "We're all going to do things sometimes that aren't great. If I do, if Daniel or Trent do, we'll apologize. What would you do if we honestly apologized and atoned for what we'd done?"

"I'd forgive you."

"Exactly. You made a mistake, sugar, and they happen. They're part of life. We dealt with it, and the second it was over, we were over it. We wouldn't keep punishing you for something we'd already handled."

She let out a slow breath that warmed his thigh. "I remember one time I snuck out. I was only eight—it wasn't like I was going anywhere bad, but I'd wanted to play with this other kid across the street. I ended up out after dinner, because I didn't realize it had gotten late. It wasn't like I ever got to play with anyone normally."

The hitch in her throat broke his heart. "What happened?"

"If I'd gotten home when my mom was the only one there, nothing would have happened. She'd never have told my father, but I stayed out too late, and he was already there."

He kept his temper in check. She didn't need his anger, not for old ghosts. There was nothing he could do about them. "Did he hurt you?"

She shook her head, then nuzzled against his thigh, the action seeming unconscious, as though she needed to seek him out for comfort. "My father didn't believe in hitting females. He thought that was beneath him, beneath any alpha. He never raised a hand, not to my mother, not to me. He never needed to. There was something so cold in his eyes, though, like a part of him had died, something that should have killed him too but somehow hadn't. He told me how disappointed in me he was, how he didn't ask much of me and I couldn't even do that one thing. He locked me in my room for two days—no food, nothing. I drank water from the bathroom faucet, but no matter what I did, no one would open the door or even acknowledge me." She trembled, and Kyle grasped her hands, pulling her up and into his lap. He stroked his hand down her back, trying to make up for the horrible memory.

Still, the tough omega kept telling it. "Two days later, my mother let me out, told me to get cleaned up and dressed and come down for breakfast. I was starving, but I was so happy to be done. I said good morning to my father at the table, and he ignored me. Sitting in that room alone for two days wasn't enough for him. He still wouldn't speak to me, wouldn't acknowledge I even existed. I gave him the card I'd made, a stupid one out of scraps of paper. I'd even destroyed one of my stuffed animals to add pieces of fur, trying to make it special. I thought if I could apologize right, he'd forgive me. He'd see I didn't mean to be bad."

Even without knowing the end, Kyle could see the train barreling for her, knew in the way she spoke that the story didn't end with some great make-up moment. "What happened, sugar?"

She curled against him. "He didn't even open the card. He picked it up, walked over to the trash and dropped it in. I'll never forget him talking to me, finally, after days of silence. *'I ask little of you, Corrine, and you still consistently disappoint me. A worthless card doesn't change it. I'm not sure why we even punish you, because it doesn't seem to make a bit of difference.'* I remember staring at the trash can, thinking about all the work I'd put into the card. I asked him what I could do, and he shook his head. *'Nothing. Some people, they're born bad.'* He left then, going to work, and I sat in my room all day, repeating that over and over again. It didn't matter what I ever did, he'd never forgive me, not for anything. Not for breaking the TV one time when I was playing in the house, not for being out when I wasn't supposed to go, not for waking him up because I was throwing up when I got the stomach flu. They were all just points against me that I was never going to be able to make up for."

Kyle purred, the soft sound strange since he never did it as a rule. He pulled her tighter against him and kissed the top of her head. "He was a dick, sugar, and we aren't him. I can't say you'll never disappoint us, that you'll never do something we wished you hadn't. Fuck, we'll do things that disappoint you, too. That's life. But I can promise that we'll make what we want clear, and we'll work it out, and after we forgive you, we will be good." He curled his fingers around her hip, knowing that the next thing wasn't going to go over so easily. "And you aren't bad. You know that, right?"

She went to push off his lap, just like he expected. *Clearly, those words have struck.*

He held her close. "I'm serious. Your father, he didn't know shit. He thought good meant someone he could control, something weak and malleable. He wanted pets, not partners. The fact that you weren't born a mindless yes-ma'am doesn't make you bad or broken. It makes him an idiot for not seeing how amazing you are."

"Real amazing," she muttered against his chest. "I keep getting in trouble."

He chuckled. "Yeah, you do, but guess what? I like when you get in trouble. Pretty sure Daniel does, too, and even though you might be sore, I could taste how much *you* liked it. Getting in trouble doesn't make you bad, it makes you human. It's just a fact of life when you've got people trying to create something together. So, yeah, you're trouble. Hell, you broke my nose the first time we met, but you're trouble that is completely worth it. I wouldn't want some girl who didn't have a backbone, who fell over at a strong word or hard look. You? You're tough, and you're strong, and you don't take shit from anyone. Those things don't make you defective or bad, they're the *exact* things that make me—" He snapped his mouth shut before he made the disastrous mistake of actually finishing that sentence.

That time she did manage to twist away, to look into his eye with more fear than she'd had when Daniel had pressed his cock to her ass.

It seemed the end of that sentence was more frightening than a bit of anal...

Kyle didn't try to pretend away what he'd almost said. He didn't make excuses, didn't try to lie. What was the point?

They both knew damned well what he'd nearly uttered.

"*This* isn't real," she said.

"You sure about that?"

She gulped, the battle clear on her face, between what she needed to be true and what actually was true.

Still, she showed that backbone when she nodded and pulled from his lap. "Yeah, I'm sure. It's temporary. As soon as the case is over—"

"You'll what? Walk away?"

"Yeah, I will."

The certainty in her voice hit him. She might hate it, she might not want to, but she had no doubts that she'd still leave.

And right then, the hollow ache in Kyle's chest that he hadn't been able to identify, the one that wouldn't go away—he finally figured it out.

It was the countdown until she walked out of his life forever.

Chapter Seventeen

"Surprises are never a good thing," Alison muttered as she sat in the back seat of the car beside Trent.

"They can be," he said.

She shook her head then pulled the seatbelt so it didn't rub against her neck. "Not in my experience. Why don't you just *tell* me where we're going? I thought we couldn't leave the house."

"Call this a much-needed mental health field trip. And don't worry, we made sure we weren't tracked."

Which explained their first stop at the large, private hospital, where they'd taken the elevator up, then the stairs down to a lower parking garage that had a different car waiting, Daniel already having the keys.

Not that any of that told her where exactly they were going.

All she knew for sure was that she'd woken up exhausted, as she had the last few mornings, and the alphas had been ready to go. They'd packed her a bag and told her to get into the car.

The auction was only a week away, now. It meant their final visit had to happen any day. As much as she enjoyed their routine, a sense of unease had plagued her, especially after Kyle's little slip-up.

She chalked her not feeling well up to that. How could she be expected to sleep or function when she had so many things running at full speed through her head?

When they arrived at the destination, she narrowed her eyes at Trent.

He only shrugged. "Figured you could use a break."

"This is Tiffany's house."

She'd never been there, at least not officially. However, after Tiffany had settled in with her mates in the home belonging to the doctor, Marshall, Alison had made damned sure to drive by, to know where it was.

She'd figured it was only a matter of time before it went to hell, before she would need to swoop in and save the young girl, and she'd much rather be prepared for that inevitability.

The fact that it hadn't happened yet amazed her.

Stranger still, Tiffany looked happier each time she saw her, as though the things Alison feared not only hadn't happened, but she somehow enjoyed her life more and more.

Then again, how have you felt these last few weeks?

She shook her head as though she could shake away the unwanted thought. *This* was a ploy, nothing else. She'd taken them up on the rest not only because it would make their cover more believable, but also because she'd never have a chance like this one again. *Not* taking advantage of it would have been foolish.

She let the half-truth sit, because examining it might make her admit to things she wasn't ready to.

Tiffany rushed from the house, her blonde hair bright in the morning sun. She'd always been effortlessly beautiful. Alison knew she was pretty, but Tiffany seemed to embrace her looks in a way Alison never really managed.

On the young omega's heels were her mates, Kieran and Kane looking as unhappy and dangerous as ever and Marshall smiling as if he liked…well, everything.

Alison left the car when it became clear there was no good way out of the get-together, even more because Tiffany had now seen her. While she'd never encouraged a relationship with the girl, upsetting her had always felt like kicking a puppy. One just didn't do it.

Tiffany hugged her, the action uncomfortable, especially with all six alphas standing around and staring. After that, she dragged Alison by the wrist, and even when Alison offered a pleading look to her alphas for some help from the overly-excited blonde girl, they only grinned.

Useless alphas.

Half an hour later, Alison sat in her bikini on the edge of the pool, her feet in, with Kara beside her.

The event had been even larger than she'd realized, and by the time everyone had arrived, she wished she had just turned around and left, even if it meant upsetting Tiffany.

Claire had come, her alphas and her infant daughter along. Tracy, her daughter, and her three mates were there. Kara, of course, and her mates, and lastly Ashley, who Alison hadn't met but whose mates she knew enough not to trust, had all attended.

Alison knew Kara professionally rather than personally, partly because she never cared for getting too chummy with others. Still, it was hard to have another omega in town who did whatever the fuck they wanted and *not* at least be acquaintances.

"Don't babysit," Kara told her quickly. "I did, and there isn't enough whiskey in the world for that nonsense."

"You gave her daughter whiskey?"

Kara laughed, leaning her weight back on her hands. "Oh, no, I drank the whiskey. Cullen is surprisingly good with kids. By the time Claire got back, I was wasted."

Alison chuckled at the irreverent blue-haired girl's story. The truth was, it was impossible to know if Kara was lying or telling the truth. Alison had learned that early, but it didn't mean she didn't trust the girl—well, as much as she trusted anyone. Kara wasn't the type to sell her out, but the details of any story she told were likely only fifty percent true—at best.

"How is mated bliss?"

Kara cast a heavy side-eye. "You thinking of settling down?"

"Well, I had figured neither of us ever would, but you went and blew that to hell."

Kara kicked her feet to splash her mate, Damon, who was swimming in the pool with Tracy's daughter. He grinned in her direction, cupped water and splashed Kara.

She laughed before turning her attention back. "What can I say? I wanted someone who had to take care of me when I'm old and gray and can't see anymore. That's why I collected the young one. He'll be able to read well past the rest of us."

Kara's flippant words didn't hide the affection beneath them. She might pretend that the alphas she'd chosen meant little to her, but the truth rested in the way she looked at them, in the way she'd unconsciously lean toward them.

Is that love? Alison hadn't ever had that, hadn't known it or understood it.

In fact, she'd written off the entire idea as a joke, as some sort of trick people used to justify the idiocy of pairing off. She'd seen how well matings worked in her lifetime, and she'd never once believed love had anything to do with it.

It was a fairytale people told themselves to excuse their bad choices.

Except…when she turned her gaze to find *her* alphas seated with Kieran and Joshua and Bryce, a pang went through her chest.

Could she ever have this sort of life? Could she ever fit into this sort of world? Smile and laugh and play with the offspring of her friends, be comfortable in a social setting? Just another person enjoying a party?

It all felt beyond her.

Even right then, the most she managed was to sit off to the side with Kara. Claire stretched out, Kaidan sitting behind her on the chair. Tracy held Claire's daughter, smiling down at the baby as if she were the most precious thing in the world. Ashley sat beside Tracy, clearly gearing up to steal the infant for her own cuddles. Their alphas all might have sat back, engaged in their own conversations, but the connections were still obvious. They'd glance over, gazes seeking their mates as if drawn. Only once they'd found them would they return to their own talks.

It was all so normal. Wholesome. Kara had never quite fit in, much like Alison, which might be why they both sat on the outskirts of the party.

Though, from the start, when Alison had walked in to find Kara holding the infant, talking with Claire, it had been obvious that the other woman, for all her faults, had found a place in the group.

And it was a place Alison doubted she could fill, even if she wanted to.

Being part of a group like this felt like tearing off a tiny piece of armor for each of them, risking herself for each of them.

Not that she wouldn't put herself at risk—she'd made her life's work taking care of omegas like these—but actually getting to know them, having any sort of lasting connection?

That wasn't her. It wasn't safe and she didn't think she even knew *how* to do it.

Her stomach rolled, telling her exactly what it thought about the entire idea.

The very idea of friendships made her want to throw up.

"Looking a little green there," Kara said, no sympathy in her voice.

"I think I've reached my limit of sisterhood."

Kara let out a laugh that said, no, she didn't feel sorry at all for Alison, the bitch. She called over to Tiffany. "Goodtime gal here needs to throw up. Can you show her the bathroom?"

Alison rolled her eyes at the way the entire party ground to a halt around her. Being the center of attention was something she *hated,* and yet there she was, the spectacle.

"Are you not feeling well?" Trent was the first over to her. He pressed his hand to her forehead as though to check for a temperature.

Alison shoved his hand off, but a sharp look made her go still. The *last* thing she wanted was to risk a punishment—or even a sharp word—in front of the others. She couldn't imagine living down the hit to her reputation if Daniel decided to threaten to spank her ass, or the way her cheeks would always heat and her breath would quicken when he did.

Trent felt her head again. "No fever." He crouched. "Are you sick, pet?"

Kara snorted at the name before walking away.

"No. I didn't sleep well, and I need to go to the bathroom. Kara's just a little…colorful."

Trent pressed his lips together, as if he wasn't sure whether to believe her or not.

However, Tiffany bumped into him as though he wasn't a good hundred pounds heavier than her and pure muscle. "Come on, I'll show you where my bathroom is. Stop hovering, Trent, she's fine. Probably too much sun, since you've all had her cooped up in that house for over a month."

Trent lifted his lip as if to snarl at Tiffany, but seemed to think better of it. Snarling at mates, even without any malice, could easily spark a fight between alphas.

Tiffany again took Alison's hand, as she had when she'd arrived, and tugged her toward the house. Tiffany guided her past the guest bathrooms downstairs, going to the second floor and into what was clearly her room.

"Don't you sleep with the alphas?"

Tiffany glanced around the room decorated with flowers and bright painting. "What? Oh, yeah. This is the room where I keep my stuff and where I usually sleep. Kieran, Kane and Marshall each have their own room, but usually one or all of them end up in here."

Which explained the massive bed. It looked as large as two kings up against each other.

How does someone even find a bed that big?

Before she could think too much about it, Tiffany guided her through the room to her private bathroom. It was bright, done in mostly whites and marble. "There's medicine in the drawer if you have a headache or anything, and feel free to jump in the shower if you just need to rinse off from the sun." Tiffany offered a sweet smile. "Or if you want a bit of privacy where people can't hover."

Alison closed the door behind Tiffany after a quick 'thank you'. Just getting away from the party had already helped settle her stomach and her nerves.

It again told her *this* wasn't a place for her. Even if she pretended she was capable of and wanted a relationship with the alphas, this entire friendship-and-family thing was something she lacked the skills—and possibly the genes—for.

She thought about her family, about her uncaring father, about her beaten-down mother, and the truth was that she didn't know anything about how to behave or form connections like the ones between these people.

Daniel, Kyle and Trent might have already become part of this group, but she never would.

Yet another reason why we'd never work out.

She opened the drawer Tiffany had pointed to, and sure enough, a pharmacy's worth of medication was there, all labeled and organized. *The benefit of being mated to a doctor.*

She found the pills for her headache, but before she grabbed them, her gaze caught on something else.

A blue box, one of six stacked together.

Pregnancy tests.

Was Tiffany trying?

She seemed far too young to be a mother, and yet some omegas got pregnant far earlier. Or perhaps they had the tests just in case, to check after a heat.

A person could wait the weeks until their period started, but the nice tests, like these, could check a bit earlier. At the very least, they could get a positive while still in the 'late period or pregnant?' stage.

Which made her stomach roll again.

Alison did the math in her head, quick and frantic. Five weeks had passed since her heat.

Five weeks and no period. She was still in the range of it being possible, since an omega could get her period between four and six weeks after a heat, but her exhaustion and headaches and all of it turned sinister.

She grabbed a test with shaking hands, reading over the directions three times when she couldn't seem to absorb the information on the first two goes.

She took the test, then set it on the counter and paced.

Please, be negative. She repeated the words like one of those stupid self-help affirmation tapes, as if she could will that into the universe by sheer belief alone.

Her stomach was worse, her breath quick. She hadn't really considered becoming pregnant to be a possibility. She wasn't the mothering type. What the fuck was she going to do if it was positive? She couldn't have a child. She had no idea what to do with a kid. She hadn't really had parents, so who the hell was she going to emulate?

And all those issues ignored that she'd be walking away from the alphas the second the case was over. The last thing she wanted was a reason for them to argue about it.

She glanced at the clock, dread settling deep inside her as the seconds ticked away until she could check.

Finally, it was time. The test sat on the edge of the counter like a trap, as though if she didn't look, it couldn't hurt her, couldn't be true.

She crept forward as though trying to avoid being noticed, like she could see it without it seeing her and that would somehow make things okay.

Her stomach rolled as she looked at it, as she read the tiny window for the answer. As quickly as she did, she bolted for the toilet and up came everything she thought she'd kept down.

Two lines. I'm pregnant...

Kyle's gaze had shifted up toward the house every minute since Alison had left.

He'd seen the look on her face, the paleness of her cheeks.

She'd needed to get away. She didn't handle get-togethers like this well, it seemed. Which he couldn't say he fully understood.

She'd known these people better and for longer than he had. Sure, she might have kept her distance from the alphas, but she knew the omegas. She'd been friends with them, even if she didn't talk much about it.

So why she couldn't just relax and have fun, he didn't understand.

"I don't think you should see her anymore," Dylan said.

Kyle jerked his gaze back, ready to bare his teeth until he realized the alpha was talking to Tracy and not him.

"She isn't that bad."

"You just told me she broke some man's arm," he deadpanned.

"To be fair," Kara said, "the man grabbed a waitress's ass. I feel like that's almost wearing a 'please break my arm' shirt."

"I broke a man's hand when he grabbed Ashley's ass," Erik added, no repentance in his voice. "Hand is better. You put an arm in a sling and it's fine. Hand? All those little bones? It's a far longer lesson."

Ashley's mouth gaped open before she shoved Erik's arm, as if scolding him.

He caught her and pulled her into his lap despite her weak protest. "People who touch what is mine don't deserve to have unbroken limbs."

Kyle chuckled at the exchange. The more time he spent with these people, the more he found himself missing this sense of family. He'd moved around with Daniel so much, been away from what little family they had for so long, he'd forgotten how much he enjoyed the feeling of belonging.

Maybe we should think about setting down some roots.

Trent had done it, creating himself a life there. Why couldn't they? Hell, maybe all of them could move forward.

"You are missing the best part of the story," Kara said, as though breaking the arm of a man wasn't the most interesting bit. "The man's friend got all upset. I think they were planning on double-teaming the girl or something, the perverts." A snort of laughter from a few of the others—given that they *all* shared women—

said what they thought about that statement. "So he gets in Alison's face, and he is huge. I mean, he makes Trent here look tiny, and Alison is just standing there, doing that blank face she does, letting him go off. He throws a punch but the idiot is already pretty drunk, so she dodges it, and when he's off balance, she's able to slam his face down into the table. I think there might have been teeth on the floor. No one *ever* grabbed Anne's ass again."

The name caught his attention. "Anne? The omega who's missing?"

That sucked the humor from the story out of the room, the reminder that while the get-together might be fun, reality wasn't so forgiving.

Claire answered, nodding. "Yeah. I met her a few times, and she was—"

"Is," Tracy said firmly, as if the belief were enough for it to be true.

Claire seemed less convinced but took the correction anyway. "Is very sweet. She's only in her early twenties, never calls any of us for anything. Any omega going missing is hard, but her? She's just the sort of person you think the world should leave alone. Like, there are those ones who are just too fragile, too good, who shouldn't have to deal with the bullshit of the world. That's Anne."

Trent again cast his gaze up, toward the house, pieces fitting together a bit more about Alison's dedication to the case, about how quickly she'd been willing to leap into something most people would take a minute or two to consider.

Worse, he thought about what would happen if they were too late…

He didn't think Alison would ever forgive herself if something happened to her friend, but he hadn't found the world to be an overly kind place.

* * * *

Daniel had pressed his lips together when Alison hadn't come down for dinner.

He wished she was storming around, throwing a fit, because he knew exactly how to handle *that*.

Hell, he enjoyed dealing with her temper tantrums.

Instead, she'd been quiet when they'd returned from the party. In fact, she hadn't really recovered after going to the bathroom. She'd assured him she wasn't sick, but she'd never engaged with anyone else. She would sit off to the side, close enough that no one felt she was left out, but far enough to not be part of the conversations.

Then again, was it that different from the start of the party? Alison didn't seem like she fitted, or at least like she wanted to fit.

She watched over the omegas, always tense when they were curled up with an alpha, as if she were waiting to need to jump in and save someone.

The best way to describe her was a lifeguard, there on duty, sitting above everything else but not a part of it.

Which seemed silly, since he'd never met a group of people who seemed happier or more content with their mates and their lives.

Still, she had watched.

When they got back to the house, after a changeover at the hospital and collection of new medical documents to prove the visit, should anyone have tailed them and asked, she'd gone to her room for a shower.

That had been two hours before and she hadn't left yet.

"She might be getting herself pretty," Kyle said, a grin on his lips. "You know women have to do all that shaving to get ready."

Daniel gave him a glare in return. "I don't think that takes two hours."

"Maybe she's relaxing, or taking a nap?" Trent, ever the optimist, said.

Maybe.

"Whatever it is, dinner is almost here. I guess I'll go let her know."

Trent pointed a finger at him. "Be nice. If you scare her, she might not come down at all."

"I am always nice."

"You fucked her ass until she cried."

Daniel spread his lips into a wide grin. "Oh, yeah, trust me, that *was* nice."

Trent growled softly but let Daniel go up the stairs without another word.

He knocked on the door, surprised when she called for him to come in.

Inside, he found her sitting back on the bed, a damp rag on her forehead.

"Hey, sweet. Not feeling good?" All those things he'd been thinking slipped away, replaced with a sudden worry and need to fix the problem.

She looked at him, and it was then he noted the dark circles beneath her eyes. Why hadn't he noticed them before? Perhaps the sun from the day had brought them out more. "I'm just not feeling great."

Her words were soft, and it didn't take a genius to hear the lie.

Or at least the omission.

Daniel sat on the edge of the bed before he dragged his fingers across her cheek. "What's wrong? And don't tell me nothing."

"Why not? If I'm not feeling good you won't punish me."

"I won't right now, but I have a long memory."

She stared him down for a moment before letting out a long breath, slow and heavy. "My heat was five weeks ago."

The first thought that popped into his head pleased him far more than it should have. He thought about the infant at the party earlier, thought about how Alison would look, a baby cradled in her arms. She'd be the fiercest mother he'd ever seen.

Before all the thoughts could go through him, before he could ask, she kept talking. "I started bleeding."

All those pictures crashed down around him. He fought not to look disappointed. His life wasn't set up for a kid. *They* weren't prepared for a kid. It was for the best, and the last thing she needed was for him to make it any harder or make her feel guilty.

He slid over beside her, then placed an arm down so her head was on it before he pulled her against his side. "I'm sorry you're not feeling well. Do you have what you need here? If not—"

"I do. Everything was already under the sink." She said the words quickly, as though she needed to get the conversation over as fast as possible. Then again, females could be strange about such subjects. Beta males tended to be as well, to be fair. Alphas? He supposed it was due to that primal part of them. Blood was a part of life and periods were only the logical conclusion to a heat when the omega didn't conceive. He didn't find much to be squeamish about.

However, she hadn't grown up around very caring people, always used to dealing with shit on her own, so he gave her some privacy. She already didn't feel good—there was no reason to torture the poor girl.

"I guess that explains why you didn't look like you felt so good today."

She nodded, melting against his side in a way that made him tighten his grip more. He didn't care for her being sick, but he loved those times when her defenses came down, when she stopped keeping him at a distance. Often it happened slowly, as if she lost the strength to fight him anymore, until the real woman beneath all those coping mechanisms came out.

Wetness dribbled down her forehead from the rag, soaking into his sleeve, but he didn't care.

"Are you disappointed?"

She tensed, her eyes closing again. Eventually, she answered. "No. I would make a horrible mother."

"I don't know about that."

She snorted. "I don't have a maternal bone in my body. I won't even hold Claire's daughter. I have no idea what a good mother even looks like."

He danced his fingers along her arm as he answered. "You're tough, and you're protective. I think you'd make a great mom, someday, when you're ready."

She sighed, then whispered a question. "Are you disappointed?"

He considered lying to her. He wanted to tell her no because that was what she wanted to hear.

He didn't lie, though, and especially not to *her*. The trust that needed to exist between the two of them was too important to risk breaking over anything, least of all this.

"A little. I hadn't even thought about it, to be honest. I'm not looking to have kids any time soon, but when I walked in, when you said it was five weeks ago, I had a moment of picturing it. If we're putting it all out there, I'm not sure I'd make a good dad, either. Kyle and I have moved around so much. What kind of life would that be?" He shook his head. "No, this is the best outcome."

She made a sound in the back of her throat, something that seemed to indicate she'd heard him, but didn't give him any idea what she thought about it.

Worse? The last thing he said ran through his head.

This is the best outcome. He fought to decide if that was true.

Because it sure didn't *feel* true.

Before he had to deal with it, the door opened and Kyle walked in, his normal smile missing.

"What happened?" Even as Daniel asked, he remined there, his arm around Alison.

"We got the call," Kyle said. "Tomorrow night is the last meeting, and it looks like they're not fucking around. They'll be sending the head of the organization."

Which meant they needed to be ready.

Shit was about to get very real.

Chapter Eighteen

Alison thought the second time they played this damn game, she'd have been more comfortable. Instead, she felt as unprepared as the first time.

Which was insane.

They had backup who could reach the house quickly and weapons hidden near at hand. They'd already done one such meeting, and yet Alison couldn't shake the unease.

It was the audience, she suspected. Kneeling for Kyle, Daniel's fingers tight in her hair, or Trent's hand feeding her were things she enjoyed, but they felt private. She didn't want them occurring in front of an audience—and worse, in front of someone she couldn't trust.

It meant she had to submit to the alphas in front of someone who would be doing the most horrible things to her if they could, and she had to put her faith in the alphas to keep her safe.

A hand set on her lower back, and she reacted without thought. She spun, elbow raised, to nail the person in the face.

Instead, a hand closed around her elbow, catching her before she made contact with anything.

"Well, aren't you in a mood?" Daniel twisted her until she faced him, though he didn't appear all that annoyed.

"You aren't supposed to sneak up on me."

"I like it rough."

"Because you're a pervert."

"Fair." He released her then stepped back, his gaze moving over her body from her feet up.

She had no shoes on—they again reminded her that slaves didn't need shoes. The bite had healed, so they didn't need to hide it. It meant she was wearing something even more skimpy, though it covered all the important parts, a short ruffled black skirt with matching black panties beneath it. She paired that with a black bra that pushed her breasts up to create cleavage enough to distract anyone.

He let out a low growl, telling her he hadn't found the outfit lacking at all.

A chill ran up her back, and it had nothing to do with her state of undress. Rather, it had everything to do with the intensity of his gaze.

"You know, I could be quick." His voice dropped low, coaxing, as he came close enough to run his fingers along the waistband of her skirt.

She wanted to give in so badly. Just a few minutes with him would take away her worries. She'd forget about the meeting, about Anne, about the pregnancy test. None of that could stand against the touch of his lips or the grip of his strong hands.

She shook her head and took a step back. "I can't."

He lifted an eyebrow. "Why? Because of the bleeding? Sweet, if you think *that* bothers me, you clearly don't know me well."

"It bothers *me*."

He let out a loud sigh. "Fine. But, in case you didn't know, orgasms help with cramps, so when you're done being stubborn, you know where I am."

After that, Alison took a deep breath, glad he'd accepted the rejection so quickly. As she'd proven time and time again, she didn't have a lot of willpower when it came to turning down the alphas, especially when she needed what they offered so much.

Her cuffs felt extra heavy on her wrists as she waited for whoever was to arrive. The alphas reviewed the details, because as much as they might seem relaxed, it was clear they still knew what needed to happen. Trent checked her cuffs, Kyle the weapons and Daniel the alarms to signal a problem to the backup who had parked a block down, far enough to not scare anyone off.

Her stomach was worse, though she'd hidden it from them. Sipping water all day and nibbling on small amounts of food had held the nausea at bay, though nothing had helped her headache.

Can't even take ibuprofen anymore. Even a single day into finding out she was pregnant, she'd realized that of all the bullshit being a female came with, *this* had to be the worst. It seemed like a personal attack, after everything else, that she had to suffer this badly. Alphas should have to carry the babies to make up for everything she'd already dealt with.

The ringing of the doorbell made her freeze. There could only be one person there.

"Come on, pet." Trent's voice got her moving, spurring her back to action.

They had to get through this, then the real work was over. Once they'd fooled the head of the slavery group, they only had to stay there for another week until the auction date, when they'd received the address and the authorities could swoop in.

Anne would be safe. The bad guys would be gone. Alison could disappear and figure out what she planned to do away from the alphas, without them hovering and clouding her judgment.

Trent didn't hook her cuffs together as he helped her to her knees on the pillow placed again at the center of the seating. She took a deep breath and placed her hands on her thighs, eyes down.

"It'll be okay," he told her, as if he knew she needed the reassurance.

Too bad it didn't help, because of all the things on her list of 'not at all okay', the meeting was only the smallest part.

He leaned in and pressed his lips to her shoulder, to the mark there. "I promise, pet. We're almost done. Nothing will happen." He ran his fingers through her hair, then pressed a hand to her back to straighten her stance before taking a seat beside her.

She strained to hear everything from the other room. The opening of the door, the exchange of words. Most of it was too soft for her to understand, and yet she tried.

The flooring echoed the steps as people came into the living room.

"Not chained?" The voice made her heart speed.

It sounds familiar…

"No. We only need to chain our merchandise at the start," Daniel said. "If she needed to still be bound to behave, we wouldn't be ready to go to auction."

"Admirable," the man said, his voice deep and aged. "We've had a lot of interest since adding her to the registry for the night. I don't usually come out myself, but I admit, I couldn't resist."

"Thirsty?" Kyle asked.

"Yes, actually. I don't drink alcohol, so water is fine."

A snap of fingers drew Alison to her feet without even thinking. *This* was why they'd done their training. She knew what the sound meant, didn't need to consider it, didn't need them to spell it out.

She couldn't see the new man because she kept her eyes on the floor as she hurried into the kitchen. She took a water bottle from the fridge and wiped the condensation from it before returning. She left it closed, knowing people who didn't trust one another wouldn't drink from something open.

No one wanted to risk poison.

She bowed low and held the bottle out to the newcomer.

"Thank you," he said as he took it, drawing her gaze up for a quick glance.

That face… The dark brown eyes, the black hair, the one she hadn't seen in so long…

She swallowed hard as her heart pounded and her head swam.

Fuck.

Trent hadn't expected Alison to freeze. He'd seen that same blank expression on her face a time or two before, when something hit her that she couldn't process.

However, she'd managed the last meeting without it happening, and this seemed far less stressful than when she'd been forced to breathe in the drug last time.

Still, understanding wasn't needed for him to react.

He snapped his fingers. The sharp sound seemed to rouse her to focus. She blinked slowly as she rose and took a few steps backward. Even as she moved, steps careful, she fell into the familiar. She knelt, not on the pillow but just before Trent, and once against allowed herself to stare at the floor.

The new man, Geoffrey, the leader of the group, sat across from her. He wore an expensive tailored suit—black with pinstripes. He had the build of an alpha, so even in his sixties, he appeared fit. Lines in his face betrayed his age, but still he spoke with the confidence of a man who had long ago grown used to people listening. He'd brought two others—large, armed men who stood on the edges of the room. While Trent didn't love that, there hadn't been a way to get around it, either. No one as important as this man would ever consider coming to a private residence without protection.

"You impressed my associate, Galen," he said.

"He didn't seem very impressed. If anything, he seemed to feel we were idiots," Kyle said.

The man didn't even chuckle. He hadn't displayed the least bit of emotion since he'd arrived. "He is loyal and has been in this business a long time, but he's also set in his ways. Most of the scouts in the area handle things in a very different way from you, choosing more of the 'spare the rod, spoil the child,' philosophy.

Rarely do I see omegas in such good condition so close to the auction."

Kyle snorted. "Who would pay for damaged goods?"

The man nodded. "I rather agree. Personally, I dislike seeing women bruised. Not only do they make a woman look unladylike, but striking a female is like someone declaring themselves king. Anyone who needs to say it isn't really. Hitting a female to prove you're in charge only proves the opposite."

Trent frowned, the words…familiar. He couldn't place them, though.

"We've had another series of tests done, to prove she's still free of any diseases or defects. When Galen forced that drug on her, she did end up in heat, but the records also prove she didn't conceive. She is currently bleeding, but that should be over by the time of the auction."

Geoffrey took the files Kyle had, though he didn't look at them. Instead, he held them out without looking, one of the bodyguards coming forward to take them.

"Not even going to check?" Daniel asked.

"No need to. We will go over them fully after we leave here, but they'll tell me what you've already said here. I'm more curious about things that won't be included in there. I understand you offer additional training when needed?"

Daniel sat back, one ankle resting on his other knee. "When they need it. Transitions can be hard, and we're fans of things going smoothly."

"She froze a bit," Geoffrey pointed out.

"She's used to the three of us. We didn't warn her about the meeting, and I think she was worried you were her new owner."

Geoffrey didn't laugh, only tilting his head and staring harder at her. "No. I'm not in the market for a new omega, and even if I were, she's too young for me."

"When you wanted to come yourself, I'd wondered," Kyle said.

"Like I said, I've done this for a very long time. It's rare in this area to get new scouts, especially ones who come so highly recommended. During the actual auction, I'll have duties to attend and won't get the chance to really see her, to ask questions. I couldn't pass up the opportunity to meet a few like-minded individuals."

Trent fought the urge to snarl at the 'like-minded' comment. Even as the old doubts crept up, as he reconciled enjoying consensual submission with loathing forced servitude, he kept his face clear.

I am nothing like that asshole.

"Well, I get that. We've done enough of these to see the trash that usually show up, wanting to get a couple grand out of some used-up omega they already beat to hell." Daniel curled his lip up as though the idea of unprofessional scouts was the real embarrassment. "Then again, that's why ours sell the way they do. That's why we always have waiting lists of people. I'm hoping for a similar turn-out here."

Geoffrey nodded as he took a drink of the water. "From the response we've gotten so far, I believe you'll have no problem finding buyers. I knew that from your reputation, but now, seeing her? Well, I believe you'll do quite well."

Trent fought the urge to touch Alison, to bare his teeth at the man for looking her way. He recalled the way he'd crashed after the last meeting and forced himself to stay quiet.

"Is there anything else you need to know?" Daniel asked. "Any concerns? As we explained before, we do not allow any testing of the merchandise, since we want them delivered to the auction in prime condition. Still, if you have any questions, we're more than happy to answer."

He looked her way. "Will she speak to me?"

Daniel eyes flashed, the rest of his face giving nothing away. "When given permission. We find omegas are better seen than heard. Go ahead, sweet. You may respond to whatever he'd like to know—honestly."

Geoffrey leaned forward, his elbows coming to rest on his knees. "Look at me." His tone left no room for denial, and Alison followed the direction. "You have lovely green eyes. I haven't seen such eyes in a very long time."

"Thank you, sir," she whispered.

He reached out before Trent realized what he would do and grasped her chin.

Fuck.

For Alison's part, she didn't panic. Somehow, she kept calm, her eyes locked on Geoffrey's, giving off that same submissive sense she had since he'd arrived.

"She'll draw plenty of buyers," Geoffrey said, voice soft as he turned her head. "I don't think we've had someone like her before, at least not for a very long time."

Trent wanted nothing more than to knock his hand away, but she hadn't used her safe word, hadn't shown a sign of needing him to step in. It meant doing so would be about him, and he wouldn't risk the case—or her friend—over his jealousy.

Geoffrey narrowed his eyes, as if trying to figure her out. After a moment, he shook his head and released her. "Everything looks good. I don't have any reason to believe there will be a problem. Expect to be contacted on the day of the auction with the time and place. Have her ready to go, because you'll only have around two hours to arrive." He rose to his feet, and Trent did the same.

He could have stayed with Alison, but he wanted to make sure the son of a bitch left. He might not have been able to break his jaw right then, but at least he could make damn sure that he was gone.

They walked to the door, the bodyguards going along as well, flanking Geoffrey. At the door, he turned, moving his gaze past them as though he was still looking to catch a glimpse of Alison. "You know, maybe after this is all over, we could talk."

"I thought this was the last auction for a while." Daniel held the door open.

"It is. However, I have plenty of contacts who I believe are looking for what you can provide. While it is too dangerous to continue the way we have, perhaps the business doesn't have to end entirely. I could work as a middleman, connecting you with buyers, still taking a cut, and we remove much of the risk that an open auction has."

Daniel nodded, as though the idea had merit. "We're just starting out in this area. We have long wait lists, usually, but I never turn down a good connection opportunity."

"It's rare I find people who understand omegas the way we do. The half-brained scouts we normally have see omegas as punching bags. I don't care for it, but it's reality. You? I believe you get it."

"I'm in it for the money," Daniel said, as though he didn't want to commit to anything.

Geoffrey lifted an eyebrow. "Perhaps, but you can't pretend you don't see the truth. Omegas need alphas to be happy. They *need* what we provide. Without that structure in their lives, they fail to achieve anything worthwhile to society. Sure, they might complain, they might fight it, but they're like dogs who don't want to be housebroken. Once we force them, they're happier for it." His gaze moved past the alphas, and there was something almost nostalgic there. "I had a mate, many years ago. When I saw her in an auction, I knew she was for me. It was back at the start of the business."

"What happened to her?" Trent questioned.

"She died. A fire broke out in our home and it claimed her life and that of my young daughter. Losing one's mate leaves a wound, and it is one that has never healed. Still, it taught me how much we *need* omegas, and how much they need us. Not everyone understands what I do, why I do it, but I think back to my mate and I know I'm not wrong. She might never have looked twice at me had I met her any other way, but because I forced her to accept me, to accept her role, she had many happy years in her proper place. Omegas are a treasure, and all treasures worth anything should always be protected, no matter whether they want that or not."

The words hit Trent like a sledgehammer. Between his story about his mate and those haunting words, it all came together.

Geoffrey, the man running the slavery ring they were after, was Alison's father.

Chapter Nineteen

Kyle took Alison's wrist and pulled her to her feet. She moved without fighting, but he could tell she was miles away.

There was no reason to yell at her right then, to question why she hadn't explained everything, why she hadn't told them the truth about her father.

The haunted look in her eyes said it all. He wrapped an arm around her and escorted her outside, to the private patio. Fresh air would do her good, and she always seemed to relax when she breathed in the scent of the honeysuckles that grew along the lattice fencing.

He sat on the swing, then pulled her into his lap. The fact that she went without complaint said she was as shaken up by the night as they were.

She trembled, so he rubbed his hands along her arms, over her bare side.

Trent came up with a mug. He pressed it into Alison's hands, cupping them around it. Steam escaped the top, and he lifted the drink to her lips so she could sip.

Chocolate. The scent was unmistakable.

She could probably use the heat and sugar

Not that they were ignoring the topic. They'd have a conversation, but her wellbeing mattered most right then.

She drank the hot chocolate slowly, sipping at it while Daniel and Trent pulled up seats.

Her barely clothed body wasn't something he could fully ignore, and he wished he could do other things to relax her as well. She'd made it clear enough with Daniel that she was not interested until her period ended, which meant he'd have to just grin and bear it with what she inspired in him.

After a good half an hour had drifted by, when she stopped trembling and had finished the hot chocolate—though she still pretended to drink—Daniel was the first to speak. "Did you know it would be him?"

No need to ease into the conversation.

She shook her head, and Kyle didn't think she was lying. Alison could lie, of course, but she had more tells. Besides, as unsettled as she still was, with how she'd frozen, he doubted she'd expected to see him.

"So go on, pet, explain." Trent leaned forward, using his gaze to trap her.

She rubbed her hands along the tops of her thighs. "I knew my father was connected to the slavery ring, but I had no idea what it was. I was raised in Texas. Why would I think he'd ever be *here*? I haven't seen him in over twenty years. Hell, I didn't even know if he was still alive."

"He mentioned your eyes," Daniel noted, not needing to finish the thought.

She shook her head. "He didn't recognize me. I think it just reminded him of my mom. I hadn't become an omega yet when he last saw me. There's no way he would still recognize my scent, either."

Trent nodded, coming to the same conclusion. Geoffrey had seemed nostalgic, but not as though he recognized her.

A small miracle.

"You should have told us about your father," Kyle said, trying to gentle his voice so it didn't sound like scolding. She didn't need a lecture.

"I did. I told you my mom was a slave. I told you he bought her. He didn't exactly bring his work home with him, so I didn't know how he fit into the group. It wasn't a part of my life, not the business of it. Of all the ways I thought tonight would go, seeing him wasn't anywhere on the radar. If it was..."

Trent reached out and tucked her hair behind her ear. "If it was?" he prompted.

"I would have told you, I swear. I'm not trying to keep anything from you. I had no idea he would show up."

Kyle took a deep breath, relieved at her honesty. After so many times when she'd blindsided them, at least they'd reached the same page on this issue. "Does this change anything, sugar? You know him, or at least knew him. Does him being here change anything we should know?"

She took her lip between her teeth, worrying it as though really thinking about what he'd asked. Finally, she shook her head. "No. He's a businessman at his core. He wasn't just spouting bullshit tonight—that's what he really believes. He honestly thinks you all are doing the lord's work, that you're putting things right for society. Really, knowing it's him, I don't think there's a chance that he wouldn't let you into the auction. You're exactly the sort of person he would want to make a deal with."

Kyle pulled her against him, wrapping his arms around her. Her bare skin was warm and soft, and he allowed himself to enjoy it. "Good. You doing okay?"

She didn't answer right away, and that pleased him. He'd rather she took a minute and really think about it instead of offering up the quick answer of 'I'm fine.' At least if she really considered the question, she might be honest.

She snuggled back against him. "I don't know. I never thought I'd see him again, and certainly not when kneeling at an alpha's feet like he always wanted. Sad thing that it might be the only time in my life he would have actually been proud of me." Her words came out bitter, but he got it.

"Is that why you've resisted this?" Trent asked.

She gestured down at herself, at how she sat in Kyle's lap. "This doesn't seem like resisting."

Trent offered a half smile. "You do. Even when it's something you like, something you want, you can't give in fully." He didn't ask why—didn't need to.

She shifted as if the conversation made her want to move, but Kyle kept his arm tight around her. "Sometimes I feel like when I give in, I've become what he always wanted me to be. It feels like, why did I escape? Why did I work so hard to be on my own if I was going to end up some brainless omega who relying on an alpha anyway? Why did I fight the way I did, suffer all I have, if I was going to end up *here* anyway?

Giving in feels like betraying all that, like betraying my mom and every omega I've seen forced into servitude."

Kyle nodded, pressing a kiss to her head. The words didn't surprise him, though she voiced them more clearly than he'd expected her to. He let Trent speak, since he was going to do it far better.

"Wanting something is different from being forced."

"Is it? Even if the actual thing is the same?"

"Sex isn't rape. You know that. Consent, that's the difference. It's everything. Just because you've seen what rape does to a person, the horror of it, that doesn't mean you turn celibate."

She frowned, as if the idea had some merit but she wasn't quite willing to accept it.

Then again, it was a hard pill to swallow. Even if they *were* different, it was far too easy to see them as the same. Hadn't Trent struggled with the same thing? Hadn't they *all* at one time or another? After watching what happened to omegas far too often, after seeing how they struggled, it wasn't so easy to take any joy out of making one submit, even if they did it happily.

Still, that wasn't the sort of thing they'd work out, not right then. It would take a very long time for her to get comfortable with it, but the more he was with her, the more he got to hold her like this, that he got to see the sides of her she showed to no one else, the more he knew he wanted that very long time.

Assuming he could convince her of that.

* * * *

The water from the pool licked at Alison's sides as she swam her laps, lost in the familiar and repetitive motions. It had become part of her routine, to rise when Kyle did, to have coffee with him, then to swim.

A clearing throat made her stop, and sure enough, crouched by the side of the pool was Trent. He didn't smile, but she'd come to find that tiny crease that appeared in his cheek was his version of it, though it didn't do much to soften his features.

He crooked his finger, and while weeks before she'd have balked at such a blatant demand, she found herself wading to him without a second thought.

Trent's lips against hers could wipe away any of Alison's good intentions. She'd always thought of herself as a strong woman, as someone who could resist anything.

Leave it to the alpha to teach me how wrong I was.

He leaned forward at a precarious angle and gave her one hell of a kiss. When he pulled back, she tried to follow like a mermaid he was luring to dry land.

Isn't that supposed to go the other way?

If there was anything she'd learned with the alphas, it was that either she was all wrong about the alpha-omega interaction or she was just exceedingly easy. She'd always thought the omegas lured in predatory alphas, that the female was the trap.

Instead, she'd found herself drawn to *them*. They could do nothing, just sit there, and everything inside her would crave just a little affection. She'd want to crawl into their laps, even as they watched television, and curl against their chests.

Worse? They'd allow it.

And here she was again, her plan destroyed, and all because of one crooked finger. Yet, even as she scolded herself, she kissed him. She *wanted* him. Four days without sex, of resisting them, of passing off all the horrible symptoms she'd started to have as nothing but her period. They were sweet, ensuring she had anything she needed, that she took it easy, that she didn't overdo anything. Even at night, when she curled against them, they didn't go past the limit she'd set.

And all of that only served to make her feel worse. It was so much easier to resist them when she thought of them as nothing but pushy, overbearing, asshole alphas. When they acted like *this*, when they treated her as though she mattered, it unsettled her.

Trent broke the kiss, a groan on his lips as though he wanted nothing more than to take her around the waist and pull her from the water to fuck her right there.

He'd do it, too. Another truth they'd proven was that modesty mattered little to them. They had no hesitation about starting anything with her anywhere, as though it were the most natural thing in the world.

And worse? She'd grown to feel that way, too. The shame she'd had at first if she kissed Trent and Kyle walked in, if she were in Kyle's lap when Daniel took a seat beside them, had disappeared. All the times she'd grown up hearing that only whores took more than one alpha, when the idea of doing such a thing was a foreign idea, couldn't keep a foothold when the alphas looked at her as they did, with such affection.

Trent sat, his legs crossed in front of him. "How are you feeling today, pet?"

She floated backward, wading in the deep water. "Good."

"Did you sleep better?"

She nodded, though compulsion forced her to add, "I'm still not feeling great once I wake up."

"I had some tea delivered. It's supposed to help. I want you to try that instead of coffee."

She opened her mouth to argue—coffee was a staple of life, after all—but his lifted eyebrow silenced her.

Except, as usual, he relented, especially once she'd given in. "Tea first. Wait an hour, see if it helps, then you can have coffee with some food."

Alison studied his handsome face—well, *she* found it handsome, but she wasn't sure if others would. He was frightening, larger than most men, covered in muscle, and the sharp lines of his face gave him a dangerous edge. "Thank you," she said, an honesty behind the words she hadn't meant. It just slipped out, as if she meant it for so much more than just the coffee.

It was about everything. It was about their entire time together.

As they neared the end, as Alison had accepted that she would lose those things, she was still grateful she'd experienced them.

Losing them would hurt, sure. She had no doubt that aching hole in her chest would never fully heal, as if they'd reached in and torn a chunk out, when she finally walked away.

Still… she couldn't regret it. Each time she tried to tell herself she wished she'd never said yes to this, she knew it was a blatant lie.

"You know," he said slowly, as if unsure. "I was thinking, after this is over, maybe you'll want to come check out my gym. I know you like the one you're at, but I think you'd find there were some perks with mine." He offered a smile that was more nerves than confidence. "Like me?"

Alison's smile fell away, a chill running through her. She shook her head. "I can't."

"Why not? I know you told Kyle the same thing, that this is over as soon as the case is. Why does it have to be?"

"Because I don't want mates."

"You've got them. Whether or not you want us, whether or not you choose to walk away, it doesn't change the fact we *are* your mates."

The words threw off her treading water, and she sank just a bit.

No. She denied it with everything she had, shaking her head as she went toward the ladder to the left of where Trent sat. That couldn't be right.

They had some sort of…affection between them? There was something, but she chalked it up to great sex and close contact.

That wasn't mates.

"You're wrong," she bit out as she grasped the ladder to climb out. "I'm not the sort of girl to go bonding with alphas, and even if I were, I told you from the start this was just temporary."

"What you tell yourself and the truth aren't always the same thing. You might not have a lot of experience with mates, but I promise you, that's exactly what we are. Do you really think I can't see the way you look at us? The way you edge toward us in any room? The way you lean against us and touch us as if you can't help it?"

She snatched her towel from the back of a lounge chair, patting herself dry with rough, fast motions. "That's just stupid hormones. That's playing a part."

"It might have started as a make-believe, but it hasn't been that for a long time. Are you really willing to throw it away? For nothing?"

"I'm not throwing anything away. I'm being clear that I don't have room for *this* in my life, even if it were real."

"Why not? Are you that happy living alone, with no friends?"

"Yes, I am!" Even she felt the lie as it escaped her throat.

She thought back to the pool party, to the way she'd wanted so badly to be like the rest of them, to be *part* of the world instead of just some protector of it. No matter how dangerous that might have been, she'd craved it with everything inside her.

"If you were, you wouldn't wrap those arms around me quite so tight when you get into my bed, pet. I wouldn't feel those nails in my skin while you sleep, like you're terrified of me leaving. You know? I got up one night to get a glass of water, and when I came back, when I looked down at you while you were sleeping, your eyebrows were drawn together. You reached across the bed, searching, and I don't know if I've ever seen you quite so upset as when you found nothing."

"You really think I should base my future on what I did while I was asleep?" She tried to keep her voice as incredulous as possible, to make it sound as absurd as it really was.

"Why not? At least when you're asleep, you stop sabotaging yourself, you stop giving up things you want just because you think you shouldn't want it."

"*Can't* want it. There's a difference."

"And why can't you? What is so different about you that makes it so you're the only person in this whole world who can't take that risk? In case you didn't realize it, it's a risk to everyone who gets involved with anyone. You could walk out and break our fucking hearts, and yet here we are, trying to convince you to stay."

Break our hearts. Alison ignored the statement, the one that meant far more than it should have.

"Because I've *seen* what happens, because I was fucked up from the start. I didn't grow up seeing this shit work out, seeing happy families with loving parents. I grew up with a father who saw my mother and me as property, and I know what it did to us. What the hell do I have to offer to mates?" She pulled the towel tighter around her, a horrible empty feeling inside her taking hold as she said the truth. Each word seemed to take another piece from her, like they all hollowed her out. "Some people are ruined, Trent, and you can't fix that. I've seen omegas who hit that point, who just breathe until they die. They can't get past things—they can't move on. They've been turned into whatever they are, and there's no coming back. That's me. Others, they had something to build on. Even Kara, for all she suffered, for all her crazy faults, she had a connection with her brother. I didn't have anything. Until you three, I didn't have a single thing in my life to keep me here. I could have fallen asleep and never woken up and no one would have known, and that was exactly the way I wanted it. You can't change that—no one can."

He tilted his head, gaze steady, standing against all her bluster and anger and hurt. "If you think you don't have any connections, you're not paying attention. Those omegas you helped, and in turn their alphas, they're all family, even if you don't want it. Family isn't always something you choose, but it's something that happens and that doesn't let go even when you want it to. You aren't nearly as broken or alone as you think you are."

She wanted to cry. Why? She wasn't sure. The words sounded so good, like she wasn't the pitiful thing she'd always assumed, but she knew better. When she watched the omegas talk amongst themselves, when she watched them smile and at ease, it was obvious.

She *wasn't* part of that, and no amount of pretending otherwise would change it.

Heavy steps stopped their argument, a voice speaking only one side of a conversation.

Daniel rushed in, phone to his ear. "Yes, I understand. Here she is."

He held the phone out to Alison.

She took it, pressed it to her ear and answered.

A male's voice responded, and it took her a moment to identify it. Marshall, Tiffany's mate. "I need you to come to the hospital, Alison."

Her knees weakened, as she let herself drop to the chair.

Wait, no, Daniel eased her into it, as if he'd known she'd needed the help.

"What happened to Tiffany?"

A pause, then a rushed, "No, no. Tiffany is fine."

Those words let her pull in a rough breath, and a hand against her nape pressed her forward so she could breathe slower.

The fright meant she took a moment to catch up to what Marshall said, to make sense of his words.

Eventually, however, they all came together.

"The friend of yours who went missing, Anne? She's here."

And if she'd felt nauseated before, it was nothing compared to right then. "What happened?"

"Why don't we discuss it when you get here." He paused, the bustle of a busy hospital behind him on the line. His next words were weighted, and she sucked in a breath at them. "Alison, you really need to hurry..."

* * * *

Daniel held Alison's hand, whether she damned well wanted him to or not. The more upset the girl got, the more she tried to pull away. It was natural for her, the desire to stand on her own.

He'd gotten to understand it more as they'd spent more time together, had realized the reason.

She worried that if she leaned on anything, when it disappeared—and she was sure it *would* disappear—she feared she'd be unable to stand on her own anymore. Instead of risking that, she'd rather never let anything close.

Too fucking bad.

She ricocheted between being shocked and angry as they drove to the hospital. They'd done all they could to ensure that no one followed them and intended to gather new paperwork to explain the hospital visit should they need to. It was easy after her heat, to blame the visit on fertility tests best done at the start of a new cycle.

Still, Daniel rubbed his thumb over her hand as they walked through the hospital.

He'd gotten a few extra details on their drive over about what had happened, though they knew little. Anne's crumpled body had been found dumped behind a convenience store, barely alive.

It was still touch and go on if she'd make it.

She hadn't woken, though the clerk said she'd been conscious for a short time before the EMTs had arrived. Instead, it was Marshall who'd recognized her, who'd known to call Alison.

Please let us make it in time. If they didn't…

He doubted Alison would ever forgive herself. She protected those around her with a ferocity that was terrifying for anyone standing in front of her, and already he worried what she might do because of this.

They had a plan, needed to wait. The auction was to happen the next day, but he wouldn't put it past Alison to throw that away and go in guns blazing herself the moment she discovered the location.

Which would be a monumentally bad idea. Not only did the FBI have a plan in place, one that had taken a very large amount of manpower to set up, but the last thing Alison needed was to be anywhere near that place.

The risk was always that some of the people could get away. Did they want to risk her being caught up in that?

The elevator doors opened on the floor where Anne was. Marshall was already waiting down the hall, his face stoic.

Which was a very bad sign.

Alison broke into a jog, pulling away from Daniel's grasp.

The doctor's flat expression said everything. He shook his head, his words quiet and just for her.

She didn't crumble, didn't tremble, didn't cry. Instead, she nodded as she listened.

Daniel neared them, catching some of it. *Did what we could. We're so sorry.*

Still, she didn't break down.

She didn't even flinch when Kyle set a hand on her shoulder, as though she couldn't feel it.

The emptiness in her eyes was terrifying, reminding him far too much of her father's eyes.

She'd just lost the reason she'd done so much, and for the first time ever, Daniel really did worry she might be broken beyond repair.

Alison stared at Anne's unmoving body. It was hard to recognize her, honestly. If she'd shown up unconscious, or dead, Alison wasn't sure she'd have been able to identify her.

Her bright blue eyes were swollen shut, and her lips—usually pulled into a smile—were pale and split.

She'd lost weight over the past months that she'd been gone, and her skin had lost the pretty glow it usually had, since she'd always been a sun lover.

She'd gone from being a bright, sweet girl to being a corpse, and after all Alison's promises to keep her safe, she'd failed.

Someone placed a hand on her back, but Alison ignored it. Suddenly all her stupid internal nonsense didn't seem like it mattered, not compared to this.

"I'm sorry, pet," Trent told her.

Alison shook her head, swallowing hard. She almost wished she could cry, that she could show the sort of sorrow Anne deserved. "I should have done more. Maybe if I'd been faster, better, I could have found her before they did *this* to her."

"You can't put this on yourself," Daniel said. "I've worked enough cases to know that. This? The people who took her did it, and we'll nail them to the wall for it, but you can't blame yourself for it."

"Why not?" She stared down at the girl, who'd been too young and too sweet for the things that had happened to her. "You know how I met her? She got my number from Claire, and when she called, I expected to have to break some alpha's nose. Instead, she called me hysterical because she was hiding outside someone's house. It turned out she'd watched some drunk asshole kick his dog, repeatedly, and wanted to rescue the dog, but she had no idea how to get past the locked gate."

Alison thought back to how worried she'd been on the phone, but how sure she'd been when Alison had arrived. No matter the danger, that girl was going to rescue the dog. She'd been optimistic and ready to take on anything. It had been a strange combination that Alison hadn't known quite how to deal with, being around someone who could honestly believe the world was a good place no matter what she saw, who could rush into a situation even though she knew the risks and knew she didn't have the skills for it.

"What happened?" Kyle prompted her.

"I went and we got the dog—and I made sure the owner understood the error of his ways with a few well-placed kicks of my own. She took the dog in, the largest, ugliest dog you have ever seen. It would have torn off the face of anyone who looked at her wrong, but it was entirely devoted to her." She sighed as she thought about how she'd placed the dog with another omega after Anne had disappeared, about how she'd have to tell that omega Anne wouldn't be coming back, that the dog was now hers.

Another part of my failure.

"You did everything you could." Kyle set his hand on her nape, rubbing along the collar. That usually relaxed her, but right then? Right then she couldn't think of anything except all the ways she could have done things differently.

Instead of waiting around and playing house with the alphas, she could have been working. She could have been off her ass and doing something.

Anne would have done more for her, but Alison? She'd failed.

Her stomach gave up the good fight of keeping anything down. It made her curse the pregnancy again, because now instead of focusing on Anne, she was again thinking about herself.

She gagged, and Kyle tugged her toward the door. Across the hallway sat a restroom with a woman's sign on it, and she bolted away from the alphas.

After hunching over the toilet, thankful to be alone for a minute, even if it did mean she'd vomited up what little she'd eaten, she flushed and stood.

Everything inside her had gone numb, heavy, as if she was dragging around a body that was nothing more than a collection of useless appendages she couldn't even feel.

She splashed water on her face, hoping the cold would shock her system, would help her wake up and get on with it.

That was what she was supposed to do, right? No time to mourn. Mourning was for better people, for friends and family. The most she could offer was revenge.

She stared at herself in the mirror, frustrated by the lack of tears, by her reflection, by everything. No matter how hard she tried, she was always falling short. Always failing when it really mattered. *So* many years of training, and for what?

She still couldn't even protect one little omega.

The temptation to smash the mirror to pieces hit her, and she curled her hand into a fist. She wanted to shatter her reflection, to break something, as if that might snap the impotent anger inside her.

Instead, a face appeared behind her, the man having moved so quietly she hadn't noticed him at all. *Galen.*

Before she could react, he wrapped an arm around her and pressed a cloth over her mouth.

She clawed and tried to scream, but it was muffled under the running sink water, and each gulp of air she drew in was tinged with something sharp and chemical.

Everything blurred, and her body turned even heavier until she sagged against his grip.

She turned her gaze toward the door, toward where she knew her alphas were waiting, but she couldn't even call out for them. Eventually, even holding her eyes open became too difficult, and darkness overcame her.

Chapter Twenty

Trent rested his back against the wall outside the bathroom. "Do you think she's sick?"

Kyle paced the hallway, being the type to move when nervous. "Just hormones and adrenaline, I bet."

Anne's body still rested in the room, Marshall waiting to see if she wanted to see it once more before they moved it.

The shit luck of it all wore on Trent. Alison had risked so much to try to save the girl, and it had all been in vain. According to the doctor, the girl's wounds hadn't all been recent. He doubted she'd have lived much longer regardless, meaning that even if Alison had managed to find her a little quicker, she might not have been able to save her.

Not that it would ease Alison's mind. The women blamed herself for everything, as if she needed to be perfect to hold the entire world together.

He'd seen it in the way the other omegas had looked at Alison, like some guardian of theirs that they were always in awe of. Alison took that to heart, put too much on her shoulders.

It was impossible to save everyone. That was a lesson Trent knew all too well, one of the reasons he'd gotten out of his work with the FBI. He'd seen too many people he couldn't save, had grown tired of seeing them die pointless deaths.

That ground a person down, and watching Alison rush to the bathroom made Trent fear she'd reached her limit.

He rubbed his hands over his eyes, the water still running.

Was she crying? Using the sink as a way to mask the sounds? That seemed a lot like her stubborn ass to do. She didn't care for anyone to see her weakness, even if they wanted to help her with that weight.

"How long are we going to wait?" Trent asked.

Daniel twisted his head, as if he could see through the door. "It's been a while, I guess. She's probably hiding."

Kyle snorted before stopping his pacing and walking over to shove open the door.

Inside, the bathroom was empty.

Terror swamped Trent. Not anger, not frustration, just sheer terror. Had she run? Was she going to target the slavers on her own? He didn't want to be back here to identify her body next.

"I swear, if she ran—" Daniel's threat was cut off when they spied a white cloth on the floor.

Kyle knelt and picked it up. He brought it to his face and inhaled, his expression hardening. "Chloroform."

Trent swallowed as he spied the other door, the one they hadn't realized was there, that opened to the emergency exit staircase.

Alison had been abducted, this time for real…

* * * *

Alison rolled, her head pounding and her stomach revolting. She heaved, gagging, a horrible taste in her mouth and down her throat she couldn't get rid of.

Nothing came up, but that didn't stop the heaving.

It took a while for her to catch her breath, and when she did, when she sat up, she found herself on a bed she didn't recognize.

The bathroom. The chloroform. It took another moment for her to realize what had happened, even she didn't know exactly where she was.

On the desk, across from the bed, sat a silver letter opener. She bolted from the bed, wanting to wrap her fingers around the make-shift weapon.

Something yanked her back, the bed groaning. A cuff around her left wrist had been connected to the bed frame. She clawed at it, but a lock kept it in place. They weren't the same ones the alphas had put on her.

"You're awake. Good." *That voice.*

Alison turned her head to find her father walking into the room, his hands folded behind his back, his chest out. It was as if no time had passed. "Let me go," she snapped.

He sighed, as though her reaction were disappointing and expected. "I can't believe you really thought I wouldn't recognize my own daughter."

Well, that answers if he knows or not…

He grabbed the chair from the desk and pulled it over until he could sit just outside her reach. "Even twenty years isn't enough time to forget those eyes. Besides, you've grown into a near-identical replica of your mother. When I saw you, for a moment, I almost thought you were her."

Alison yanked the chain again but made no progress. Anger was no match for steel. "Is that what this is? Some creepy replacing-mom thing?"

He lifted his lip in disgust. "I am not some pervert, even if you wish to paint me that way so you can sleep at night knowing your father was a monster. No. You may look like your mother, but you are my daughter, and I have no such inclinations toward you."

"So why am I here?" She sat on the bed when it became clear she wasn't going to get free by pulling. *Conserve your energy. Look for an opportunity.*

"I suspected someone would try to infiltrate my auction, but I didn't suspect it was them, not at first. They came highly recommended, and perhaps I was naïve due to liking what they said."

"Are we doing father-daughter catch up time?"

He lifted his dark eyebrow, a look so similar to when she'd been a kid. Why had it terrified her then? Why had she cared so much back then? "I'd hoped you would have settled over the years. In fact, seeing you behaving yourself yesterday gave me hope for the first time in your life that you had learned your place. I see it was part of the ploy, however."

"I guess neither of us is all that happy with the family we have left."

"Indeed. Still, it wasn't easy to catch you alone."

Alison lowered her gaze as she worked through it. The realization hurt down to her bones. "Anne? You used her?"

"The scouts who took her were not careful. She would have brought almost nothing to the auction, assuming she survived to that point. I didn't put it all together, not at first. I had heard some blonde woman had been asking questions about her. Once I realized it had to be you, the trap was only too simple to bait."

The anger inside Alison burned through her. Anne had ended up dying because Alison had asked questions, because she'd been a target?

Geoffrey was either unaware or uncaring of Alison's internal struggle, because he waved over someone from outside the doorway. Galen approached, a pair of bolt cutters in his hands.

Dread settled inside her. She wasn't an idiot. She *knew* that people holding bolt cutters around prisoners was a bad thing. She drew her hands into fists out of instinct.

Galen came closer, and when he reached for Alison, she moved.

Being one-handed made her struggle weak, but she adapted. She swung her elbow out and caught him in the jaw, then reached for the cutters. He was stronger, larger, and he had use of both his hands.

The fight didn't last long, though the blood leaking from his mouth still pleased her, especially when she thought back to the things he'd said about her before. He pinned her to the bed, his weight enough to keep her still, his body above her chest to keep her arms locked to her sides.

"Careful, now. He could cut something on accident if you struggle too much."

"Wouldn't want to mar the goods," she choked out, Galen's weight enough to make taking full breaths hard. Still, she settled.

Escape was more important than pointless fighting.

The bolt cutters neared her throat, but it wasn't until they closed over the small padlock there that she realized the plan.

And it set her off, again. The snap as he cut through the lock, as the collar Trent had put on her was pulled free, ran through her. She felt truly naked without it, the skin below cold in a way that sank into her.

"I can't have you wearing a collar with the wrong name, or one I lack a key to," he explained.

The collar was tossed to Geoffrey, who caught and examined it. "The odd thing is, I would have believed them. You weren't faking, not entirely. I can tell, of course, the difference between a woman who submits and one who pretends. It is a valuable skill that has helped protect me from being stabbed by women biding their time."

Galen got off her, and she managed a hard kick to his ribs before he could quite get away. He snarled back at her, but Geoffrey waved him gone. "I think the funniest part is that all I ever really wanted for you was to find your place."

"No, you wanted to put me in the place you liked. Not the same thing." She sat up, drawing deep breaths now that she didn't have a heavy man sitting on her chest.

"You have always been stubborn, always too quick to suffer needlessly to prove some foolish point. Let's not pretend, Corrine."

Her old name grated, something she hadn't been called since she'd escaped.

"You are my daughter, my flesh and blood, my legacy, and the last part of my mate. You do not belong out there doing whatever you have been for the last twenty years."

"So you'll sell me, like I'm just a used car you found?"

"You aren't livestock, not like the others being sold. Will money exchange hands? Of course. That is the best way to ensure you end up somewhere where you will be properly taken care of. People who pay a great deal for their things tend to take better care of them. I will choose the correct alpha who can handle your…" He hesitated, as though trying not to insult her. "Your spirited ways."

"If you think I'm going to just give in and be a good little omega for you or any asshole who thinks he can own me, you really don't know me."

He waved off her argument. "Everyone says that at first. I *saw* you, Corrine, and even if you don't want it to be true, you were made to submit. Even when it was supposed to be a ploy, even when you were supposed to be acting, I watch you react on instinct. You were born to kneel, and the sooner you accept that, the better your life will be. Fight it, if you must, because it won't change a thing. This is who you are, and it is who you will always be." He rose, and even when she lunged at him, even when she tried to grab him, nothing worked.

He walked out as though her fight were a temper tantrum, one he would accept because she couldn't help herself.

Too quickly, the energy ran out, and she sat on the bed. The collar sat on the table like a dead thing, forgotten, used up and tossed away.

And for the first time, a real tear ran down her cheek.

* * * *

Kyle couldn't stop pacing. Everything inside him was on edge, frustration eating away at him.

The auction was today, and they still had no damn idea where it was. Clearly, they'd been found out, so it wasn't as though Geoffrey would be sending them an invite with the details.

And Alison was out there, somewhere, alone, and there wasn't a damn thing he could do about it.

"Sit down," Kieran snapped from his computer, them having all gathered at Tracy, Sam, Mason and Dylan's place.

"When *your* mate is missing, *you* can sit down. Until then, shut the fuck up," Kyle snarled back.

Kane responded from his spot in a chair that he balanced on two legs. "Don't mind him. Trust me, he was a bitch when Tiffany went missing."

Kyle shook his head and resumed his pacing. They needed to do *something*.

The FBI had promised to help, but so far hadn't come up with anything. They were at the same dead stop they'd been at before Alison had agreed to join.

And now Alison was gone. What if the auction went on as normal? What if they sold her? What if he never saw her again, never even knew what happened to her?

He drew his hands into fists, the tension inside him making him want someone to do something to let him lose his temper. Blowing off a little steam would be perfect right about then.

Instead, he kept pacing and let everyone work. Sam was at the police station trying to find anything he could, especially since the murder was local, and he was on the special division for omega crimes. Kieran and Joshua were working tirelessly on their computers.

Kane, Kara, Torrin, Liam and Erik had gone after every contact they could, trying to discover anything.

It had led to fuck-all.

The only people who knew about the auction were those attending, and *those* people wouldn't be breathing a word of it.

The front door opened, and a moment of stupid, baseless hope made Kyle turn toward it.

Sam.

He was breathless, as if he'd run all the way there. "I've got something." He held up a small bag, then pulled the folded paper from it.

Kyle snatched it from him, unfolding the page and frowning at the messy, sprawling handwriting. "What's this?"

"Anne wrote it before she passed out, when the clerk was calling nine-one-one. He didn't find it until after everyone left."

Red splotches over it could only be blood, but he ignored that as he made out the words. An address?

And a time.

He lifted his gaze to Sam as Daniel snatched the paper from him. "She knew where the auction would be?"

Sam nodded. "It has to be. I bet they didn't expect her to wake up, let alone be able to tell anyone. She must have wanted to get out one last message."

Daniel was on his phone a moment later, stepping away from the group, no doubt contacting the FBI for backup.

Suddenly, Kyle wished he'd gotten to know her. He wished he'd had the chance to meet her, because right then, she might have been the only thing that stood between his mate and the same fate that Anne had suffered.

Daniel walked back in, his lips twisted into a grimace. "They won't do anything."

"What?" Trent was the one to rise that time, his voice nothing but fury. It was one of those times Kyle had to remember that Trent wasn't one to push too far.

"They said they would set up outside the auction and wait, picking up people as they left so they could get as many as possible."

"What if they miss her? What if they miss grabbing the person who has her?"

Daniel ran his tongue along his teeth, his voice calm even though his face wasn't. "They don't consider Alison a high priority. She doesn't have any special information and she isn't an agent. They see her as an acceptable casualty."

Kyle bared his teeth at that. *Acceptable casualty?* It was a good thing no one had said that to his face, or he'd have decked the fucker. "They really expect us to just sit outside and hope they find our mate? That we're going to leave her there for one fucking second longer than she has to be?"

"They've taken us off the case officially. We were ordered to fly back home and let them finish it."

"Well, fuck that." Trent's voice left no room for debate. "There's no way I'm sitting this out. She'd never do that if it were any of us."

Kane rose and walked out of the room, silent, which was rare for the man.

Kyle narrowed his eyes, thinking about what Alison would have done if it were Tiffany who was missing.

"I'm not waiting to see if this turns out okay," Kyle said. "I don't give a shit about what they want. I'm damn well going to get my mate."

Trent nodded. "Me too."

Daniel didn't move at first, as though it was the hardest choice for him. It was, though., He'd been devoted to his job forever, and now he had to actually pick between it and her. If they went, if they disobeyed the order, they were done as FBI agents. That life was over.

And they had no idea if Alison even *wanted* them.

Daniel shook his head. "Fuck it. Let's go."

Kane walked back in, a bulletproof vest over his black shirt, a gun strapped to his hip. At Kyle's stare, he lifted an eyebrow. "What? She's annoying as fuck, and I am constantly afraid she'll castrate me for funsies, but she's family."

It was then that Kyle really looked around. He'd been so focused on his conversation with Trent and Daniel that he'd stopped paying attention to the others. The commotion was quick, but steady.

Anyone able-bodied was already preparing, with the few who were less able to fight helping to pack and prepare.

As he gazed across the room, the alphas and omegas willing to ignore any risk in order to protect one of their own, Kyle sucked in a deep breath.

This was what Alison had created, even if she never realized it, and anyone who dared to hurt her had just called hell down on themselves.

Chapter Twenty-One

Alison's wrists itched from the new cuffs they'd put on. No collar—that would be for her new owner to choose.

When women had come to clean her up and get her dressed, Alison had tried her best to convince them to help her. They weren't mean, but it became clear they'd never do a thing for her.

Fear was a powerful motivator, and these women had been beaten down for too long. Besides, Galen had hovered, staring *far* too intently when she'd changed.

They'd given her a dress that reminded her of what her mother used to wear. Knee length, buttons up the front, black with a tie around the waist to show off how narrow she was there. It was the perfect outfit for a little homemaker, as if it would somehow turn her into what her father thought she needed to be.

Hell, what her father thought she *was* deep down.

And yet his words stung. They stuck with her as they always had. No matter how many times in her life she'd told herself to ignore what he said, that all those jabs delivered without inflection were just his own fuck-ups and not her problem, they'd always managed to dig into her.

And these were no different.

Even as she tried to think about what the alphas had told her, about how different it was to submit to them, of her own free will, she feared her father was right. Was she just like any omega? Something born and made to be trampled? Was it written in her very DNA?

Her heels clicked against the floor, the noise of people floating through it despite her not having seen many. Galen escorted her, and she played her part by following him quietly until she saw an opening. Her hands were cuffed together in front of her, and she hadn't got a weapon.

Well, the idiot put me in heels. They could be useful.

Through the long hallway, they passed a door that opened into an office. A large window overlooked the main area, and her stomach again lurched. This time it had nothing to do with the pregnancy.

Cages and other areas to chain up woman were all over the room. Already omegas were bound inside, some quiet, some sobbing, some screaming. Men moved through the space as though shopping at a mall, as if they were picking out furniture rather than living, breathing people.

"You see, you should be thanking me," her father said. "You could have been down there. Others, they'd have thrown you onto the floor to be bought up by the highest bidder, like the rest of the merchandise here. I didn't do that—won't do that. You should show some gratitude."

She swallowed down the bile in her throat and closed her eyes, not wanting to see it anymore, wishing she could shut out the noise.

For a brief moment, she was almost thankful for Anne not being there, that her suffering was over. Without the alphas coming, Alison was on her own, and she wasn't confident she could do a damn thing to help anyone.

"She's beautiful," a new voice said.

Alison turned to find the man who'd spoken, who was dressed nicely, much like her father. He was younger, perhaps in his thirties, and had blond hair pushed back from his face. No matter how nice he looked on the surface, however, the cruelty in his eyes wasn't something he could hide.

Geoffrey nodded toward the man. "This is Howard Lostern, your new mate."

Mate.

She shivered at the word, the immediate denial. Even her nose, able to pick up the scent of the alpha, knew he was all wrong.

That was the moment she accepted that Trent had been right. Even if she fought it, Kyle, Daniel and Trent *were* her mates. Her body knew it, even if she hadn't wanted to admit it.

Howard crooked a finger, similar to what Trent had done. Where with Trent, she'd followed the demand without hesitation, drawn there by a pull she didn't understand, she didn't move a muscle for this man.

His expression hardened.

Galen shoved her forward, then hooked a leash to her bound cuffs and handed the end to him.

Howard yanked the leash until she was just in front of him. "You have a lot of learning to do, but I think you'll be worth it. I'm not sure I've seen such a pretty omega before." He took her chin between his fingers, grasping it tightly. "And I'll enjoy training you."

No panic rose with the touch. Instead, anger swelled inside her. *Train me?*

She swung her face forward, striking him in the nose. The crunch was like music, even if she knew she'd pay for it.

Sure enough, he swung his hand, striking her across the face. With the heels and her mind still fuzzy from them drugging her before, she couldn't keep her balance and fell to the floor.

Wetness dribbled from her lips, and a red spot appeared below her. She remembered the bright red lipstick the women had put on her, and she had to laugh at how they were the same color.

"Do you think this is funny?" Howard asked.

"Yeah," she said, still on the ground. "I do."

Howard came forward as though to get in another strike, but froze before contact. She turned to find her father, his hand lifted, palm out, as a warning to the other alpha.

Howard growled lowly. "She's mine. You don't tell me what to do with her."

"She isn't yours *yet*. The money hasn't come through, and until it does, you will not harm property you do not yet own."

Again, she laughed, uncaring that she looked insane. "You know, you almost had me, *Dad*."

He leaned down and pulled a handkerchief from his pocket, using it to clear the blood off her face. "How so?"

"I thought for a minute, maybe you were right. Maybe I'd been fighting this whole time to avoid something I was never going to escape. Maybe I was meant to be *this* person." She met his gaze head on, truly defying him for the first time in her life. She didn't just snap, didn't offer pointless hissy fits, but stood toe-to-toe with the man who had ruined so much of her life. "You were wrong, though. I'm not something to be owned by whoever pays the most. I am not property."

"I saw you kneeling for those other alphas. If you think that didn't come naturally, you're fooling yourself." His words were soft, as if she were naive and he were trying to help her understand, gently.

"That's what you don't get, what you'll never get. You can't *force* someone to submit. It isn't possible. Trying is like declaring you're king. If you have to say it, it isn't true." She threw his words back at him. "Do you know why I knelt for them? Why I willingly gave up my power to them? Because I trusted them. Because they earned it. Because at the end of the day, it was still *always* my choice."

He titled his head but said nothing.

"Mom never loved you. How could she? You were just some man demanding he was king, and in the end, she killed herself rather than spend another fucking day with *you*."

That got to him. His face darkened in a way she'd never seen before, and the man who rarely showed any emotion had fury written there across his features.

Still, she didn't relent, didn't back down. She was *done* letting him control her.

"You will do as you're told," he said, voice steady and dark. "You will behave yourself or you will find your life very unpleasant. You will listen to your mate, you will do as you are expected, you will have his children and care for them."

Another groundless, crazy laugh left her at that all. All sorts of *fuck that* ran through her mind at all the ways that would never happen.

"What's so funny?" Howard asked.

"I'm already pregnant," she said. "Sorry, buddy, but you're buying damaged goods. Whatever little power fantasy you have, it's never going to happen. I'm never going to submit to you, and I'll spend my entire life trying to end yours. Hope you're up for the long haul, buddy, because this will *never* get any easier."

Geoffrey grabbed her chin, forcing her eyes to his. "You think you've won?" he *tsk'd* softly. "You have *no* idea what I am capable of. You will behave, because you will be chained until you learn to. Trust me, no omega has ever outlasted me. And you're pregnant? *That* is a very simple problem to fix. Perhaps when we take care of that inconvenience, it will also remove this pointless infatuation you have with those alphas. You will never see them again, not only because you'll be gone, but because I expect they won't live long enough to cause me any more problems. I dislike loose ends and they have seen my face."

The world went away as she stared into her father's dark eyes. His words slithered through her, casting away the sounds of the people downstairs, the guards in the room, Howard. None of it mattered.

He reached forward and set a hand on her stomach. "You will have offspring with who *I* decide. Perhaps one of them will actually make for a proper omega. Not this one, of course. Lucky for you, we can take care of it easily tonight."

The touch was what did it, what snapped loose whatever control she had. Something dark inside her spread out, filling her, twisting her. She'd done a lot of things in her life that weren't good, a lot that might shock a better person, but she'd never enjoyed them.

She'd done them because she'd needed to, because she logically knew they were necessary.

Whatever it was that took over her wasn't logical. It didn't care about what needed to happen, or what should, or what was right or wrong.

It only cared that he had threatened her mates. That he had threatened her unborn child.

She moved forward so fast that her father didn't even have the ability to scream. She had no idea if anyone else reacted, since her focus was entirely limited. She brought her hand down against his face, only three times, but he stopped moving. A yank to her hands made her growl.

The leash.

She wrapped her fingers around it and yanked back, moving Howard off balance. Still, that fury inside her didn't abate. Everyone in that room had proven a threat to her mates, to her child, and at that moment she had no idea what mercy was.

She came forward, knocking Howard down and twisting behind him. She got her bound cuffs around him and used them against his throat, her knee in his back. Sickening gurgling noises left him, but she didn't let up.

Something struck the side of her face.

She snarled at Galen, amazed he hadn't shot her. Then again, she was worth a pretty penny.

They should have shot her.

She yanked again, hard enough for a snap from Howard's neck, for him to go unnaturally lax.

She tried to extract herself from him, but Galen did most of the work when he grabbed her arm and yanked, hard. She was nothing compared to him when it came to weight. Her cheek hurt where he'd hit her, and it took a moment to realize he'd used some sort of stick.

Coward.

He grabbed her around the throat, hauling her against his chest, trying to restrain her. "What should I do with her?"

"Chain her up," her father snapped, his precious composure gone. "We'll take care of the pregnancy tonight and train her before we sell her off again."

A crash outside the room floated by her, like a detail she didn't give a fuck about. Her father still stood there, the threat, the thing she needed to get rid of.

Everyone else turned their heads toward the window, but she didn't care what happened down there.

She swung her elbow down and into Galen's gut, then twisted and kicked him as hard as she could. He flew backward, tripped by Howard's body, before he crashed into the window.

The cheap single-pane glass was no match, and he toppled down. Screams from downstairs filtered in, but her brain was full of rage and red and something old and primal. It had no room for that.

Only she and her father were left in the room, and the widening of his eyes, the fear there, was the first time she'd gotten to see the real coward beneath all those layers of practiced civility he wore, the ones he used to hide what he really was.

He wasn't strong. He wasn't in control. He was a little boy who knew the only way he could get what he wanted was to try to bend others to his will.

Too bad. Whether he'd meant to or not, he'd raised a daughter who wouldn't bend, and he wasn't nearly strong enough to break her.

"Alison, let's talk about this," he said, as if he could explain away what had happened, what he'd said.

No words came to her. She couldn't even recall words right then.

"You can go. Leave and never come back. I won't look for you—I'll leave you be."

She didn't believe him. This sort of man had an ego that couldn't let something go, and even if he *could*, she wanted blood for what he'd have done if he had the chance.

She rushed forward, leaping at his chest to knock him backward and onto the floor. She snarled down at his face, wanting nothing more than to feel his flesh between her teeth, than to rip out his throat to make sure he was never a threat again.

Whatever this was, whatever she was, it was the last thing her father would ever see.

Trent stopped short at the doorway. After a body had crashed through a window from the upper floor, he'd known damn well where his mate was.

The rest of the place—a large open building set back in the middle of nowhere—didn't matter.

With all the alphas who had come, with Kara and Claire and even Tiffany, there weren't a lot of places for the slavers and the buyers to go.

It was chaos, but that worked in their favor. Those who tried to escape were met with Kieran's rifle outside, since a bullet to the kneecap sure did slow down those who thought they could run.

None of that mattered, though, as Trent took the stairs with Daniel and Kyle behind him.

But at the top was a sight he was pretty sure was the herald of death.

Alison was above her father, another body unmoving on the ground. Blood dripped from her face, her teeth bared and a growl a grizzly would be proud of rumbling from her chest.

The woman he knew was gone. There was nothing of her in that body.

Omega rage was the sort of thing one wished to never see in their entire life, and he could happily go another forty years without ever seeing it again.

There were times when he had to admit he wasn't at the top of the food chain, and nothing could remind an alpha of that faster than what Alison had been reduced to.

"Pet," he said, flinching at how *not* appropriate that name might have been right then.

Still, it made her turn her head toward him, even as her eyes didn't seem to recognize him.

"Get her off me," her father shouted.

"I'd shut up if I were you," Daniel said. "Because if she decides to tear out your throat right now, well, you better get right with your god because no one will be able to stop it."

Geoffrey paled more but thankfully shut up.

"Come on, sugar," Kyle tried. "We're here now. We brought some friends of yours, too. It's all over now."

She swallowed, slowly, but when Geoffrey shifted, her gaze zeroed back in.

Fuck, it was like trying to talk down a snarling wolf who had already tasted his prey.

"No, pet, it's fine. Don't worry about him. He can't do anything, now." Why they were trying to save him, Trent wasn't quite sure. The fucker deserved whatever she did to him.

But she wasn't herself, and the last thing she needed was to live with the guilt of killing her father.

She wrapped a hand around his throat, squeezing for a long, terrifying moment before she moved off him.

He went to rise, but a sharp look from Daniel made him think better about it.

Alison came up slowly, her steps careful, studying Trent like she almost recognized him.

Her cheek was swelling, and her lip had been split. It seemed that was where the blood had come from. All in all, she wasn't in terrible condition.

When she stood just before him, she inhaled, slowly. *Good. Scents are written deeper than anything else.* If anything could reach into that rage, could settle her, could draw her out of it, it would be smell.

Sure enough, her eyes fluttered closed and she crossed the last bit of space, wrapping her arms around him.

Blood soaked into his shirt, but he didn't give a damn. He pulled her against his chest as Kyle and Daniel came closer, both doing the same, running their fingers through her hair, touching every visible inch as if to ensure she was okay.

He breathed her in deeply, unable to believe she was really safe.

Chapter Twenty-Two

Alison sat on the hard hospital exam table. Despite not being far along, she already felt unbearably uncomfortable.

The past two weeks had passed in a blur. FBI, police, the news. Everyone wanted her story.

They'd saved forty-eight omegas and had taken down the largest slavery ring in the country. With how well it had all gone, no one dared to come after any of them for something unsanctioned.

Kyle and Daniel had left the FBI—or they were let go, it wasn't entirely clear. Or, at least, that was what Alison had heard.

She hadn't seen them, not since Marshall had checked her out just after the warehouse, when he'd suggested she stay with him and Tiffany so he could keep an eye on her for the night.

She'd gotten a few text messages from the alphas, but they hadn't tried to see her.

Was she an idiot? Had she misread everything? Maybe they'd been playing the entire time, enjoying an available omega who provided easy access.

She'd been the one to constantly say it would end after the case, so the last thing she'd expected was for them to pull back.

And yet…they had.

She hadn't asked to see them, because the thought of being directly rejected by them was too damn scary.

So she waited, frustrated that when she finally knew what she wanted, she couldn't have it. She wasn't scared of it, had perfect clarity and now they decided to get cold feet.

Assholes.

The morning sickness had grown worse, and while she didn't have to hide it anymore, she missed having them look after her. As much as she'd balked about the hovering, when she was crouched over a toilet, she would have given anything to hear Trent call her pet and run his fingers through her hair. Without Trent feeding her small bites, without Daniel growling out a threat when she didn't drink enough, without Kyle wrapping her in a hug and forcing her to sit down and relax, she discovered she didn't take great care of herself.

Staying with Tiffany for a few days had meant she still had alphas trying to order her around, but she could easily ignore them. It seemed she couldn't get more than an hour or two before some alpha or omega was in her space, bothering her and trying to help her.

And yet the more she thought about those things she was losing, the more she sank into hopelessness at losing it.

Marshall came in, a file in his hands. Alison had to admit that Tiffany hadn't done too terribly. Besides, it seemed Alison and the doctor would spend plenty of time together, as he had taken over her prenatal care. She hadn't even had much of a choice in it.

After all the alphas and omegas had showed up for her, it seemed they didn't plan on letting her sit on the outskirts anymore.

And she couldn't deny they were family, not when they had all risked themselves for her.

"Your numbers look good," he said, gaze down. "Strong. You've lost weight, though."

"Well, when the little spawn makes me throw up constantly, I'm not surprised."

He chuckled. "Try candied ginger and eat small amounts all day. If you've got nothing in your stomach, you'll feel sicker."

She waved off the advice.

"Okay, lie back." He set the file aside and rolled over an ultrasound machine.

They hadn't done that before, hadn't heard the heart. Thus far the baby had been nothing but a parasite that made her nauseous. Maybe seeing it would make her feel a little more maternal?

Then again, she *had* killed two people and nearly her father to protect it, and that had to give her some mothering points.

Marshall moved her sweater up, revealing her stomach that was not quite as flat as it had been. She was around nine weeks, and even though she was sure it was just bloating, the change in her body unnerved her.

The thought of doing this all alone terrified her. Could she really be a mother without any help? She pictured trying to care for a child, trying to get everything right.

What did she even know about that?

Marshall picked up a small bottle, then frowned. "I'll be right back. This one is empty."

"I'll be here," she muttered and closed her eyes.

Just her luck for there to be a problem. It seemed to be the way her life went.

She tucked her hands into her sweater, playing with the thing she'd bribed Kara to steal for her, the thing that never went far. How it could hurt her as much as it helped, she had no idea, but she'd known she *needed* it.

The door opened, and Alison kept her eyes closed. "Men should learn that if they need it, it's best to keep lube close."

"Not sure I care for you making that joke to another man, pet."

She bolted upright at the sound of Trent's voice. Sure enough, Daniel and Kyle stood beside him, and all three stared at her in a way that said…

They know.

Trent couldn't breathe. It had been too long since seeing Alison, and each day had felt like some cruel torture.

She'd been so…unsure after the warehouse, after she'd been checked by Marshall. As much as Trent had wanted to take her into his arms and kiss her until he could relax, he'd forced himself to give her space.

She didn't *have* to stay with them anymore. They couldn't take that choice from her. No matter how much it hurt, how much he wanted to walk into the place she was staying, throw her over his shoulder and bring her back to where she belonged—with *them*—he had to give her the space to make her own choices.

Except, when they'd backed off, she had, too. She'd become more evasive, and when Tiffany had let slip that she had an appointment with Marshall today, Trent couldn't shake the fear.

What if she's sick? What if those fuckers at the auction hurt her?

The last thing he'd expected was to walk in and find the ultrasound machine pulled up beside her, her sweater raised.

She's pregnant.

He didn't even need to ask. It was written all over her face. The guilt. The fear. It was all there.

"What are you doing here?"

"Wrong question," Daniel said. "Did you really think you were just not going to tell us?"

She reached into the large pocket at the front of her sweater, fidgeting with something there. "I didn't know how to tell you."

"You could have gone with, 'Hey, you know how I lied to you about getting my period? Well, guess what, I'm actually pregnant,'" Daniel said, voice rough.

She winced, her shoulders curling in. "I was going to tell you, but then you seemed like you'd changed your minds."

"What?" Trent asked.

"After the warehouse. You agreed I should go to Marshall's, then you didn't come see me."

"You didn't ask us to visit," Kyle pointed out.

"I thought you realized it was all just some game, that maybe I was stupid because I'd never been in love before." Her bottom lip quivered the tiniest bit, and still she played with what was in her pocket.

Stupid woman.

Trent came up and rested his hip against the bed. "We backed off because you always said you were done after the case. I didn't want to push you, to make you feel trapped. I thought maybe a little time on your own would let you realize you actually liked us. I guess I underestimated how stubborn you are."

She didn't even smile, though she did lift her face to his.

I miss her collar…

"I'm afraid," she admitted. "What if you change your mind?"

He looked down at her, waiting until she met his gaze, until those stunning green eyes of hers were locked on him. "I've been alone for the last eight years, pet. I never figured I'd have a place again, that I'd ever find one worth wanting. You? You're home."

"My father was selling me off to the dead man in that office. I realized right then that I didn't want to go back to my old life. It made me finally able to see the difference between what I was afraid of and what I wanted."

"Oh yeah, and what did you decide you wanted?"

She reached out and cupped his face, pulling him in to whisper against his lips, "you," before she kissed him.

And that was the best thing Trent had ever heard.

Kyle couldn't quite take his gaze from Alison's stomach.

Pregnant?

How could he be a father? How had everything changed in the last few minutes?

Still, when she looked his way, he offered her a smile he knew he always would, his way of reassuring her, of telling her something his words were no good at. "Got to say, I missed you."

"You're sure about this? Because I'm not trying to force you into anything."

He laughed, taking Trent's spot when he moved. "You couldn't force me into anything. In case you've forgotten, you're the one who gets tied up, not me. And, sugar? There's no one I want to spend the rest of my life tying up more than you." He set a hand on her stomach, gentler than he needed to be, before leaning in and setting a kiss there.

Without jobs, Kyle and Daniel had taken it easy for the past two weeks. He had no idea of their direction, but something had felt better when they had moved into Trent's place. They'd been missing Alison, of course, but the fracture that had run through him since the falling-out with Trent finally felt healed. He couldn't imagine going back to being separated, no matter how their lives fell into place together.

Kyle had never wanted anything, content to take things as they came. Nothing had ever mattered to him enough to care. Then he'd met her, the feisty woman who had been more trouble than any female ought to be, and for the first time he'd not only wanted but needed something.

He had a family, one he cared about more than anything, one that he'd damn well do anything to keep, and it was all thanks to the omega who had broken his nose.

Daniel waved Kyle off, taking the spot. He slid his fingers into Alison's hair and tightened his grip. "I don't like that you lied to me."

She wrinkled her nose at him. "Liar. You just want to punish me for it."

Her humor made him laugh, and he leaned in to take a kiss that was far rougher than what Trent had given her. Then again, Daniel wasn't a gentle person. It was something he'd accepted about himself, but something no one else had ever been able to.

And Alison? She didn't pull away, didn't hesitate. She moaned against his roughness, against the way he tugged at her scalp with his grip in her hair.

She was breathless when he pulled back, when she tried to follow him as though that taste wasn't enough, a desperate little whine on her lips.

"You know, my life has been nothing but work. I've always picked my job over everything else, thought nothing was more important. Hell, I turned my back on one of my best friends because I'd convinced myself my job was all I had. When I had to decide between that and you, though?" He shook his head. "Never made an easier choice."

"And you won't regret that? You won't resent me for it later?"

He shrugged, his lip curled into a grin. "I figure if I ever miss the FBI too much, well, I know a certain omega I can use my handcuffs on."

"I didn't need to hear that," came the doctor's voice from behind them.

Daniel laughed and rose, giving Marshall room to work.

"I assume you're okay with them being here. I won't even bother to ask how they knew."

Daniel lifted an eyebrow in Alison's direction, but she assured the doctor it was fine.

Marshall lifted her sweater, and when she moved her hand, something fell from the pocket, the thing she'd been fidgeting with since they'd come in.

Her collar.

He'd assumed it had gotten lost at the warehouse, but it seemed she'd had it the entire time. Hell, she'd carried it with her like a prized possession.

He picked it up, then pressed it back into her palm. "We'll buy you a new one, sweet," he promised as he kissed her forehead, even as Marshall moved the ultrasound probe on her stomach. For all Daniel cared, the doctor could work around him.

"Well then," Marshall said, his eyes on the screen.

Trent turned a glare on the doctor. "Doctors are not supposed to say that or sound surprised when doing exams."

Daniel looked at the ultrasound screen but he couldn't understand it. It was all just black and white and meaningless to him. "What's wrong?"

"Wrong? Nothing. She's healthy and so are they."

He drew in a deep breath in relief. She was fine. So were they.

They?

That forced a double take so obvious it was almost funny. "Excuse me?"

Marshall grinned, looking even younger than he was. "She's carrying twins."

Marshall said a few other things, but Daniel didn't catch any of it. He stared at the screen, then at the picture Marshall printed out and handed to him.

Twins.

Not just a father, but he'd have two children?

He wrinkled the image from holding it so tight, but fuck, he didn't care.

When Alison sat up, Daniel pulled her against him. He pressed a kiss to her head. "You're going to do every damned thing Marshall says you need to. We clear?"

She lifted her eyebrow, mischief across her features. "I don't know. I'm not very good at following directions."

Daniel set his hand around her throat, where a collar would be by day's end if he had anything to say about it, a sign that she was *theirs*.

"That's fine. I don't mind punishing you when you get out of line. I've got some extra time on my hands right now, and I can't think of a better way to spend it than training you again."

The press of Daniel's hand against Alison's throat was a sensation she'd expected to hate. It was a claim, and she'd always seen that as a choking leash.

Revulsion didn't come, however, and she finally understood why.

She'd spent her whole life running away from *this*. She'd thought risking herself was a foolish choice that only idiots made. Each time she'd seen a friend of hers fall for the pretty words of an alpha, she'd rolled her eyes and waited for the horrible outcome.

Yet, in Trent's harsh features that softened only for her, in Kyle's smirk and humor, in the grasp of Daniel's hand against her throat, she didn't find the stifling claustrophobia she'd feared.

Instead, she'd found freedom—from loneliness, from expectations, from her own past. The alphas she'd run from—even before she'd realized she was running from anyone—had ended up being her own leap into a future that held more than she'd ever thought she could have.

They weren't just any alphas—any men. They were her partners, her protectors, her mates, *her* alphas.

Alison smiled up at them, at the only men who had been brave and tough enough to match her, to make her face her own demons, to face theirs in response. She happily accepted that they needed one another, that they were bound.

She might be theirs, but they were damn well hers right back, and that would never change.

Want to see more from this author? Here's a taster for you to enjoy!

Ready or Not?: Enemies Closer

Jayce Carter

Excerpt

Charlie squinted through the falling snow visible in the glow of the headlights of her car, but she could see next to nothing.

"This was a waste of time," she told Darren on the phone.

"You always say that."

She should have never agreed to this damn meeting in the middle of nowhere. Of course the secretive author would live out past any sense of civilization. He'd refused to come into their office, one located in the main city a few hours away.

No, he was far too busy and eccentric for *that.* Instead, Charlie had taken a short flight then rented a car to drive up into the mountains in the dead of winter, all because the great Skylar Tafferton needed a new firm to represent him.

She'd done the work, gotten together every resource and contact she had to prove to him she was the best choice. Her firm might not have been the largest courting him, but *she* was the right lawyer. Even still, the way he'd looked at her said he hadn't agreed.

How often had that happened in her life? People saw her—her youthful face, her sweet demeanor—and they thought she wasn't capable.

"I became a lawyer so I didn't have to do this anymore, so I could prove myself." She tightened her fingers on the steering wheel. "But no one gives me a chance."

"You have proven yourself. Just because one client doesn't get you isn't reason for you to doubt your entire life path. Come on, Charlie, you're being ridiculous."

She thought back to the years she'd struggled as a waitress, as a bartender, as whatever second or third job she had to work just to get herself through school and into the job she'd always dreamed of. She'd done it to be respected, and what had happened?

She was still the same girl trying to prove to people she was worth a damn. Her bosses, her clients, everyone.

Her car slid, the tires losing traction for a moment. "Fuck, fuck, fuck," she muttered as she took her foot off the gas. Thankfully, the tires caught again. "This snow is horrible."

"Pull over. You sure as hell won't get the client if you end up dead in some ditch."

"I don't have time to wait on the storm and hope everything works out. I need to get home and try to move on to the next potential client on my list before you-know-who gets there first."

She refused to even say the name of the asshole who had managed to steal nearly every good client from her over the last year. Maybe if she didn't say it, he wouldn't be real. He worked for a larger firm than hers, and he'd leveraged that position well.

They hadn't come face-to-face because she rarely did trail work. Mostly she handled client relations, both obtaining them and keeping them happy. Her rival did the same, only he seemed to do it better.

No rest for the wicked.

The car shuddered, then slid again. This time, however, her excellent driving didn't do anything. The car careened to the side, over the slick ice-covered road, and struck a berm of snow that the plow how driven off the road earlier.

Charlie's seatbelt kept her in place and the airbag didn't deploy, but when she pressed on the gas, the tire spun.

"Great," she said, letting her head hit the backrest of the seat.

"Are you okay?" Darren's voice came out frantic.

She'd forgotten he was even there. "Yeah. Looks like you were right, though. I don't think I'm going to be making that flight."

"Do you need to call someone? Where are you?"

Charlie peered through the darkness and white to spot a neon sign in the distance. A motel?

It wasn't that far, only a couple blocks at most. Even though she wasn't dressed for hiking in the snow, she could make it that far.

"No, I'm fine. There's a motel up the street."

"Right, because a creepy motel in the middle of nowhere during a snowstorm isn't the start of every horror movie out there?"

Charlie rolled her eyes and gathered her things from the backseat. She needed her files, her phone, her laptop and her chargers. "Well, at this point I'm either in the horror movie where the motel gets me or the one where the snow beast who lives in the woods gets me. I'd prefer a nice warm bed if something is going to kill me."

Darren laughed softly. "Fine. Text me when you're settled in, so I don't worry."

She agreed before ending the call and sliding the phone into her briefcase.

Walking in heels through the snow in below-freezing weather wasn't how tonight was supposed to go, but at least there would be a bed at the end of it.

* * * *

"What do you mean there aren't enough rooms? I booked one yesterday," Ryder said, keeping his temper in check as the motel clerk went through the paperwork.

"I understand that, but it looks like it wasn't ever confirmed. The snowstorm meant we had more unexpected guests than we were planning. All our normal rooms are taken."

"Normal? So what *abnormal* room do you have?"

"The honeymoon suite."

"Fine. I don't care what it is so long as it has a bed and a heater."

"There is a slight problem." The clerk spoke with halting words, but Ryder was used to that. It had to do with his suit, with the expensive watch on his wrist. People assumed he was a grade-A prick, and yeah, sometimes he *was*.

Not to clerks just trying to do their damn job, though, even if he was exhausted and wanted nothing more than to crawl into a bed that they wouldn't give to him.

"What's the problem?"

The clerk sighed. "We have another guest, and both of you are trying to rent the last room."

"Well, tell them to go elsewhere."

"The roads are impassable, and their car went into a ditch."

"What do you mean I can't have the room?" The voice of a woman caught his attention, and to his left, at the same checkout counter, stood a young woman in a black suit.

She couldn't have been thirty, and her suit was cheap. A stray piece of thread hung down from the knee-length skirt and her leg showed from the slit in the back.

Ryder ran his finger along his bottom lip while he stared at her.

Well, maybe things are looking up…

"Miss?"

She turned, and the stunning freckles on her dark cheeks astounded him. She had eyes so dark they looked black in the dim lights of the lobby, and a cherub-like pointed chin.

Though, her expression was anything but heavenly. "Yes?"

"It seems there's one room left. Given it's a suite, it's probably large enough to share."

Not that he wanted to share it with too much space between them. What had seemed like a necessary but ultimately useless stop might have just borne fruit. He wouldn't mind a day or two cooped up with this woman.

She pressed her lips together, but a glance at the clerk—who only shrugged—seemed to solidify her lack of options. She blew out a slow breath before nodding.

TOTALLY
BOUND
Home of Erotic Romance

About the Author

Jayce Carter lives in Southern California with her husband and two spawns. She originally wanted to take over the world but realized that would require wearing pants. This led her to choosing writing, a completely pants-free occupation. She has a fear of heights yet rock climbs for fun and enjoys making up excuses for not going out and socializing.

Jayce loves to hear from readers. You can find her contact information, website details and author profile page at https://www.totallybound.com

www.ingramcontent.com/pod-product-compliance
Lightning Source LLC
La Vergne TN
LVHW050930080826
845145LV00001B/283